CHIMERA
SCOURGE OF THE GODS
MATTHEW DENNION

SEVERED PRESS
HOBART TASMANIA

CHIMERA: SCOURGE OF THE GODS

To my two daughters, Serene and Savannah, who are always willing to watch a giant monster movie with me, especially if it has Godzooky or Frankenstein Jr.

PROLOGUE
GERMANY 723 AD

Hundreds of people had gathered around the mighty oak. They had come from as far north as Norway, and as far south as Scotland. Most of these people were Vikings, warriors from the time that they were born, until the time that they hopefully died on the battlefield, and ascended to Valhalla. The people gathered at the oak had seen dozens of battles, ranging from small skirmishes to massive armies clashing across miles of land.

Despite all of this battle experience, none of the gathered warriors had witnessed an event of this magnitude. The wars that they had lived through had all been wars between men, but on this day, gods would clash!

The oak the masses had gathered around was Thor's Oak! The focal point of the entire Norse Religion. The tree was the one spot on Earth where Thor consistently showed his power by causing his fearsome lightning to strike the tree. For centuries, sacrifices have been made at the tree in Thor's honor. Usually, the sacrifice came in the form of a ram or a bull. On rare occasions, a human was sacrificed to Thor. The stakes today were much larger than human sacrifice. Today a god and entire religion would fall.

The Christian Winfrid had declared that he would cut down Thor's Oak. In doing so, he hoped to prove that Thor and the Asgardians were nothing more than a myth, and that the Christian God was the only true God.

As Winfrid picked up his axe and approached the tree, a gust of wind struck the crowd. Several of the war-hardened Vikings gasped as they were sure that Thor was soon to strike down this man and prove his power over the Christian God. Winfrid made the sign of the cross over his body and then approached the tree. He lifted the axe above his head and struck the mighty oak. Most of the crowd winced, expecting a bolt of lightning to descend upon them but to their surprise nothing happened. With each swing of the axe, more and more of the Vikings lost their faith in Thor and the Norse gods.

Through a portal, Thor watched and seethed with anger as the Christian cut into his tree. He roared and grabbed his Hammer preparing to strike down the human who dared to challenge his power!

Thor lifted his Hammer to call upon the thunder when Odin stayed his hand, "No my son, despite the lack of respect shown by this Christian, this is the moment we have been waiting for the humans to mature to. They have moved passed the need for our stewardship. Their civilization has reached the point where they can become the caretakers of the planet. The Olympians and the Mesopotamian gods have already moved onto another planet. It is time that we joined them."

Thor took a deep breath and relaxed his arm, "Father, long have I fought to protect this planet from the frost giants and other races that would threaten it. Is this how I am to be rewarded for my efforts? Am I to be mocked by this human as he cuts down the symbol of my power? Is this how I am to leave this world, as a coward and weakling?"

Odin placed his hand on his son's shoulder as they began to walk toward the rainbow-colored dimensional portal that connected their world to the rest of the universe, "My son, your words are accurate; we protect this planet, not the humans specifically. Our race has vowed to protect all planets which sustain life within the universe. This planet represents one of our greatest successes. The Earth is rife with life. These humans represent a shining example of the potential that life has on this planet. We have given the humans agriculture, mathematics, and language. We have taught them how to live on Earth without overusing its resources and threatening the viability of the planet."

Odin gestured toward the rainbow portal, "Come my son, there are other planets that require our protection and supervision, our brothers and sisters have already begun working with the native populations of those planets to fight off the demons and monsters that would threaten them. Let us travel there now and assist our brethren in their efforts. We shall return to Earth in due time to evaluate the humans and their stewardship of the planet."

As father and son entered the portal, Thor took one last look over his shoulder as Winfrid delivered the blow which sent his tree crashing to the ground, "Indeed father, we shall return."

CHAPTER 1

Colonel Conner kept his men moving at a quick pace as they ran through the countryside. He stopped them one mile from the base of the mountain. Connor was not sure exactly what he and SEAL Team Omega were going to encounter today but one thing that he was sure of was that this was the most important mission he had ever led. The threat made by the enemy was both direct and absolute, not only to the US, but to the entire world. Like most of his missions, this was one that had to be kept secret. Given the gravity of the situation, the Greek government was assisting the US in helping to cover up the truth behind the current threat that they were facing. The enemy has set up their base of operations at the top of the largest mountain in the area. The government had concocted a story about a chemical spill around the base of the mountain that would require an evacuation of a twenty mile radius around the mountain. With that kind of clearance, Colonel Conner and his team were free to operate without fear of drawing the attention of the local population.

Conner surveyed his men, all of them looking at him for orders as to what they needed to do. He felt a sense of pride in himself and his team in that they would again be taking steps to make the world a safer place. Connor cleared his throat and then began addressing his team. "Men, our mission is as follows. A threat of the highest magnitude has set up its base of operations at the top of Mount Olympus. The enemy has a powerful electro-magnetic pulse weapon in their employ. An attempt to bomb the top of the mountain was stopped when an EMP hit the bomber squadron when they were on route to the target, causing them to fall into the sea. As such, this is a low-tech mission. No enhanced targeting apparatuses and no radio. It's just us and our firearms against whatever is on top of that mountain. Our mission is to scale the mountain and destroy the hostiles and equipment that we find there."

One of the SEALS raised a hand to ask a question, "Sir, what exactly are we expecting to find up there?"

Connor shook his head, "We are not exactly sure. When the hostiles set up their base of operations on top of the mountain, they also began utilizing some form of a moisture condenser to cause heavy cloud cover to shroud the top of the mountain. Even satellite is unable to see exactly what's up there." Connor took a deep breath, "I may not be able to tell you what's up there, but one thing I can tell you is, that whatever is up there, we are going to kick its ass!"

A roar of approval went up from the gathered SEALS and Connor felt that his team was as ready as they could be for the mission ahead of them. Connor raised his rifle above his head, "SEAL Team Omega, let's move out!"

Connor led the jog across the open field toward the mountain. Within seven minutes, the team had reached the base of the mountain and they had yet to encounter any resistance. Their timing was good. It was nearly dusk and with night vision not being available, scaling the mountain at dusk was their best option of not being seen while still being able to see the mountain that they were climbing.

Connor waved his men forward to the base of the mountain. When they were within one thousand feet of the base of the mountain, Connor saw three large shapes begin to emerge from a cave on the mountainside. He pulled out his binoculars to get a better view of the objects. When he looked through his binoculars, he could not believe what he saw. The shapes were three incredibly large wolves. Connor estimated that each of the wolves was at least thirty feet in height. The wolves sniffed the air then began to move in the direction of his team.

The wolves were charging at the group and running in a tight formation. Connor gave the order for his men to fire. Rifle fire ripped through the air but the bullets seemed to have no effect on the massive wolves. Connor watched in disbelief as the three wolves seemed to merge together and form one massive wolf with three heads. The merged creature was well over one hundred feet high. Most men would have turned and run when facing this supernatural adversary, but Connor and his men were SEALS. They held their ground and continued to fire. The three-headed horror continued to charge forward as if the bullets pelting its hide were nothing more than rain drops. When the monster reached the SEALS, all three of its heads reached down and began devouring the men.

Seeing that his team was being slaughtered and that their weapons were having no effect on their target, Connor ordered his team to retreat. The team turned around and began to run when they saw another massive shadow that seemed to be gliding across the ground and blocking their retreat. With the three-headed wolf massacring their comrades, the remaining SEALS risked running into the slithering shadow. As the SEALS approached the shadow, they saw a long thin form begin to rise into the air revealing the face and torso of a hideous gigantic woman with the lower body of serpent. The giant snake woman hissed at the men and then quickly used her body to encircle several of the SEALS. The men screamed in pain as the snake woman constricted her body and crushed them. Connor soon found that he and his remaining men were trapped between the two giant monsters. He knew that his team was on its last mission. He took small comfort in the fact that since he had no radio, as a precaution he had left two members of his team to watch what occurred from a safe distance. These men were held in reserve so that if the mission was a failure they could report what had happened to Connor's superiors. Connor took a deep breath and shouted, "Tight formation everyone. We are SEALS if we are going to die, let's die like SEALS." The men replied in unison with, "Sir, Yes Sir." The men then quickly formed a tight circle and began firing in vain at the monsters that surrounded them. Thirty seconds later the gunfire ceased and the countryside was silent once more.

CHAPTER 2

Faster, he kept thinking that he had to run faster. This was literally a matter of life and death and Luke Davis had to be faster. He pushed his legs harder and was sure that he felt something pull in his hamstring, but he pushed through the pain. Terrance was only about twenty feet from the door and the oncoming rush of buses was just outside. If Terrance made it outside, he would run right in front of the buses without fear of being run over.

With about ten feet left between Terrance and the door, Luke finally caught up to the fleeing student. Safety protocols dictated that Luke could not grab Terrance from behind; it had to be from the front or the side. Luke side stepped in mid sprint and felt his already tweaked hamstring tweak a little more. He slid in front of Terrance and caught the force of a two hundred pound fifteen year old slamming into him at a full sprint. Luke was pushed back several steps but he was finally able to halt Terrance's elope attempt toward the door.

He didn't say a word to Terrance. He just pointed back to the classroom. After trying to push through Luke as if he was sumo wrestler, Terrance finally relented and went back to class. As they were walking through the hallway, Luke thought to himself that this was the last time he left Terrance with a particular assistant when he went to lunch.

Luke walked back into the classroom to see the rest of his students preparing for dismissal. Jack was skipping around the classroom singing a Wiggles song; Lester and Brian were sitting at the computer. They were glued to a SpongeBob YouTube video. Things were going well until the YouTube video froze. Luke could see that Lester was having difficulty dealing with the crashed video. Lester screamed, ran to the table in the middle of the room, and flipped it over before anyone could stop him. Luke directed Lester to pick up the table, and then he asked the three staff members who were standing around watching the event to start taking the other students out of their buses.

After Lester had sat down at the table in an appropriate manner, Luke pulled a social story out from his desk for the student. The social story was a printed up PowerPoint that gave Lester directions on what to do when he got angry. Lester worked through the story just prior to having his bus called over the loud speaker. Luke held out his fist to Lester who gave him an excited pound. Luke smiled and pointed to Lester's bag. Lester picked up his bag then Luke walked him out to his bus.

Once Lester was on his bus, Luke jogged back inside and collected the daily behavior data for his students. Lester had hit someone five times that day and he had flipped the table twice. Terrance had eloped four times, causing Luke or one of his assistants to sprint after him and chase him down. He had also stripped naked on two occasions. Jack had hit himself in the face twenty two times today and Brian had bitten three people.

Most people would have looked at these behaviors and been horrified but as Luke was reading the data, he actually smiled. Luke smiled because the interventions that he had put into place were working. All of the student's behaviors were down from yesterday and trending down from the previous week.

Luke was teacher of students with autism. He had a Master's Degree in Education and was a Board Certified Behavior Analyst or BCBA for short. He was well-trained in using Applied Behavior Analysis techniques to modify students' behaviors. Basically, the theory of Applied Behavior Analysis was that you found what motivated someone and used that motivation to reward the behaviors you wanted that student to exhibit. At the same time, you give as little attention as possible to the behaviors that you do not want someone to exhibit. In the case of Lester, Applied Behavior Analysis stated that you don't say much when he flips the table over, as it is the behavior that you don't want to see him exhibit. Conversely, you want him to read through the directions in the social story about what to do when he gets mad, so when he reads the story, you give him pound and a smile.

Luke thoroughly understood the concepts of Applied Behavior Analysis and, more importantly, he was able to effectively utilize those concepts in his classroom. Luke was good at what he did and he took great pride in that fact.

Teaching was a difficult profession to accurately gauge effectiveness in and teaching students with autism was another story altogether, but Luke had the data to prove how effective he was at his job. Every year, for the past ten years that he had been teaching, he had been given students with some of the most severe behaviors in the state, and in nearly every instance he had significantly reduced the behaviors of those students. Luke participated in yearly presentations where other teachers of students with autism presented interventions that they had utilized. Luke had won the award of best presenter in every presentation format that he had attended.

That he was able to attain such high level of professional success, and the fact that he was making a difference in the lives of students who were in dire need of help, pleased Luke tremendously. He loved working with the students; yes he was hit, kicked, and bit on a daily basis, but none of that mattered if those same kids gave you a pound at the end of the day or asked if you were still their best friend. As much as Luke liked the students, he had to admit to himself that he was starting to get burned out. First, there was the fact that he had been around long enough to know that there was not much out there for his students when they finished their schooling at age twenty one. Most of the progress that he had made with his students would be lost in programs that lacked the man power and funding to run a successful program for adults with autism.

The state was also making his job more difficult by the year. They had no idea how to assess special education students in the general population, let alone the students that Luke taught. As such, they dumped a ridiculous amount of paperwork on teachers. At the beginning of his career, this would not have mattered but that was before he had a family. He had a wife and two daughters that needed his attention as a husband, father, coach, teacher, and dad.

Aside from the psychological burnout, there was the physical toll that his job was taking on his body. Blocking and redirecting students when they were running at full speed or hitting you was one thing when you were twenty-two years old. That type of punishment was something else when you were thirty-five. Luke had been talking to his wife about finding a new job but the same issues kept coming up. Luke needed a job that generated as much, if not more money than he made as a teacher, and even with his Masters and BCBA, that job did not exist. He could switch to a new school but with the current climate he would be pushed way back down the pay scale and with two young children that was unacceptable. Despite these factors, he kept his resume up on several employment sites. He received plenty of offers for part time consulting jobs, which would have been fine if he was retired and was collecting his pension as a supplemental income. Luke was on his way out the door when the classroom phone rang. At first, he was content to let a parent phone call go to his voicemail and to respond to it tomorrow. However, when he checked the caller ID, he saw that it was his principal.

Luke picked up the phone, "Hi! Luke Davis's room."

The principal was quick with her reply, "Luke, I need you to come to my office immediately. There are some men here to see you."

The teacher put down the phone and walked toward the office. He was wondering exactly who these men could be. Typically the principal would give him a clue as to who needed to see him, saying Mr. Blank is her to talk about his son or that a therapist needed his advice. Luke's principal was unusually quick and cryptic with her phone call.

Luke entered the main office to find his principal waiting by the secretary's desk for him. She grabbed him and whispered, "The men are in my office. They are from the Department of Defense and they have asked me to step outside so that they may talk to you in private."

A shocked look appeared on Luke's face, "The Department of Defense? Why on Earth would they want to talk to me?"

The principal shook her head, "I don't know, but if you need any help, I am right here for you. All you need to do is open the door and call for me. I'll do whatever I can to help you."

Luke was surprised to see two men who looked like they were Will Smith and Tommy Lee Jones from the film Men in Black.

One of the men stepped forward and flashed a badge, "Mr. Davis, my name is Agent Scott and this is Agent Jackson. We work for the Department of Defense. I will be brief. We are currently looking for a BCBA with experience in dealing with subjects who exhibit aggressive and destructive behaviors. This is a full-time position with full benefits for you and your family, as well as continuing to pay into your pension at your current rate. This position within the Department of Defense would require you and your family to relocate to a military installation in Virginia. We came across your resume and you appear to be one of the most qualified people for this position. You have the credentials for the position and the field experience to deal with the subject that we have in mind. For reasons of National Security, I cannot divulge any further information about this project until you have accepted the position. I also understand that this is short notice for the offer but we need to know if you will be accepting this position within the next twenty four hours."

Luke was still in shock over the entire situation, "I am definitely going to need to go home and discuss this with my wife."

Agent Scott nodded and handed him his card, "Of course, if decide to accept this position call this number within the next twenty four hours. Thank you for your time, Mr. Davis."

The agents left the office with Luke staring down at the card still trying to process what had just happened.

CHAPTER 3

Felicia Cally and her friends entered the night club and headed straight for the bar. As a blonde in her early twenties with extremely well-developed attributes, Felicia usually did not have to wait long before some guy approached her and asked to buy her a drink. She was scanning the bar for potential suitors when she saw a guy who had businessman written all over him. The man came up to Felicia and started talking to her. He was not bad looking so she began chatting with him. The conversation carried on until she looked further down the bar and saw another man staring at her. The man was tall. He was at least 6'5 and extremely well built. Through his T-shirt, she could see his muscles rippling with each movement that he made. His face was chiseled and tanned. He looked like he could be a movie star. Felicia walked past the first man who had approached her as he was still talking to her. Her eyes and her mind were set on the man at the end of the bar.

Felicia was completely transfixed on the man. It was as if every move that he made was perfectly timed. He was like a living work of art. When the man looked at her and smiled, she felt a rush of energy course through her body. She couldn't understand what was happening to her. She had just noticed this man and she felt as if she was back in 7th grade, and this was the first time that a boy asked her dance at one of those silly middle school dances.

The man put down his drink and started walking toward Felicia. He put his arm around her and Felicia could feel her body quiver. He leaned forward slightly, "My name is Aiden. May I be so bold as to inquire to the name of the vision I see before me?"

Felicia was almost hypnotized. She stood silent for a moment before her brain screamed for her to wake up and say her name. She stammered, "Fe, Felicia. I am Felicia."

Aiden smiled, "Felicia, meaning one of fidelity." He grabbed her hand and kissed it, "I could not think of a more fitting name." He gestured toward the bar, "Can I buy you a drink?" Felicia smiled, "Sure."

After sharing a drink, the two of them hit the dance floor. Felicia could not believe what a good dancer Aiden was. Most of the big muscular guys that she had met were stiff and awkward when they were dancing but Aiden moved as if he were one of Usher's backup dancers. When they took a break from dancing, Felicia briefly noted that she had lost track of her friends. She was looking around for them when Aiden leaned in and kissed her. She found herself lost in his kiss. At first her entire body tensed up, and then gradually it began to relax. She quickly realized that this was the best kiss that she had ever had.

Aiden pulled his lips away as Felicia was still caught up in the ecstasy of it. He looked into her eyes, "Do you want to get out of this place?"

Felicia nodded as Aiden put his arm around her and they walked out of the club. Felicia's friend Nicole saw her leaving with the stranger and she was a little surprised. Felicia was not above hooking up with a guy at a club but she was not prone to leaving with a stranger no matter how good looking he was. Nicole made a move toward the entrance when a wave of people suddenly blocked her way. She called out to her friend but she was sure that Felicia did not hear her. She watched Felicia and the tall stranger walk out into night.

As they walked into the cool night air, Felecia could hardly believe what she was doing. One of her first rules about clubbing was to never leave with a stranger, but she found herself unable to pull herself away from Aiden. She was starting to doubt what she was doing until they had to stop at an intersection and wait for the light to change. As they stood there, Aiden leaned in and kissed her again. With his kiss, he erased any doubts that she may have had. Felicia quickly decided that rules were made to be broken and that Aiden was certainly rule- breaking worthy.

She wrapped her arm around his waist and together they crossed the street when the light changed. When they had reached the other side of the street, Aiden led her down a dimly lit alley way. Normally, this would have stopped Felicia in her tracks but she felt surprisingly safe with Aiden. She attempted to initiate a conversation with Aiden to help ease what nerves she did have about the dark alley," So where exactly do you live?"

Aiden took a quick look around the alley and saw that is was empty of any other people. He smiled. "You might say that it's the most luxurious high rise in the world. Would you like to see it?"

Felicia was about to answer him when from the corner of her eye, she saw a bright light beginning to glow. She turned to see a bright white light emanating from Aiden. She started to scream when he reached out and grabbed her. Then in a flash they both disappeared.

CHAPTER 4

Diana Cain stopped for a moment in front of the door to her Community College Class on Folklore and Myths and looked into the door at the students eagerly awaiting her arrival. She had a degree in English Literature but she had always loved mythology. For a girl who grew up as devoted fan of Hercules the Legendary Journeys and Xena: Warrior Princess, teaching a class in mythology was a dream come true. To a girl who saw herself as frail when she was young, seeing a heroine, even a fictional one in the form of Xena, gave her a reason to believe in her own abilities as woman.

Diana wanted to learn more about her heroes, and while she was glad to learn that Hercules was indeed a mythological character, it took a little wind out of her sails to find that Xena was a creation of Sam Rami. Despite this, she still fell in love with mythology and she was pleased to find that myths and folklore were filled with numerous other powerful women. The Greeks told stories of the Amazons and Athena. The Vikings had the Valkyries, and most of the more powerful deities in Hindu mythology were goddesses.

She took a deep breath and tried to channel the power represented by those women into her. While she was not exactly going to fight a war on an ancient battlefield, for a woman who grew up with self-esteem issues teaching a class full of college freshman was a daunting task.

Diana pulled open the door and immediately approached the SMARTboard. As a tall and athletic strawberry blonde in her mid-thirties, Diana usually got the attention of the male students in their twenties as soon as she entered the classroom. Even though she was a confident single woman, there was a small part of her that appreciated this attention. Overall though, she had much greater desire for her students to look forward to seeing her because of the knowledge she possessed and the manner in which she taught her course as opposed to her looks.

Prior to greeting her class, she picked up the pen for the SMARTboard and began outlining a giant bird. She smiled as she was pleased to see that the bird was pretty much a reproduction of the symbol used by James O'Barr in his Crow novels. She was fan of all forms of mythology after all. She returned the pen to its holder and picked up the remote control for the SMARTboard so that she could conduct her lecture and be free to move about the room.

She turned to the class and began her lecture, "We have covered multiple mythologies, and as we enter the last few weeks of the semester, it is time that we look at connections between many of the myths that we have covered. There are some obvious and easily identifiable examples of how and why some myths are similar. For instance, the Greek god Zeus and the Norse god Thor. Both gods are powerful warriors who control thunder and lightning. The basis for these two characters to have similar backgrounds is easy to identify. Thunderstorms are a common occurrence everywhere on Earth. If you are an ancient Greek or a Viking, a thunderstorm would both enthrall and terrorize you. Prior to Ben Franklin inventing the lightning rod, lightning strikes were known to burn entire city blocks to the ground, so if you lived in ancient times, you were probably well aware of a home or settlement that had been destroyed by a lightning bolt. Given the power of this natural phenomenon, it was only logical to assume that it took a powerful male god to control this power."

Diana stopped talking and took a long look at her class to see if her words were sinking in with them or not. She observed a few students nodding their heads, several jotting down notes, and two or three of them were sleeping. The young professor took a deep breath and then continued with the introduction to the day's discussion, "With that in mind, I present to you the symbol of a giant bird. The Roc in Persian myths, Garuda in Hindu mythology, the Peng from Chinese Mythology, and the Thunderbird from Native American folklore. There are countless other examples of a massive bird represented in various myths. Often the birds are said to be able to carry off the largest land creatures found in that area. The Roc was said to be able to lift an elephant off of the ground and the Thunderbird was reported to do the same to bison on the American Plains."

She stopped again to see that she still had the attention of the majority of the class, "Now, why would so many different people all develop almost exactly the same story?"

Hands shot up all over the class. Diana pointed to an overweight young man sitting in the front row. He put down the coffee he was chugging on to offer his thoughts, "Is it possible that one group of people co-opted another groups myths and slightly changed it to be their own? The Persians and the Hindu's are close enough geographically where the Persians could have taken Garuda and changed him into the Roc."

Diana nodded, "It is almost a certainty that the Persians took some of their myths from the Hindu's, but how does your theory account for the Thunderbird and the Peng? The Chinese and the Native Americans were completely separated from both the Persians and the Hindu's."

The student shrugged and quickly went back to slurping down his coffee. An older woman in the back of the classroom raised her hand and Diana gave her the floor, "Is it possible that the legends are based on factual creatures which are common around the world? Birds of prey for instance, eagles, falcons and such."

Diana smiled, "Excellent deduction!" She then hit her remote opening up the first slide of the presentation which she had constructed, "Ladies and gentlemen, I give to you the Teratorn! A massive eight foot tall bird who hunted our cave-dwelling ancestors. Fossil evidence shows that this massive raptor would use its claws to crush the skulls of our ancestors and then devour them. Luckily for us, the Teratorn went extinct thousands of years ago. In fact, their extinction is thought be one of the factors which allowed our ancestors to leave caves and start forming villages. It is a lot easier to build a hut without having to worry about a giant bird crushing your skull." With the exception of the still two sleeping students, Diana could see that all of the students were focused on what she was saying.

She hit the next slide on her presentation, "Clearly, even the Teratorn was not the size of the Peng or the Roc and it was long gone by the time the Persians, the Chinese, and others that made these myths. With that in mind though, we can see how from the time of the Teratorn until the time of these great civilizations, word of mouth recalled these once true threats to humans and turned them in them into exaggerated myths. My point is that the myth of the giant bird, like all myths, has some basis in truth." Diana saw some of her students nodding and she advanced the presentation to its next slide. She was about to speak when she noticed her supervisor enter the room with a man dressed in black from head to toe. Thinking that this was some surprise observation, she continued her lecture, "This is the basis for your final paper. You are to choose a mythological character, idea, or event and write a paper explaining a possible real world connection to the myth."

Diana looked over to see her supervisor gesturing that he needed to talk to her. She nodded in reply and then spoke to her class, "Okay everyone, pair up in groups of three and start brainstorming ideas for your papers. I will be around to check with each group in ten minutes."

Diana was walking over to her supervisor when the man in black stepped forward and held up a badge, "Mrs. Cain, my name is Agent Raymond and I work for the Department of Defense."

CHAPTER 5

Luke had made it home and was going through the usual hectic process of feeding his youngest daughter, cooking dinner for everyone else, and packing lunches for the next day. While this was a lot to squeeze into a half hour period, he was quite proud of himself that he was able to it. He turned around to pull dinner out of the oven when he heard his wife walk in through the front door. Like most men, he did not always show it but that opening of the door, signaling that Melissa had made it home, was the sound that he most looked forward to each day.

On the surface, it meant that he would have some assistance with the dozen different things that his daughters needed help with. More importantly, though, it meant that he could see the love of his life. Luke and Melissa had begun dating in high school and even back then anyone who was acquainted with them knew that they would end up together. Their story was right out of a teen romance movie.

In school, Luke was a lanky kid who sometimes tripped over his own feet, but his sense of humor and sparkling personality made him fast friends with almost everyone that he met. In many ways, he was one of the most popular kids in school. While not the most athletic student on the varsity sports team, he was by far the hardest working. That combined with his ability to deliver quick quips won over almost everyone. He was friends with all of the different high school groups of guys - the jocks, the nerds, etc.

Luke's personality was such that he could talk to any girl in school and hold their attention as if he was their best friend. Despite these qualities, in high school Luke did not have much luck in the way of dating. All of the girls thought he was great and loved him as friend but they did not see him as boyfriend material. All of them, except for Melissa. Melissa was the prototypical teen movie girl. The quiet girl who had those very pretty 'girl next door' looks that no one noticed because she was not a cheerleader or star soccer player. Luke himself really didn't notice Melissa until the day that she asked him out.

Luke was surprised but he accepted her offer and from that point on their relationship went forward. Melissa and Luke were a good balance for each other. They were the perfect example of opposites attracting. Melissa, the quiet person who always considered other's feelings, but who was also afraid to push her limits or to accept a challenge. Luke was an outgoing individual who was always looking for the next way he could challenge himself and validate his abilities. Together they helped each other grow as individuals, and as a couple. Luke helped pull Melissa out of her shell and pushed her as much as he could, while Melissa tempered Luke's sometimes overzealous need to challenge himself.

They were married as soon as Luke graduated with his teaching degree. Ten years of fun and the occasional argument were ahead for the couple as they built their careers and enjoyed each other. Finally, they had reached a point in their lives when they were ready to move forward and be real adults. It was at that point, that their first daughter was born. The couple had waited three years until their first daughter had crossed the threshold from toddler to little girl when they decided to have their second child. Shortly thereafter, their second daughter came into their lives. Their nights of fun quickly changed from staying out all night to getting up early to coach and run off to different sports and activities with the kids. It was a busy life but they were happy with the life that they had made and with each other.

All of these thoughts cascaded through Luke's head as he thought about the conversation he was about to have with Melissa. A new challenge had been presented to Luke, a challenge that he knew almost nothing about, and here he was about to ask Melissa to move away from everything that they had done and to accept this new challenge with him. While the pressure would be on Luke, he knew that the moving to Virginia and embarking on a new direction in life would be difficult for Melissa. She was comfortable where she was and, while the thought of leaving that behind for the unknown was exhilarating for Luke, it would be terrifying for Melissa. There was one part of Melissa's personality that Luke could appeal to in this instance. Above all else, Melissa was a practical person and the suggestion of three times his current salary would weigh heavily on convincing her to agree with him to take the offer from the D.O.D.

Melissa walked in and kissed him, "My day was terrible, we were down two people and I had to work through lunch to get everything taken care of." She continued to fill Luke in on her day while he washed the dishes and half-heartedly listened to her tale. His mind was too busy organizing his thoughts about how discuss the mysterious but lucrative offer from the D.O.D.

When Melissa had finished talking, Luke took a deep breath and then filled her in on his visit, "I had a very strange visit from the Department of Defense today at school."

Melissa raised her eyebrows in confusion, "The Department of Defense! What on Earth did they want with you?"

Luke smiled, "They wanted to offer me a job for three times my current salary and full benefits for you and the kids."

Melissa ran over and hugged him, "That's tremendous! I told you that if you just kept trying something would come up for you! What is the job about? I can't image what the D.O.D. would want with someone who teaches students with autism. I know you tell me how tough those kids can be but I don't see them being on the front lines in Iraq or anything."

Luke took a deep breath, "That's one of the two catches to the job. I don't exactly know what it is that they want me to do." Melissa stood there waiting for the second catch. Luke hesitated for a moment and then he filled her in the second stipulation to the job, "If I accept the job, we would have to move to Virginia. They have offered to move us at no cost to us and you and the kids would be coming with me as well."

Melissa rolled her eyes, "So I would have to quit my job and we would have to pull Stacy out of school and away from her friends. What about our families? Everyone that we know lives up here."

Luke had been prepared for this discussion and his response was slow and measured, "Honey, you have been talking about leaving your job for years. You have also often said that you wish you could spend more time with the kids. This is the chance that you have been waiting for. With the money that I will be making and with our housing paid for, you won't need to work anymore. You can stay home with the kids! Stacy is only in kindergarten and she has her dad's personality. She makes friends quickly wherever she goes. She will be fine. Sally is still a baby and it won't make any difference to her. With the money that I will be making, we will have the ability to send the girls to any college that they want to attend when they graduate high school. As for our families, Virginia is only a six hour drive from here and an hour flight. They will be able to fly us right into Maguire Air force base whenever we have free time." Luke waited for his words to sink in then continued with his thoughts, "I feel like this is the chance that we have been waiting for. The chance to take the next step in our lives. I think we should go for it. I know you are scared of the unknown, but I feel that together we can handle anything this world can throw at us! I am asking you to take this chance with me, but at the same time I am telling you that I won't take this chance without you. If you feel strongly that we should pass on this offer, I am okay with that. Like you said, something else will come along."

Melissa smiled with joy. She knew Luke and she knew how much a chance like this would mean to him and still he was willing to pass it all up for her no questions asked. How could she say no to him in this instance? This offer appeared to be everything that they had ever wanted. She was scared of the unknown but more than anything she loved Luke and their kids. This position at the D.O.D would secure all of their futures. She hugged Luke again, "Of course I will go with you. I would go with you to the ends of the Earth."

While her response was something that wives typically said to their husbands, Luke knew that when she said it she actually meant it. What Luke did not know is how true her words would come to be.

Chapter 6
The Atlantic Ocean

The Merchant ship, the Mockingbird, was making its monthly trip of taking American made cars to Africa. The ship was the size of a city block and housed nearly as many people. The crew worked around the clock in three separate shifts. One crew was on duty running the ship and checking the inventory on a regular basis, one crew was off duty, and the third group of crew members was sleeping soundly.

Tony Johnson was a former naval man who had had left the military and taken to the life of a merchant marine. He loved being on the water and, while he was a brave man who had served his country with pride, he was happy to be on a ship that was not heading into a war zone. He found that it was much easier to live on the water he loved so much when his life wasn't in danger from a foreign enemy.

Tony had just finished his shift and was currently off duty. There were literally dozens of things to do on the ship when someone was off duty. The ship had a movie theater, a night club, and a full gym amongst other things. Still, with all of the comforts that the modern ship offered, Tony preferred the classic method of playing cards to pass the time when he was off duty. He and several other shipmates had a bi-weekly poker game that Tony was heading to. He had been on a hot streak the past several weeks and he was looking forward to continuing it. Tony walked into the mess hall where the game was going to take place to find several of his shipmates waiting for him.

John Harmon turned to Tony and smirked, "There's the hot hand! The other guys were wondering if you were going to show up or not. I told them that a smart man would take a few weeks off and keep the money that he had won until we got to shore where he could use it. I told them that with you they have nothing to worry about because not coming is what a smart man would do."

The three other men burst out laughing at John's comment. Unfazed by their jeering, Tony confidently walked over to the table and sat down, "I don't to need to be a smart man. I just need to smarter than you knuckleheads. Now, let's play same poker."

Tony sat down and John shuffled the deck and started to deal the cards out. He was in the middle of dealing when he looked down to see a strange blue light emanating from the floor below him. He tapped John on the shoulder, "What the hell is that?"

The light appeared to be coming right through the floor and it almost seemed as if the light itself was spinning as it rose. The light touched John's boot and he began screaming in pain, "AHHHH, my foot! It feels like it is being cut to pieces!"

The other sailors jumped onto the poker table as John's foot gave out underneath him causing him to fall to the floor. Tony watched in disbelief as the blue light continued to swirl around John, dissolving his body but leaving his clothes seemingly unaffected. In mere seconds, John's body was simply erased from existence.

Tony and his remaining friends shrieked in terror as the light began to wash over the sides of the table that they were standing on. A moment later, Tony's feet felt the pain that John had described when light had touched him. Tony's scream changed from a shriek of fear to a bellow of anguish as the light dissolved his foot within his shoe. He began to fall and he reached out to grab one of his fellow sailors for support. Tony and his friend both tumbled into the swirling blue light. The last thing that Tony saw was the brilliant blue light and then his eyes were torn to shreds. His scream was cut short as his throat suffered the same fate. Tony felt three more seconds of agonizing pain before he felt nothing at all.

Ten minutes after Tony had passed away, the entire crew of the Mockingbird had shared his fate. Piles of clothes were all that remained of the over three hundred crew members onboard. The Mockingbird continued to float across the ocean as ghost ship while the blue light that surrounded it began to expand.

Chapter 7

In the past twenty four hours, Diana had been put onto a military flight to Virginia and driven to an instillation in the Appalachian Mountains. She was put in a small briefing room where she was told that she would need to await the arrival of a second person before she could be completely filled in on why the D.O.D. needed her "expertise" as they put it. She was unsure exactly how her skills as an English major could help out National Security but the agent who spoke to her made the situation seem pretty grave. The generous package that they offered her was also a pretty good incentive to accept the new position.

Her phone had been taken from her when she entered the facility. All that she was afforded were a few magazines to look at to pass the time. The room had four white walls with no windows and no pictures. It was the dullest room that she had ever found herself in. After an hour or so of waiting, the door opened and a tall, athletic-looking, middle-aged man entered the room and stood in the doorway assessing the room as she had when she entered it. Diana looked the man over and thought that, while not model good looking, he was still attractive. As she was assessing him, she noticed the wedding ring on his left hand and she immediately rushed the thoughts of how attractive he was or was not out of her mind.

The man had the same confused look on his face that Diana was sure she possessed when she was ushered into the room. Never one to be shy, Diana walked over to man and introduced herself, "Hi, I am Diana Cain. From the look on your face, I guess you were offered a mysterious position with the D.O.D as well."

Luke shook hands with the attractive professor, "Yes. I am Luke Davis. Do you have any idea what all of this is about?"

Diana shook her head, "All I know is that they are bringing me in here primarily as a consultant. I work as a professor of myth and folklore at my local community college. Why the government needs my services, I have no idea. I was told that I would not be heading into a currently active combat zone."

Luke shrugged, "I am Board Certified Behavior Analyst. I work as a teacher in a school for students with autism. I was approached only yesterday about this position and today my family and I were flown down here from New Jersey. Other than that, my story is pretty much like yours. I have no idea why the D.O.D needs me." Luke scanned the room again and smiled, "Well, at least they have placed us in a stimulating environment while we wait."

Diana giggled at her fellow teacher's dry sense of humor and responded quickly, "Yes, it appears that the interior decorating techniques of the D.O.D. are second to none."

Her comment caused Luke to laugh and she was sure that each of them could feel some of the tension from the situation ease out of the room.

The wall on the far side of the room from them suddenly disappeared revealing a two way mirror. A tall and muscular man with a uniform on, which identified him as a general, stood behind the mirror. Next to the general stood a short, overweight man wearing a lab coat who Diana guessed was a scientist. The wall-length mirror slid open and the general stepped forward with the scientist behind him.

The general approached them and started speaking, "Please excuse the theatrics. I just wanted to get a quick look at the two of you prior to introducing myself. I am glad that you two seem to be getting along so well. You two will be working together for the foreseeable future on what is likely the most important operation since the Manhattan Project."

Diana was shocked by the man's claims and from Luke's facial expressions she could see that he shared her surprise. Before either one of them could speak, the general continued his introduction, "My name is General Sam Parsons. Please have a seat. We do not have much time to waste. I will explain to both of you why you are here and the situation that your skills can help our government address."

Diana and Luke sat down with their eyes fixed on the general as he continued to brief them on the situation, "Let me first start by explaining why we recruited Ms. Cain and then I shall address Mr. Davis's role in the situation." The general took a deep breath, "Ms.

Cain, would you please enlighten us as to the nature of your Master's thesis?"

Diana's mind was awash with confusion. In her mind, she was thinking how a thesis on real world explanations for myths fit in with the D.O.D. The general asked her again, "Ms. Cain, as I said time is of the essence, please inform us as to the nature of your thesis."

She took a deep breath, "The gist of it is that many of the ancient myths were based in reality. For instance, the discovery of the giant squid seems to have given credence to the Vikings legend of the Kraken. There are other examples of animals, either living or extinct, that explain many of the beasts that appear in mythology. I also explored the possibility that people with peak human abilities or attributes could have been the basis for the myths of ancient heroes." She paused for a moment as she would were she speaking to one of her classes to ensure that everyone was following her, "For instance, the giant warrior Ajax might have been a real person who suffered from gigantism such as the professional wrestler, Andre the Giant. Achilles perceived invulnerability can, to a much less exaggerated extent, been seen in someone like Cal Ripken Jr. who is highly resistant to injury." She smiled, "To use professional wrestling as an example again, didn't anyone else think that The Rock was the perfect person to play Hercules in a movie?" She laughed, "I mean, a world class athlete with his physique would surely have been seen as a demi-god in ancient times."

The general prompted her once again, "What of the gods themselves Ms. Cain? How did they fit into your hypothesis?"

Diana sighed, "The gods themselves are the most difficult part of my thesis to account for. I, of course, turned to the works of Erik Von Daniken and others who suggested that the ancient gods were extraterrestrial beings. I did deviate from his idea though in that I offered the idea that the gods did not come from another planet. Physics is not my field of study but I did find that what little theoretical data we have on interstellar travel suggests that, while possible, it is highly impractical." She paused for a moment. It had been a while since she had to defend this section of her thesis and she wanted to make sure that she had her information correct, "To travel through interstellar space, you would need to travel at the speed of light. Einstein proved that as a body approaches the speed of light, time slows down for that object but remains constant for everything else in relative time and space." In her mind, she was thinking that she must sound like one of the Doctor's companions from a late night BBC marathon. Diana refocused then continued, "With that in mind, even if an advanced civilization existed that could travel at light speed, they would know that do so would be a waste of time. Let's say that a ship of aliens had left their planet and traveled at light speed for two years, worked on another planet for a year, and then traveled back to their home planet for two more years at light speed. From the perspective of the aliens on the ship, they would have been gone for six years but from the perspective of the people on their home planet they would have been gone for over six thousand years."

She stopped once more to make sure that everyone was following her. She felt reassured when she saw the man in the lab coat nodding his head. She had no idea what he did but he looked scientific and he seemed to agree with what she was saying. Before the general could ask her to continue again, she finished her explanation, "Think of what a difference six thousand years makes. We are talking about the difference between today and four thousand B.C.! Anyone who knew of them and their mission would be long dead, and society would have advanced to the point that the aliens who had left on the mission would no longer recognize it. Then there is the possibility that in six thousand years their entire society would have gone extinct. Then you need to consider what exactly would the aliens on the ship have accomplished on their mission?"

General Parsons and the scientist hung on every word that she said while Luke continued to just stare at her with a quizzical look on his face. She guessed that, much like herself, he was even more confused than ever as to why they were here. She looked back at the general and finished reviewing her thesis, "I speculated that the ancient gods may have indeed come to Earth and helped shape early humanity, but I suggested that instead of coming from another planet, they may have made the much shorter trip from another dimension. Honestly, I would need to look at my thesis again to explain the theoretical science behind it but I know that it was feasible."

General Parsons nodded, "Thank you, Ms. Cain. I am sure that you are wondering why I would have you recite a research paper that you wrote fifteen years ago. The answer quite simply is that you were absolutely correct on almost all of your points."

Diana grimaced," You mean that the ancient gods are real?"

Parsons sighed, "They are more than just real. What I am about to tell the two of you is currently classified information, but over the next few weeks it won't matter because the entire world will soon learn the horrifying truth that is facing our species." He took a deep breath and then continued, "The Ancient gods are real. Specifically, The Asgardians, the Olympians, and the Mesopotamian gods. All three pantheons are members of the same interdimensional race. One month ago, members of this race contacted several world leaders in secret to discuss their plan for humanity."

Parson's grabbed a nearby chair and sat down, "It seems that these beings see themselves as protectors of planets capable of sustaining life. By human standards, these creatures are extremely long lived if not downright immortal. We don't really know for sure. When they met with our world leaders, the beings had informed them that centuries ago they had left the Earth with the idea that we humans would become caretakers of the planet. They felt that through the skills that they claim to have taught us that we would be capable of caring for the planet in their absence. After inhabiting other dimensions for several thousand years, the gods have returned to check on the Earth. When they saw how we are destroying the planets eco-system and over populating it, they decided that we needed to be exterminated."

Parsons was beginning to sweat. He removed a handkerchief from his pocket and wiped his brow. He folded it neatly, then continued with his briefing, "They even went so far as to explain to our leaders that they would replace humanity with hybrids of our two species and that they would soon be abducting our planet's most desirable young males and females to mate with. The plan is that, once the rest of humanity had been erased, the offspring of these interactions would become the new dominant species on the planet. They claim that since these hybrids will have the god's blood in them, they will be better able to care for the planet rather than destroying it as we are. To avoid mass panic, the leaders of the various countries who attended the meeting have all agreed to keep this information from the public."

Luke finally spoke up, "If this is true, then surely our government would have responded to such a threat quickly."

Parson's nodded, "We tried to respond. The gods are just as arrogant as their myths claim them to be. The Olympian faction boldly proclaimed that they would be stationed on top of Mount Olympus itself. Naturally, a squadron of jets was sent to turn the mountain into rubble. As the planes were approaching the mountain, the Olympians unleashed an EMP that shorted out our jets in mid-air causing them to crash into the sea. After the failure of sending in jets, we decided to take the low tech approach of sending troops to scale Mount Olympus and engage these beings in close quarter combat. That turned into another disaster. A naval destroyer brought several teams of Navy SEALS to the shores of the Aegean Sea. The SEALS landed and then headed for Mount Olympus but when they reached the foothills near the mountain, they ran into what in today's terms would be referred to as two kaiju."

Luke shook his head in disbelief as Diana tried to clarify the situation, "You mean giant monsters? Like in the Godzilla or Pacific Rim movies?"

Parson's smiled, "Yes, exactly like in those movies. The team ran into what they said looked like a giant woman with the body of a snake and a three headed dog. Both of the creatures we estimated to be about 50 plus meters in height. They slaughtered the SEAL team in under three minutes. To emphasise their power, the gods sent a kaiju that was reported to look like a massive bull with the tail of a fish to attack the destroyer that brought the team to Greece."

Diana quickly spoke up, "The snake woman must be Echidna and the three headed dog is obviously Cerberus. From the description of the sea monster, I would say that it was an Ophiotaurus." She paused for a moment, "General, I am sorry to reference a movie again but given what is happening it almost

SCOURGE OF THE GODS

seems appropriate. Are these gods pulling a Pacific Rim on us? Are they going to use giant monsters to destroy humanity?"

The general shrugged, "We don't know what they are going to do, and that is why we need you. You seem to have a better grasp on how ancient gods fit into the real world better than anyone else and you have a deep understanding of various forms of mythology. To at least partially answer your question though, the kaiju currently seem to be utilized to protect specific targets such as Olympus. I had mentioned that the gods were arrogant and that in the next few weeks none of this would be classified anymore. It won't be classified anymore because when the gods met with our world leaders last month they told them that they would give humanity one month to put our affairs in order before they began wiping us off the face of the Earth. As you can imagine that means whatever they are going to do will start any day now."

Parsons placed his hand on top of Diana's, "Ms. Cain, I don't like the idea of working with civilians and while you may be a long shot to help us, at best I am out of other options. Up until this point, the Olympians have been the most active of three sects of gods. We suspect that they may be the most active of the three sects because we attacked them since we know where they are. In the next few weeks, all three sects will begin initiating their attacks. From our attacks on the Olympians, it seems that they are utilizing methods and monsters from what we thought were mythology. The first step in fighting back is identifying what the threats are, moving as many civilians away from it as possible, and then retaliating. I need you to work with me and my team on sifting through information on strange occurrences and determining if they may fit into the mythology of any of three sects. Identifying a threat after it has attacked is not nearly as useful as seeing it beforehand. Will you help us?"

Diana placed her other hand on top of the Generals, "Of course I will, General. What other option do I have? To sit around and wait for the world to end?" She removed her hands from Parsons's and leaned back in her chair, "What is the response that we are going to take if I find something. Machines are useless against EMP's and soldiers can't battle Kaiju."

Parson's looked to the scientist, "This is Doctor Jonathan Toombs, and he has something that might be able help us battle these gods and monsters."

Toombs smiled at Diana and she smiled back, well aware that the doctor had been undressing her with his eyes ever since she had first entered the room.

Parson's then turned his attention to Luke, "The issue is that Doctor Toombs is going to need Mr. Davis's help to activate our counter offensive."

Luke shook his head, "I don't know anything about weapons systems."

Toombs smiled, "This weapon is not a system! Mr. Davis, Ms. Cain, please follow me. It is time that you both met Chimera."

CHAPTER 8
THE ATLANTIC OCEAN: CRUISE SHIP HORIZON

Dave stumbled over a lounge chair by the pool in a drunken stupor and barely managed to stop himself from falling into the water fully clothed. He laughed at himself and took another swig of the expensive imported beer that he was drinking. He shuffled away from the pool, took out his phone, and opened the app that helped him track all of the beers that he tasted while on the cruise. His body swiveled as he attempted to steady himself. He squinted in an attempt to straighten out his eyesight so that he could see the label of the beer that he was enjoying.

As his eyesight came into focus, he saw a shapely silhouette standing alone and looking out over the ocean. Dave knew that he was more than a little buzzed but it almost looked as if the ocean was giving off a light blue glow that outlined the woman's body. Dave was a very good looking man in his late twenties and, aside from taking this cruise with a few of his buddies to try new beers, he had also taken the trip to try new women. He took a moment to compose himself and then he walked toward the woman leaning against the railing.

As he approached the woman, he casually initiated a conversation, "Excuse me, are you shooting a scene in a movie or something? Because other than some scene in a movie where a beautiful woman is standing alone and staring out over the water, I can't think of any reason that you are out here by yourself. "

The woman slowly turned around. She was about five foot five and half feet tall and thin. Her body was perfectly proportioned and she had blonde hair and bright blue eyes. She giggled, "I was just enjoying the view." She smiled and ran her tongue over her lips. The slight move sent Dave's imagination running wild. She took a step closer to him and ran her eyes up and down Dave, "Now I can see that there are much more interesting things to check out on deck."

She took a step closer to Dave, "Can I interest you in some other interesting views back in my cabin?"

Dave's eyes opened a little wider and that was when he noticed the blue light that he thought was in his imagination was getting brighter and moving toward the ship. He pointed out to the water, "Hey do you see −"

Before he could finish his sentence, the woman stepped forward and kissed him. Dave immediately lost track of what he was saying. He was now totally involved in this stranger. She pulled her lips away from his and grabbed his hand, "Come with me, handsome."

Dave was letting himself be pulled along by the woman. As they were passing through the party deck and the mob of people dancing and drinking, he realized that he didn't even know this woman's name. Normally, he was all for a one night stand, but this was a cruise after all and he would be out to sea for the next two weeks with this woman. He could tell that she was something special. If there was any chance of hooking up with this woman for the next two weeks straight, he was going to take it and the heck with all the other women onboard. He finished his beer and tossed the bottle into a recycle bucket, "I am Dave by the way, what's your name?"

She stopped and kissed him again, "You can call me Allison." She looked behind Dave at the ever growing swirling blue light vortex that was coming closer to the ship. Several other people on board had noticed the light as well and they were walking over to the railing and pointing at it. Allison tightened her grip on Dave's hand and rushed toward her cabin. She pulled him into the room, pushed him onto the bed, and then climbed on top of him. She whipped off her shirt and Dave smiled from ear to ear as he stared up at her perfect breasts. She bent down and began kissing him when they suddenly heard horrible screams coming from on deck.

Dave tried to sit up but Allison held him down. He screamed at her, "What the hell is going on out there? It sounds like the end of the world!"

Allison laughed as the blue light began to creep through the walls of her cabin, "Trust me handsome, those good looks of yours have just saved you from hell and brought you a one way trip to heaven." She reached down and kissed Dave once more and in a bright flash of white light they vanished. A second later, the bright blue light washed through her cabin and floated into the cabin next door. The people in the cabin screamed in agony as their bodies eroded into nothingness.

CHAPTER 9

Toombs turned and motioned for the group to follow him. Diana, already aware of her role in the situation, stood and followed him without question. Luke, however, was still as confused as ever. He wanted to ask more questions but what exactly would he ask now that he knew not only that the ancient gods and giant monsters were real but that they were going to initiate the genocide of the human race. The information was currently classified but was he allowed to tell Melissa, and even if he was allowed to tell her, should he? Would letting her know that everyone on the planet was about to die going to make her life any easier? Luke suspected that it would be just as hard for her to hear the news as it was for him, but he had only made it this far in life by sharing his problems with her and he would do so with this issue as well. Then Luke thought about his girls. God in heaven, he could not put this burden on them. Luke decided that he would have to wait until he and Melissa were alone to discuss the matter with her. He also had to make sure that she had enough time to process the information and determine how to keep it from the girls for as long as possible.

One thing he did know was that in order to talk to Melissa about it he needed more information. He was about to start asking his questions when Dr. Toombs starting talking. As a teacher, Luke knew when he was best served to shut up and listen, and this was one of those times.

Toombs spoke with a touch of enthusiasm in his voice as he led the group down a long corridor, "This facility houses the top geneticists in the world, including me. As such, most of the activities that occur here are kept from the public. You may recall a few years ago when the cloned sheep Dolly was first announced to the world?"

Toombs waited for a moment but no one said a word. He shrugged and continued, "Well, we were cloning horses and cows long before that sheep was ever placed in his mother's womb."

They reached a wall with a keypad. Toombs reached down and typed in a code that opened a retinal scanner. He placed his eyes into the scanner and a light flashed across them. Toombs turned toward Luke and Diana, "We will get you two scanned soon so that you have unlimited access to this area as well." A second later, the door opened and the group was hit by the most ungodly odor that both Luke and Diana had ever smelled. The two of them jerked backward at the smell and lifted their hands toward their faces. Luke had to take a moment for his stomach to settle to keep from vomiting on the floor.

Toombs and Parsons winced a little at the smell but clearly they were prepared for it. Toombs laughed, "You never really get used to Chimera's odor but it gets easier to bear each time you are exposed to it. A word of advice though, try taking shallow breaths through your mouth."

Luke and Diana both nodded and as Toombs and Parson's begin walking down the long corridor the two of them followed. Luke took a shallow breath and finally managed to ask the question which was foremost on his mind, "What exactly is Chimera?"

Toombs stopped walking and turned around to look Luke in the eye, "Chimera is not a what, he is a who. That is why we need you, Mr. Davis. It does not do Chimera justice to try and explain who he is until after you have seen him."

Luke nodded, noticing once again that Dr. Toombs clearly felt that he had a flair for the dramatic. With little other choice, Luke indulged the man and refrained from asking any further questions until they saw Chimera.

After walking for a good ten minutes, the group found themselves in almost total darkness. The horrid smell which they had encountered as they entered the corridor had gotten exponentially worse as they got closer to their destination. Toombs suddenly stopped walking causing Diana to bump into him. Luke was sure that the nerdy plump scientist had planned things to happen that way. Toombs half-heartedly apologized to the attractive professor and then once more got on with his over the top theatrics. He shouted as if he was a circus ringmaster, "Lady and Gentlemen, I give you Chimera! The Eighth Wonder of the World!"

With his King Kong quote out of the way, he pulled a lever turning on the lights. The warehouse they were in was enormous.

The entire interior of the building was set up like a forest with a large lake in the middle of it. Luke was unable to see how far the forest extended. He looked up and saw a sign that said one hundred meters at the top of it. Luke did that math in his head and realized that the roof was over three hundred feet high.

Luke returned his eyes to the forest and noticed a large gray-black hill next to the lake. When he saw that the hill was slowly rising and falling, he quickly realized that the hill was a living creature! Luke's eyes opened wide as he took in exactly what he was looking at. The creature was massive. At a quick glance, Luke guessed that it had to be about two hundred feet long. The creature, which took Luke's stunned mind a moment to realize it must be Chimera, was the oddest thing that he had ever seen. It had thick black skin that looked as smooth as ice. Its body and limbs had an overall primate look to it like a gorilla or a chimpanzee. It had long powerful arms and hands, and opposable thumbs. The head and tail were the two aspects that really looked out of place in conjunction to the rest of the body. The face was elongated in proportion to the body. Luke, at first thought that it was a dog-like face, but somehow that description did not seem to fit. Around the neck of the beast was a long shaggy mane similar to that of a lion. Luke's eyes drifted to the monster's tail. It was long, ending in a flat fluke-like tail. The tail reminded Luke of the tails of the porpoise that he and the girls often saw close to the beach when they were at the Jersey Shore.

Toombs was smiling like a smart kid who had just won first place in the school science fair. He stepped in front of Luke and Diana to make sure that they were looking at him as he spoke, "To answer all of the questions that are currently swarming through your minds, Chimera is kaiju that was genetically engineered from the DNA of a Mountain Gorilla, a Lion, and a Sperm Whale." He gestured toward Diana, "I am sure that Ms. Cain can explain the significance of his name."

Diana kept her eyes on the monster as she answered, "In Greek Mythology, the Chimera was a monster that had the combined attributes of a goat, a lion, and a serpent."

Toombs giggled, "Hence the name Chimera and given the threat that we are currently facing, I think that his name is more than a little ironic. Through genetic manipulation of his cells he is a shade over two hundred feet tall when he is standing upright. He also has similarly proportioned strength and muscle density. Most conventional artillery fire will not be able to penetrate his hide. In addition to that, his genes have been altered to help him heal quickly. Even a serious wound will heal within a few days."

The overweight man took a moment to catch his breath before he continued, "He also has all of the attributes of the animals that he is made from. He has the proportional strength of a gorilla his size. Which means he is literally the strongest creature to ever walk the face of the Earth. While he has the hands and feet of the gorilla, he also has retractable lion-like claws in his fingers and toes. Again, these are proportional due to his size. His claws can cut through six feet of solid concrete like it was paper. Lastly, he has the reinforced skull of a sperm whale. His head is a massive battering ram. He can smash through a building without injuring himself! Coolest of all though is that he is able to narrow his sonar beam and use it to disrupt his enemy's sensory organs! It's like getting hit by a sonic boom!" He turned toward Diana and grinned, "The test footage is awesome! I would be happy to screen it for you!"

Parson's interrupted the over exuberant Toombs, "In the interest of getting through this conversation today, please let me finish explaining Chimera's history." He took a slow breath, "As you know, and as the ancient gods have rightly noticed, humans are constantly making the world a more violent and dangerous place. The United States is often put in situations where military action on our part may be needed to intercede in a given situation. Take for instance the recent situation in the Ukraine where Russia has all but taken a large part of it. Given their success in that endeavor, the Russians may decide to repeat this process. Even if protecting its own interests, the US could not directly intervene without causing a war."

Parson's turned his gaze toward the monster, "That is where the idea of Chimera came into play. We took three of the most aggressive animals in the world and used parts of them to engineer a monster."

Toombs quickly interjected, "It's important to note that only three animals were chosen and that they were all mammals! If you try to mix animals from different classifications, the DNA starts to reject the additional parts. Similarly, if you try to use more than three animals in a composite, the DNA becomes too junked up and will not combine properly."

Parson's sighed, "Yes, thank you, doctor. As I was saying, the thought process was that Chimera would be the first of many kaiju that our government could unofficially use to attack a hostile nation. For instance, if our intelligence was indicating that Russia was going to invade Georgia, they might suddenly have a Chimera attack St. Petersburg. The monster would appear from the ocean, attack the city and return without any connection to the US. With a kaiju wading off their shores, Russia would be forced to desert its efforts to invade a neighboring country. If the Taliban starts stirring up trouble in Afghanistan, a giant monster wades through their camp grounds, again with no connection to the US government."

Luke could see the pieces of the puzzle regarding his involvement in this project slowly coming together. He finally ventured to ask his first question, "You are talking about attacking specific targets. How were you planning to take a kaiju composed of three naturally aggressive animals and have it attack a specific target?"

Toombs excitedly jumped into the conversation again, "The idea is really cool. Technically speaking Chimera here was going to be a cyborg. The next step in his evolution was going to be to surgically interface a computer into his brain. That would have allowed us to program instructions into his mind from a secure location. The idea was sound and would still work except for the fact that the threat we are facing uses EMP's as one of their first methods of attack. If Chimera was utilizing an interface, the EMP would short circuit the computer interface. At that point, we would have ancient gods attacking us and a rampaging kaiju on the loose as well."

Luke sighed, "A Behavior Analyst with field experience in dealing with highly-aggressive subjects. That's why I am here isn't it? You need me to train Chimera to attack specific targets using

Applied Behavior Analysis based techniques. That way an EMP will not be able to disrupt the commands he has been given. Am I right?"

Parsons smiled and nodded as Toombs excitedly pointed at Chimera, "It's possible for that approach to work! Chimera is intelligent! In fact, he is very intelligent when compared to most animals! He is far more intelligent than the sum of his parts, which by the way are composed of three very intelligent animals to begin with. We keep him sedated for the most part for obvious safety reasons but we have tested his IQ level. It falls around thirty-five or in roughly the same area as many of your students."

Luke was staring at the colossal beast when Parsons placed his hand on Luke's arm, "Mr. Davis, say hello to your newest student. You have less than two weeks to train him to save the World."

Luke's hands began to sweat and become clammy. It was one of the reactions that his body had when he became stressed or worried. He shook his head and thought that Melissa worried when he was working with a large aggressive student with autism. What was she going to say about him working with King Kong's big brother?

CHAPTER 10

It was nine o'clock at night and Luke had finally gotten the kids washed up and put to bed. Melissa had spent the majority of the day registering their oldest daughter for her new school on the military base. They were both exhausted as they headed to the family room to catch up on the day's events.

Luke let Melissa go first. When she was done describing all of the things that she had accomplished during the day, she asked Luke what he had learned about his new position. Luke composed his thoughts. He then leaned forward, kissed Melissa, and held her hands in his as he spoke, "Honey, I need you to brace yourself. The scope of this position is much greater than we could have ever imagined."

Her face changed to a look of concern, "What's up? Are the hours going to be significantly more than you had thought?"

Luke forced a smile, "The hours don't really matter." He took a deep breath, "Honey, events have unfolded which are quickly leading to the end of the world occurring in the next few weeks and it is up to me and small team of people to keep it from happening."

She looked at him and then burst out laughing, "The end of the world! That's pretty funny! You almost had me there for a minute."

Luke's face was stoic, "It's no joke. The world will quickly come to an end unless we can stop it."

Melissa's face quickly lost its color, "You are serious. What the hell is going on? Is there some kind of pending terrorist attack?"

Luke shook his head, "The truth is far more outrageous than that. What I am about to tell you is currently classified but over the next few weeks events will begin to unfold and the entire world will become aware of the danger that we are in." He stopped talking and looked directly into her eyes. The same eyes that he had looked into and loved for his entire adult life, "Please listen to me on this point. I know that it is a lot to handle, but promise me that for as long as possible we will keep this information from the girls. Heaven forbid if we are not able to prevent this from happening. I do not want their last days with us to be spent in fear about what's coming."

Tears began to well up in Melissa's eyes as she nodded in affirmation of Luke's request. Luke hugged her then continued to fill her in on the situation, "The ancient gods are real and they have returned to Earth. I am talking about the stuff we saw in movies and TV. Zeus, Thor, and others whose names I can't remember. The deal is that they see themselves as protectors of the planet and from their perspective we humans are destroying it."

Melissa was still trying not to cry. Luke kissed her again as he himself tried not to cry. He rubbed his eyes and then continued to explain how he was going to help address this threat, "The government has tried to attack these gods but they can control EMPs. Any weapons that we can use against them the gods simply shut down before they can attack. The government has also tried ground troops to attack these gods but it seems that monsters from mythology are real as well and the gods are using the creatures to protect themselves. A Navy SEAL team was killed by monsters when they tried to storm Mount Olympus."

Melissa sobbed, "Then how are you going to help? You're a teacher for God sake!"

Luke smiled in an attempt to reassure her, "You're right. I am a teacher and that is exactly what they need. The government has made its own kaiju, a giant monster. It's a massive creature over two hundred feet long and they need someone who has experience with aggressive subjects in shaping this monster's behavior so that he will attack the gods and their beasts without going Godzilla on any town that he comes across in the meantime."

Melissa leaned back in her chair, "Train a monster. How are you going to do that?"

Luke squeezed his wife's hand tightly, "That's both the easy part and the tricky part at the same time. The method is easy, using food and positive verbal praise from me we are going to train the monster to attack targets that I direct him to. We are also going to associate images of monsters and giants with negative stimuli to access the monster's natural aggressive tendencies and focus them on acceptable targets."

Melissa stood up and her voice began to increase in volume as the tears streamed down her face, "Targets that you direct him to! Are you telling me that not only will you be working with this monster but that you will also be out there with him fighting these things?"

Luke looked away from her for a minute. He knew that he could not look into her eyes as he delivered the next bit of news. He cleared his throat, "As I said, the gods can control EMPs so any electronics within range of their attack will be knocked out. I am training the monster to respond to my voice using an old fashioned speaking horn. It is sort of like a megaphone without batteries." He laughed a little, "I also get to learn to ride a horse because I have to keep up with the monster while he walks and there is no way I can run that far or fast anymore."

Melissa slapped him across the face and screamed, "Don't do that, Luke. Don't you dare do that to me! You said that you would not be on the front lines of any fight, that this would be a safe job, and that this was the opportunity that we have been waiting for! Now it's the end of the world and you are going to ride a horse as this monster you are teaching tries to fight God knows what."

Luke hugged her and began to cry as well, "Melissa, what other choice do I have? The end of the world is coming. Everyone on the planet is going to die. I have been given the chance to make a difference, to save you and the girls! I can't pass that up no matter the danger to me. I can't just stay here and wait for the end to come or hope that someone else can try and stop this!" He kissed her with all of the emotion that was building up in his body and she responded in kind.

Suddenly, they heard a voice from across the room. Their oldest daughter had been awakened by the argument. The five year old shuffled forward and spoke in a voice barely above a whisper, "Mommy, Daddy, is everything OK? You guys woke me up."

Melissa looked at her little girl and smiled, "Yes honey, we were just talking about how Daddy is going to save the world." Melissa looked up at Luke, "Now you go, Daddy. Go and save the world."

Luke smiled at his wife as their daughter came running over and hugged them too, "I always knew that you were a rescue hero, Daddy!"

CHAPTER II

Diana took off her glasses, titled her head down, and rubbed the back her neck. She took a look around at the room full of computers and the team of five analysts that were sending any of what they had designated as vital information to her. She took a deep breath and then she walked around the room that had been her home for the past ten days. She had accepted her role in this operation but she was still unsure of what exactly she was supposed to do. She knew that her directive was to look for strange occurrences that were transpiring around the globe and to then determine if these phenomenon could be related to one three mythological sects of gods.

It was clear that the government was grasping at straws when they came to her but with the fate of the world in the balance she knew that she had to do all that she could to help out in this crisis. The issue was that she was a professor of mythology not a meteorologist or climatologist. There were literally dozens of natural weather patterns that looked strange to her but in all actuality were totally normal. So far the only unnatural phenomenon that she could identify was Dr. Toombs's inability to accept that she was not interested in him. His comments to her were starting to border on sexual harassment and despite letting him know that he continued on with them. He knew that with the apocalypse looming, a sexual harassment complaint was not a high-level priority.

Diana shook her head to refocus her thoughts and then returned to the data streaming across her computer screens. She read about an earthquake in Chile, a typhoon that had hit Japan, and a sighting of a Sea Serpent off of the coast of South Africa. She thought to herself that according to myth Poseidon could be responsible for the earthquake, the hundred-handed Hekatoncheires could have caused the typhoon, and the sea monster could be any one of a hundred monsters. Of course, they could also have been simply the shifting of tectonic plates, a big storm, and whale seen by drunken people on a yacht. The question was how in the hell was she supposed to figure it out?

She moaned in frustration when she noticed a report about a ship calling in an SOS about a blue vortex in the Atlantic Ocean. It had caught her eye because she was sure that she had seen a similar report before. She began pouring through the stacks of papers which she had flagged as possible events involving the gods. She checked and there was another SOS that had come in! The first call had come from a merchant ship called the Mockingbird and the second ship was a cruise called the Horizon. She looked at the data and as far she could tell the reports had come in from a within a fifty mile radius of each other. She ran over to one of the analysts assigned to help her, "I need you to reposition a satellite to take a look at this area of the Atlantic Ocean."

Luke held his breath as he picked up one of the one hundred pound slabs of squid, beef, and bamboo that had been put together as food reinforcers for Chimera. Luke carefully placed the slab into one of the pouches on the side of Jason the Clydesdale horse that been assigned the task of being Luke's method of transportation when working with Chimera. Agreeing to train a kaiju was difficult enough but Luke didn't think that he would have to train a horse as well. Luke kept a supply of carrots and apples in his pockets to reinforce Jason for working with Chimera. The horse's natural inclination was to run away from the kaiju. To have the horse accept working with the monster, it had to be constantly reinforced as well. The past week of training Chimera had gone well. Toombs had been slowly reducing the amount of sedative that the kaiju was being given. The training started by having Luke ride around Chimera on Jason and using his speaking horn to send positive verbal praise to Chimera. Basically, Luke rode around the kaiju and shouted things like. "Good boy, Chimera," or "Good Morning, I am glad to see you." After riding around beast and delivering the praise, Luke would leave one of the reward slabs near Chimera's mouth.

During this process, Chimera was still barely awake and Luke was in little danger, but these first steps were extremely vital to the kaiju's training. Luke was establishing that his voice meant positive things for Chimera. When this was established, the sedative was lessened again and Luke started placing simple demands on Chimera prior to delivering the verbal praise and food reinforcer. The first set of directions was to have Chimera follow Luke and Jason for three steps prior to praising him and giving him the food slab. By the end of the first day, Luke had been able to space out the reinforcement enough that Chimera was able to follow Luke for three trips around the compound prior to receiving a food slab.

After establishing simple commands such as, "Follow me!" Luke introduced more difficult commands. Several large trailers and farm equipment were placed around the compound and Luke would direct Chimera to pick up a piece of equipment and then place it down. Luke found that the best method for Chimera to learn a new task was by modeling it for him first. If Luke wanted Chimera to pick up a forklift, Luke would first pick a toy forklift. He would then point to an actual forklift and direct the kaiju to pick it up. Luke was amazed at how intelligent the beast was and how quickly that he learned new skills. Luke found that he only needed to model a new direction on the first trial. Once he had shown Chimera something once, a verbal directive would suffice to get him to repeat the move again. During this process, Luke had gained an appreciation for what a truly magnificent creature Chimera was. Additionally, Parson's and Toombs were also impressed at how well Luke's behavior modification techniques were working for Chimera.

Today would be one of Chimera's most important and most dangerous tests. Today was the day that Chimera would be instructed to attack an enemy and more importantly cease attacking after destroying his target. Given the natural aggressive tendencies of the animals that comprised Chimera, getting him to attack should not prove difficult but making sure that he did not destroy everything else in sight after defeating his enemy was crucial to his effectiveness in the field.

Toombs had made up a mock adversary of steel beams and canvas. It looked something like a giant upright turtle. Luke had heard Diana say something about a Gamera movie. Luke didn't really care; as the long as the target served its purpose, it could like a giant Cookie Monster for all that he cared.

Luke had a human-sized dummy placed in front of the target. He rode Jason up to the dummy and commanded Chimera to follow him. The kaiju lumbered after the horse as Luke rode up to the dummy. Luke jumped off of the horse, lifted up his speaking horn, and then shouted "Attack!" Luke then charged at the dummy and began hitting and kicking it. He then lifted his horn and yelled "Stop!" Luke then backed away from the dummy. He quickly moved Jason clear of the danger zone, then he pointed at the massive mock turtle, and screamed, "Chimera, attack!"

Upon hearing the command, Chimera savagely beat his chest and unleashed a roar that shook the entire compound. The kaiju then charged at the target. When he reached the turtle, Chimera first lifted both of his fists above his head and then brought them crashing down onto the target's shoulders, crushing them instantly. Chimera then grabbed the target by its arms and dug his claws into them. With his grip locked on the target, Chimera roared again and began smashing his bulky head into the target's chest causing it to cave in. The kaiju finished the attack by biting into what was left of the model's head and tearing it off.

Luke raised his speaking horn and shouted, "Stop!" At hearing the command, Chimera immediately backed off of the monster, sat down on the ground, and looked toward Luke. Luke shouted through his speaking horn, "Good job attacking, Chimera, and even better job stopping!" He then tossed the kaiju one of the food slabs which Chimera quickly devoured.

Luke returned Jason to his stable and then he took the elevator up to the observation deck where Parson's and Toombs were observing the training session. He was surprised to see them speaking with Diana. When Luke walked over toward them, Parsons quickly spoke up, "Ms. Cain believes that she has identified the method that the Olympians are using to attack us. Everyone get yourselves and supplies ready. Chimera goes into action in six hours."

CHAPTER 12

Diana sat in the briefing room of the massive ship and put together the last few pieces of her presentation to review with the team prior to mission launch. The last twelve hours had been a whirlwind of activity and she was already exhausted. Their target was in the middle of the Atlantic Ocean and the process of transporting Chimera to the location was a vast undertaking. First, Luke, had to ride his horse and have Chimera follow him to an area where the kaiju could be loaded onto the Argos. It was the largest ship ever constructed and like everything else that was part of this mission it was given a name with a mythological connotation. While the team took the most remote route possible, literally hundreds of people still saw Chimera and had recorded his walk through the forest on their phones. Those videos were then quickly posted to the web.

The government still had no official comment on the giant monster that had just lumbered out of the woods of Virginia. Once they had reached the naval base, Luke led Chimera onto the Argos. The Argos was equipped with a cargo bay that served as Chimera's holding cell on the ship. The Argos was a nuclear-powered ship but in addition to its nuclear reactor, it also was home to the world's largest sails. In the event that it was hit by an EMP, the sails would still provide the ship with some manner of propulsion.

Diana's thoughts refocused on the present when the door to the briefing room opened and Parson's, Toombs, and Luke entered and stood behind their seats. Luke took the seat next to Diana. Having him next to her for support gave her confidence a small boost. While the interactions between the two of them had been limited, Diana had found that Luke had a quick wit and the same dry sense of humor that she possessed. She also found that the two of them were quickly becoming good friends.

Prior to sitting down, Parsons turned on one of the massive viewing screens set up in the room. Diana was almost overwhelmed when the visage of the president appeared on screen. Parson's saluted and then spoke to the president, "Good morning,

Mr. President. This is Ms. Cain, she will be briefing us the on the threat that we are currently on route to engage. Following that briefing, Mr. Davis will apprise us of how Chimera will deal with the threat."

The president nodded and said, "Thank you, General. Ms. Cain, if you please."

Diana took a second to think about how that a few short weeks ago she was addressing a group of college students on an elective course and now she was talking to the president about how to save the world. She took a deep breath and then started her briefing, "Thank you, Mr. President. Gentlemen, the information that we have gathered suggests that a mysterious blue vortex has appeared in the center of the Atlantic Ocean. The vortex seems to be hovering at a height of roughly three hundred feet off of the surface of the ocean. It is also expanding in diameter." She clicked a key on her computer and brought up several satellite images, "The first image is from ten days ago and at that point the vortex was roughly ten miles in diameter." She moved to the next image, "This slide is from five days ago at which point the vortex was fifty miles in diameter." Diana moved to the third slide, "Today the vortex is roughly one hundred miles in diameter. Since the Vortex has appeared, we have had at least two ships reporting an SOS that a light blue light was approaching their ship. After the SOS was received, there was no more contact from either ship. Satellite tracking systems show that the ships are still floating on the ocean but there is still no communication from either vessel. We have sent several military planes to fly around the perimeter of the vortex. They have reported that whales and other sea animals are clearly seen to be entering and exiting the vortex without any negative effects."

Diana clicked another slide and the form of a gargantuan cone shaped creature with a huge circular mouth filled with teeth appeared on the screen, "Everything that we have encountered thus far seems to be from Greek mythology. One thing that is consistent within the mythology of all three sects that we are facing is that they are extremely arrogant and proud. The fact that so far we seem to only be facing threats from the Olympians seems to indicate that the three sects have opted to at the very least to not coordinate their efforts. As such, we may be able to deal with each sect individually instead of facing them as a unified front. I would suggest that the three sects may even see who can destroy the human race as some competition between themselves to prove whose methods are most effective. While there is no precedent in mythology for different sects interacting, there are multiple examples of gods within the same sect having competitions amongst themselves where they use humans as their pawns. Since, so far at least, we seem to only be dealing with the Olympians, I feel that we would do best to look at current threats through the scope of Greek mythology."

Diana looked at the gathered group of men as she would her students to see that she had their attention. From the looks on their faces, she was sure that they were hanging on her every word. Even the president seemed enthralled by what she was saying. She took a sip of water and then continued, "Using Greek mythology as guide, it is my belief that this vortex is being created by the mythological creature known as the Charybdis. It is a sea monster whose inhalations form a deadly whirlpool which pull in any ships that come near it. I would suggest that what was thought to be a whirlpool by the ancient Greeks was actually an energy vortex which they lacked the understanding to properly describe as such. My theory is that the Charybdis is generating a vortex that is specifically designed to affect humans. Which is why there are reports of sea life entering and exiting the vortex. My analysts tell me that if the vortex continues to grow at the rate it currently is, that it will blanket the entire Atlantic Ocean within the next five days. At that point, the vortex will reach the coast of Europe, Africa, North America and South America. We suspect that anyone who comes into contact with the vortex will most likely vanish and presumably die as it seems that the crew and passengers of the missing ships seem to have done."

Diana took a few steps away from the screen that she was using to display the images behind her, "There is one more thing to consider if indeed this vortex is emanating from the Charybdis. In mythology, the Charybdis is paired with the Scylla. The Scylla is a giant six headed serpent with razor sharp teeth. Given how we have seen the Olympians use monstrous creatures to protect other targets such as Mount Olympus, I would suggest that we prepare ourselves for the possibility that the Scylla may be guarding the Charybdis." Diana walked back to her seat. "That is all I have regarding the possible mythology for this mission. I will know turn the briefing over to General Parsons who will review the tactile approach that will be employed." She sat down and felt a wave of pressure pour off of her body as she hit the chair. Luke leaned over toward her and whispered, "Good job."

General Parson's stood up and loaded his presentation onto the screen, "Thank you, Ms. Cain. Satellite images show that a new island seems to have sprung up in the middle of the Atlantic Ocean. The Island seems to be comprised of a beach-like terrain with a large lake in the center of it. The island itself is not shrouded in the blue vortex. This eye of the vortex is why, when the vortex was first noticed on radar, most meteorologists classified it as a hurricane. It was not until we utilized military satellites that we were able to see the new island. We believe that the Charybdis is settled in the lake located in the center of the island and that it is using the terrain as a tuning fork of sorts to control the specifics of the vortex. The plan is to launch Chimera from this vessel near the edge of the vortex. Since the vortex does not seem to be affecting sea life, we feel confident that Chimera will be able to swim through the vortex without being harmed by it. The fact that the vortex itself does not seem to affecting the island itself is also a benefit to us. With no vortex on the island, we feel confident that we can get a low flying non-military helicopter to fly above the vortex and over the island. Mr. Davis will be on the helicopter and we will tow one of Chimera's food reinforcers from the helicopter so that Chimera will follow us to the island. The helicopter should be able to land on the island and with no vortex on the island itself Mr. Davis will be able to direct Chimera to attack the Charybdis. The hope is that by using a non-military helicopter that the machine will not be hit with an EMP. However, should it be hit with an EMP, Mr. Davis will be strapped to a paratrooper in a glide suit. The trooper will attempt to jump out of the helicopter and glide to the island if need be. Are there any questions?"

The president spoke up from his monitor, "Just one. Mr. Davis, are you and Chimera up to this task? You are a civilian and we have yet to see how Chimera operates out of a controlled environment."

Luke stood up, "Mr. President, I have seen Chimera's strength first hand. If Satan himself were at the center of that vortex, I feel that Chimera could handle him. He has responded very well to his training and I am confident that his performance in the field will follow suit. As far as I am concerned, my family is currently on the east coast that the vortex is heading for. There is nothing I will not do to save them."

The president nodded, "Then Godspeed to you son. Lady and Gentlemen, go and show those gods whose planet this is!"

CHAPTER 13

Luke looked down from the helicopter to see the blue vortex swirling roughly one hundred feet below him. The vortex obscured his view of the ocean, but with the food reinforcer trailing from the helicopter, Luke was sure that Chimera was following them and that thought gave him some comfort. His words to the President were not just hollow bravado; he truly did believe that Chimera was capable of facing anything that awaited them at the center of vortex. He squirmed a little to try and make himself more comfortable but being strapped to another man was just awkward no matter how he positioned himself. The man introduced himself only as Sergeant Waller when they were being harnessed together.

Luke's thoughts were interrupted as a bright white flash filled the sky. He heard the pilot scream, "We've been hit by an EMP. The copter is going down! We are going to have to jump for it and try to glide to the island! We are about seventy feet from the shore of the island! I will keep the copter as steady as possible so you two can make a jump for it."

Sergeant Waller jammed Luke's speaking horn into his chest and shouted, "Just hold on tight!" Waller then jumped out of the side of the helicopter and spread his arms open. Luke could feel the wind rushing by his face and trying to pry the speaking horn out of his hands. He forced his face down to take a look at the pilot attempting to make his jump. The pilot jumped from a much lower altitude than Luke and Waller had. Luke watched as the pilot attempted to readjust his body to gain altitude but he only managed to slowly drift downward. Luke and Waller cleared the vortex and saw the shoreline of the island in front of them. Waller forced his head down and the two men went streaking toward the beach. Seconds later, they landed hard on the sand. Waller pulled a chord which separated the two men and they both turned around to see the pilot fall into the vortex just short of its edge. He screamed and then seconds later his empty flight suit landed on the beach. The pilot himself had been totally disintegrated.

Waller shook his head, "Poor bastard he was- ARGHHHH!"

From the side of his vision, Luke saw Waller being yanked into the air. Luke spun around to see Waller in the grips of one of six gigantic serpentine heads. Luke watched in horror as a second head also bit into Waller. The soldier screamed for a brief moment before the two heads tore Waller's body in half. Waller's blood rained down on Luke as he stood still with fear staring up at the horror before him.

The creature's size was immense. Each of the six heads was easily one hundred feet in length. The six snake-like heads were dark gray in color and their mouths were filled with long rows of hooked teeth. The shape and form of the kaiju's necks and heads reminded Luke of specials he had seen on the Discovery Channel about the pythons that were taking over the Florida Everglades. The six heads converged into one long and thin body with squat alligator-like legs and a long lizard-like tail protruding from the end of its torso.

The Scylla lumbered forward and hissed as it moved toward Luke. Luke turned to run and only made it few steps before he reached the shoreline and the deadly blue vortex that formed at the water's edge. Luke was trapped between two forms of agonizing death. He lifted his speaking horn in front of him like a club in a vain attempt to defend himself. The Scylla took a step toward Luke when a ground shaking roar emanated from the swirling light blue vortex. A second later a long snout emerged from the vortex followed by the awesome form of Chimera.

The Scylla stopped moving forward as its heads continued to writhe and its many forked tongues shot in an out of its mouth as its senses tried to comprehend the beast that stood before it.

Luke didn't hesitate to act. He lifted his speaking horn to his mouth and screamed, "Chimera, attack!" Chimera eyes flared wide as he lifted his front paws off of the ground and pounded his chest as he roared a challenge at the Scylla. The Scylla's heads hissed in unison as the two behemoths charged each other.

Luke watched in awe as the two kaiju crashed into each other on the empty beach. The Scylla's necks began to wrap around Chimera's arms, legs, throat, and torso as his hook-like teeth dug into Chimera's flesh. Chimera roared in anger and attempted to lift his arms above his head but the strong necks of the Scylla held the beast's arms in place. Chimera quickly changed tactics by leaning into the serpent and using his massive claws to dig into the Scylla's torso. With his claws sunk into the Scylla's body, Chimera pulled his head backward, stretching the Scylla's necks as far as he could. When he could pull the Scylla's necks no further, Chimera thrust his head forward, adding his own strength and weight to the force of the Scylla's necks pulling him. The move sent his whale-like snout crashing down into the Scylla, driving the monster into the sand. Chimera repeated the move two more times before the Scylla was finally forced to relinquish its grip.

The Scylla's head slithered forward and as one they dug their teeth into Chimera's legs. Chimera roared again and, in a show of unbelievable strength, he lifted the torso of the Scylla over his head. The Scylla maintained its grip on Chimera's legs even as it hung upside down. With another roar, Chimera slammed the Scylla into the sand. The serpent's entire body was jarred from the impact, once more forcing the monster to release its grip. Chimera placed one of his powerful back feet on the torso of the Scylla to pin the foul beast to the ground. Chimera then lifted his hands above his head and brought them down into the Scylla's exposed stomach. Chimera continued to pound on the Scylla and Luke could hear sounds of bones cracking as Chimera reigned blows down onto the serpent. The Scylla's necks were waving wildly in pain at the pounding it was taking. Chimera's head shot forward and his jaws clamped down on two of the Scylla's necks. Chimera pressed down with his leg and pulled up with head, ripping the two necks from the Scylla's torso. Blood sprayed over the entire beach as the Scylla' necks writhed in the agony of their death throes. Within thirty seconds, the Scylla's body had stopped moving and the fountain of blood spraying from its torso slowed to a trickle. With the creature dead before him, Chimera lifted his head to sky, roared and beat his chest in triumph!

Luke could see that Chimera was still in an enraged and battle ready mode and so he quickly gave the kaiju another command. Luke could see the lake roughly about a half mile up the beach. Luke lifted up his speaking horn, pointed to lake and screamed, "Chimera, attack!"

The kaiju roared once more, placed his forepaws on the ground and began running toward the lake as a gorilla would toward an invader of its territory. Luke sprinted after Chimera who was quickly outdistancing him.

Chimera stopped at the edge of the colossal lake and looked down into the crystal clear water to see the massive form of the Charybdis filling the majority of the lake with its grotesque body. The Charybdis had the shape of a huge ice cream cone with numerous rows of razor sharp teeth that ringed its mouth. The teeth were spinning around its mouth like a buzz saw and Chimera could see the bright blue light surging forth from the rotating teeth. Chimera again reared up on his hind legs, roared, and beat his chest as challenge to the beast below it. The Charybdis made no reply; it simply continued to rotate its teeth and send its deadly vortex through the island and out into the ocean.

Luke arrived at the lake just in time to see Chimera dive into the water. He gazed down into the water and he was awed by the size of the Charybdis. Chimera was huge but the Charybdis was easily five times the size of Chimera. One thing that was plainly evident to Luke was the fact the Charybdis was virtually defenseless. Luke could see why the Scylla was left to guard it; if the Charybdis was attacked directly it would be an easy target. For thousands of years, the Scylla had been a creature without equal and Chimera had destroyed it in mere minutes. Luke almost pitied the Charybdis for what Chimera was going to do to it. Chimera had battled the Scylla but his encounter with the Charybdis would be a massacre.

Chimera swam down to the center of the Charybdis's body and then he began using his claws and teeth to tear into the bloated behemoth. The clear water turned red as blood gushed out of the wound created by Chimera. An odd gurgled roar escaped from the Charybdis's jaws as its body moved from side to side in an attempt to flee from its attacker. It was a useless attempt. The Charybdis had nowhere to escape to. Its only hope was that Chimera ended its suffering quickly. Within thirty seconds, Chimera had torn a wound roughly the size of his body into the Charybdis's side. Chimera climbed inside the Charybdis and began tearing the beast apart from within. The Charybdis continued to emit a painful wail and then finally it was silent. As the Charybdis's teeth stopped rotating, the blue vortex that they were creating ceased to emanate from its jaws. Luke turned around to see the blue light disappearing from over the ocean. A moment later, Chimera climbed out of the Charybdis's corpse and swam to the surface of the lake. When he broke the surface, he roared in triumph again. Luke lifted his speaking horn to his mouth and delivered the much deserved praise to the kaiju, "Good work, Chimera! Let's go back to the ship where we can get you something to eat! Follow me!"

CHAPTER 14
PHILADELPHIA

The line to enter to World Café in the heart of Philadelphia's University section was long and only the most attractive and best dressed patrons were being allowed to enter the club by the door man. The band Vinyl Crush was performing and they always packed the building when they were on the bill. Allison and Aiden walked past the long line and right up to the door man. Typically this type behavior would have been met with anger from the crowd lined up at the door, but the young men and woman were all enthralled by the pair as they walked passed them.

Allison smiled at the door man who quickly opened the door to the club without saying a word to them. They entered the club and took a moment to listen to the band playing on the stage. Aiden turned to Allison, "Thousands of years have passed and still not one musician exists that even comes close to Orpheus."

Allison smiled, "Dear brother, you really must open your musical horizons some. Surely you enjoy the music of Elvis?"

Aiden nodded, "He is not without his charm but still I long for the poet musicians of old." He sighed, "Anyway, back to the task at hand. How many more breeders do the gods require?"

Allison smiled, "At least a dozen more males and females." She scanned the crowd for a moment, "I see my target, have you identified yours yet?" Aiden looked over the crowd, "I see a couple of candidates. Perhaps I shall mingle a little prior to choosing which one shall have the pleasure of accompanying me today."

Allison slid her coat off of her shoulders revealing her perfect frame. The subtle move caught the attention of every young man in her vicinity. She waved at her brother and then she began walking toward a young man standing the bar. He had not yet noticed her when she slid up next to him and ever so slightly touched his arm. He turned around and he was immediately entranced by her. He smiled and offered to buy her a drink to which she grinned and ordered a vodka on the rocks. The young man introduced himself as Tyrone and several minutes later he and Allison were leaving the club together.

Aiden walked up to an athletic looking young woman who was the favorite of all of the young men in the club. Aiden made his way onto the dance floor and began dancing with the young woman. As the music blared on, Aiden leaned in close to her, "What's your name, love?" She giggled and answered that her name was Ann. Aiden put his arm around her waist and whispered to her if she would like to leave this place and head somewhere else. She was lost in his voice and agreed to go wherever he wanted. They walked out of the back of the club in time to see Allison and Tyrone kissing and then in a flash they vanished. Ann went to scream but Aiden placed his lips on hers and began kissing her and then they also were gone in a flash of light.

CHAPTER 15

Luke was sleeping in his cabin when his alarm suddenly woke him up. After Chimera had slain the Charybdis causing the blue vortex to dissipate, the Argos had been able to pull close to shore. Luke then directed Chimera to swim into his holding cell where he found a generous serving of food ready for him. A small ship was sent out to the beach where it picked up Luke. When he arrived back on deck, Luke was given twelve hours to shower the combined blood of Waller and the Scylla off of himself and rest prior to meeting with the team in the briefing room. After a very long shower, Luke found the adrenaline rush that had coursed through his body on the island had worn off and as a result, he was exhausted. He laid down for a short nap but from his perspective it seemed that he had no sooner closed his eyes than his alarm was telling him that it was time to head to the briefing room. Luke quickly threw on some jeans and T-shirt. He pulled a flannel shirt on over his T-shirt, slapped on his sneakers and then jogged down the briefing room. Everyone else would be in formal attire but given what he had already been through that day, he figured that he had earned the right to dress comfortably.

Luke entered the briefing room to find Diana, Toombs, and Parsons all there waiting for him. The president's face was also filling the screen that linked him from the White House to the Argos. Parsons looked at Luke and the way he was dressed and frowned. Luke sat down next to Diana and then the president addressed him, "That was fine work you and the monster did today son! Very fine work indeed!"

Luke nodded, "Thank you, Mr. President."

Parsons cleared his throat, "Yes, excellent job, Mr. Davis. Now to bring everyone up to speed. The blue vortex that was coming from the Charybdis has totally vanished. Chimera has been fed and is resting. Dr. Toombs has examined him and has found only minimal superficial puncture wounds. It seems that Ms. Cain's suggestion that the Scylla would be protecting the Charybdis was accurate. The Scylla in fact attacked Chimera and, from what Mr.

Davis tells us and the corpse of the Scylla confirms, is that Chimera was more than up to the challenge of battling the beast."

Luke whisper to Diana, "Damn right he was up to the challenge."

She smiled in reply as Parsons continued his update, "With the pending threat of the Charybdis eliminated, and the images of Chimera that were taken during his journey to the Argos, the public has been made aware of both Chimera and the threat facing the world. This was done primarily to keep local police and military from attacking Chimera as he approaches new targets." Parsons hit a key on his laptop and the screen changed. "This brings us to our next mission. With the primary threat the Olympians were posing addressed, we are going to attack Olympus itself. It is imperative that we take this action now before the Olympians can regroup and form a new plan of attack or the other sects who have declared war on the human race begin to act. We are currently two hours from making landfall in Greece and then proceeding to Mount Olympus itself." Parson's turned toward Diana, "The SEAL team that was first sent to scale Olympus met two mythological kaiju that ended their mission at base of the mountain. I will now turn this briefing over to Ms. Cain to explain the threat we are currently facing."

Diana stood up and straightened her blouse. She then hit her laptop and brought the visages of two horrifying creatures onto the screen, "From the reports we received from the missing SEAL team, I feel that the two monsters which are guarding Mount Olympus are Echidna and Cerberus. In terms of mythology, these two creatures are real heavy hitters when compared to the Scylla. Echidna is the half woman, half serpent on the left side of your screen. In mythology, she is referred to as the mother of all monsters. She is believed to be the mother of most monsters in Greek mythology, including her fellow guardian of Mount Olympus, Cerberus." Diana did her customary pause and check to make sure that everyone was following her presentation. Confident that everyone was with her she continued, "Cerberus is the dog of the death god Hades and the guardian of the underworld. It is his responsibility to ensure that the deceased remain in the underworld. In addition to his size and power, in some myths he is reported to have the ability to spit fire."

Diana hit her laptop and another image filled the screen, "It should also be noted that the ship which brought the SEAL team to Greece was attacked and destroyed by a kaiju matching the description of this creature." She gestured to image of a large creature with the front half of a bull ending in a fish like tail, "This creature is known as the Ophiotaurus. Honestly, other than a description of the beast, there is little other mention of it in mythology."

Diana had just finished her thought when a high-pitched sound was heard throughout the Argos. A second later, the lights in the briefing room shattered and the screens went blank sending the briefing room into darkness. Parsons pulled out his cigarette lighter and flicked it on. When everyone was looking at his face silhouetted by the thin flame, he spoke to them, "The emergency power should have kicked in by now. We have been hit by an EMP. It seems that the Olympians know that we are coming for them."

There was silence for moment and then a loud crash which shook the briefing room from side to side. No one said a word until a moment later when a second crash shook the ship again. Toombs voice cracked as he spoke, "This ship is the largest vessel in the world. It would take Tsunami to rock the ship like that."

Diana spoke without thinking, "Jaws! It's just like the boat scene in Jaws!" The others were lost but Toombs knew exactly what she was talking about. He shouted, "She's right!"

Parsons moved his lighter in Diana's direction as a third crash rocked the ship again and sent everyone falling out of their chairs. Diana stood up and shouted, "We need to get on deck now!"

Parsons held his lighter in front of him to light the way and then he began to lead the group through the dark passageways. A minute later, they were on deck and standing in the sunlight next to hundreds of sailors who were all looking out at the sea and pointing.

Diana followed their gaze out to sea and watched as two large horns broke the surface of the water to reveal a bull like face that was the size of a two story house. She looked toward Parsons, "The Ophiotaurus! It's trying to sink the ship!"

Parsons handed his lighter to Luke and then he grabbed Toombs, "Davis, get that speaking horn of yours out of your cabin and head to Chimera's holding bay! Toombs, get a team of sailors to the holding bay. We are going to have open Chimera's door manually!" The boat was rocked as the Ophiotaurus struck the ship again. Parsons regained his balance and then he finished giving his orders "I want Chimera in the water and engaging that beast ASAP before it sinks the ship!"

Luke and Toombs sprang into action. Luke was racing down the dark hallway to his cabin as Toombs was grabbing sailors from the deck and leading them to the holding bay.

CHAPTER 16

The light from the cigarette lighter danced in front of Luke as he sprinted through the pitch black corridors of the ship. He was going down a flight of stairs when the entire ship shook beneath him and caused him to tumble down the stairs. The flame of the lighter burned his hand but he made sure that he held onto it. He knew that if he dropped the lighter that he would be lost in the never ending darkness inside the ship. He took another second to get his bearings and then he continued to run toward his cabin.

On the deck, Toombs ran from sailor to sailor directing them to follow him to the cargo hold. The hold had access from the deck so it was easy for the gathered sailors to get to the giant wheel crank that they had to use to open Chimera's hold. Toombs and the gathered sailors grabbed a hold of the crank and slowly their combined strength forced the wheel to turn a few times. Toombs yelled out to the men, "Only open the cargo bay halfway! We want to have it as open as possible when Luke gets here but we don't want Chimera to enter the water until Luke gives him a command! We don't know how Chimera will react without directions!"

The sailors grunted in response and continued the back breaking task of manually opening a door designed to hold a kaiju. Diana and Parsons were watching from the center of the deck as the Ophiotaurus circled the Argos and prepared to ram it again. Until now, the Ophiotaurus had directed its attacks at the base of the ship, but this time Diana watched as the creature lifted its entire bull like front of its body out of the water. Its forepaws bucked in the air as it reared back its head and then drove its horns into the center of the ship. The impact of the blow sent everyone who was standing on the deck sprawling to the floor.

Luke had almost reached his cabin when the wall to his left exploded and a gigantic horn the size of a city bus filled the hallway in front of him. The horn shook twice and then freed itself from the ship's hull. Luke quickly peeked through massive newly-formed hole to see the Ophiotaurus shake its head and then dive back into the ocean. Luke's heart was beating a mile a minute as he realized that he came close to dying for the second time in the past twenty four hours. To Luke's advantage, the newly-formed hole let in enough sunlight to illuminate the entire hallway and his cabin. He quickly darted into his room, grabbed his speaking horn, and then he sprinted for Chimera's holding bay.

Luke entered the observation deck above Chimera as the Ophiotaurus rocked the ship with another attack. He placed the speaking horn to his lips and called out to Toombs, "Toombs, I am in place, open the gate!"

Toombs heard the request and he directed the sailors to finish cranking the hold bay door open. The door slowly opened and ocean water began to spill in over the floor. Chimera looked at the slowly opening door with eager eyes and he saw the form of the Ophiotaurus glide by the ship. Luke yelled through the speaking horn, "Chimera, attack!" Chimera roared, ran forward and then dove out of the cargo hold and into the ocean as Luke ran up on deck with the others.

Chimera splashed down into the water and started to right himself when the Ophiotaurus slammed into his side. The Ophiotaurus's horns dug into Chimera's flesh. While the horns dug into the thick whale blubber that surrounded Chimera's body, they were unable to reach any of his vital organs. The Ophiotaurus attempted to further gore Chimera, but when it sensed that he was only managing to push Chimera through the water, he broke off his attack and circled around to charge again. When he had entered the water, the sperm whale instincts in Chimera's brain took over. Following his instincts, he spun around in the water and charged directly at the Ophiotaurus. The two monsters crashed into each other in a head on collision with the force of two nuclear submarines going at full speed. Chimera had positioned his maw to slide between the Ophiotaurus's horns so that he connected with the beast's skull instead of impaling his face on its horns. While the bull-like skull of the Ophiotaurus was thick, Chimera's sperm whale head had a sack filled with spermaceti which allowed it act as a battering ram. Chimera plowed through the Ophiotaurus and sent him tumbling through the water.

The Ophiotaurus shook his head to clear away the effects of the collision and then he once more swam toward Chimera. Chimera attempted to meet the bull-like creature in a second head on collision but at the last second the Ophiotaurus veered to the side and used his horn to rake Chimera along the left side of his body. Blood streamed from Chimera's side but once more the attack failed to reach his internal organs.

The Ophiotaurus was charging Chimera again; however, Chimera was prepared for its method of attack. Instead of trying to meet the beast head on, Chimera waited until the Ophiotaurus was within reach and then he used his powerful arm to backhand the creature across the face. The blow shot the Ophiotaurus up toward the surface. Seeing his chance to finish off his opponent, Chimera swam deeper into the water and then he turned to face the Ophiotaurus. Chimera quickly unleashed a narrowly-focused sonar blast at the Ophiotaurus. The sonar impact rocked the mythological monster's body causing blood to seep out of its eyes, ears, nose and mouth. The Ophiotaurus was stunned and helpless in the water. Chimera shot his body up toward the Ophiotaurus and when he reached it, he sank his canines into the cow-like throat and used his claw to slice open the monster's stomach. The force of Chimera's attack carried the two kaiju to the surface. Luke, Diana, Parsons and the hundreds of sailors on deck watched as Chimera breached the surface with the wailing Ophiotaurus trapped in its jaws. Blood gushed into the air and the water. The monsters arched through the air and then they crashed back into the water. Chimera continued to force the Ophiotaurus deeper into the water as he tore at its throat and ripped out its intestines. The Ophiotaurus struggled for a few agonizing minutes before its heart finally gave out.

Sensing that he had slain its opponent, Chimera released the beast and let its body float slowly to the surface. As the blood from Ophiotaurus spread, sharks and fish off all manners attacked the carcass in a feeding frenzy. When Chimera returned to surface of the water, he heard Luke shout, "Good work, Chimera! Return to the ship for your reward!" As Chimera swam back to the cargo hold, Luke quickly ran over to it and dumped several of Chimera's food bars into the hold.

Diana ran over next to him and looked down into the hold as Chimera climbed aboard and enjoyed his meal. She whispered to Luke, "Eat up, boy. You certainly earned it."

Chapter 17

As Chimera settled down to enjoy his meal, Luke and Diana walked over toward Parsons and Toombs. They had made it halfway across the deck when the majestic sails of the Argos unfurled over their heads. Both Luke and Diana stood still for a moment and enjoyed the grandeur of the spectacle before them. Luke turned toward his friend, "With all of the horror we have seen the past two days, it is nice to take a minute and enjoy something beautiful like this."

Diana gave him a playful punch in the shoulder, "Who would have thought that underneath the tough exterior of kaiju trainer that there was such a softy."

He laughed, "I am man of mystery."

She smiled at him and they both looked up as the sails caught the wind and the Argos started moving forward. Diana placed her hand on Luke's shoulder to gain his attention and then she gestured to the clearly impatient Parsons. Luke whispered, "Let's start walking away from him and see what he does. He looks like he could use a laugh."

Diana grimaced, "Normally, I would be all for it but I am not sure anything in the world can make that man laugh." She grabbed his hand, "Come on."

She jogged over to Parsons and he followed her. As he ran after her, the thought crossed Luke's mind exactly how close he and Diana were becoming. Melissa was the only woman in the world for him, but he could see that he and Diana were kindred spirits.

Parsons didn't waste time with small talk, "The EMP and the monster did significant damage to the Argos. The EMP fried every circuit on the ship and the kaiju caused serious damage to the hull. We took on some water that the sailors are now pumping out by hand. Once the water is out of the hull, we can start repairing it. In the meantime, we are at the mercy of the wind." He held his hand out to Luke, "If you are done with my lighter, I would like it back." Luke handed him the lighter. Parsons removed a cigar from his pocket, snapped the end of it off, lit it and placed in his mouth. He turned toward Toombs, "Doctor, as soon as Chimera is rested, I want you to examine his wounds. As long as he is not seriously injured, we are still making our move on Olympus."

Toombs nodded, "Between the battle and eating, he is already starting to doze off. From looking at him as he reentered the ship, I think that again his wounds are probably only superficial." He looked toward Diana and a sly smile crept onto his round face, "However, I am unfamiliar with the mythology of the creature that attacked him. Perhaps if Ms. Cain could accompany me, she could fill me in on any specific wounds that the creature may have inflicted on Chimera."

Diana shrugged, "Other than a description, there is not much written about the Ophiotaurus. I am really not sure that I would be all that much help to you."

Toombs looked to Parsons, "Still, I would feel better having an expert on the attacking creature along to assist in the examination."

Parsons looked at Diana, "Just go with him. It can't hurt."

Diana smiled, "OK doctor, it seems that I am your woman."

Toombs ran his eyes over her, "Yes, you certainly are."

As Toombs began walking toward Chimera's holding bay, Diana turned to Luke and mouthed the words "Save me." Luke smiled at her and shrugged. She responded with a less enthusiastic gesture then followed Toombs.

As they approached the holding bay, Diana was hit by the smell of Chimera. As if being in Toombs' company was not repulsive enough, she had to deal with the odor of the kaiju as well. The doctor entered the observation deck and checked to make sure that Chimera was sleeping before entering the holding bay. Once he was sure that Chimera was not going to decide to start walking around and accidentally crush him, he approached the creature with Diana behind him. He walked around the kaiju and stopped on the side where the Ophiotaurus had grazed Chimera with his horn. He pointed at the wound, "Does the mythology say anything about the horns of Ophiotaurus having poisonous properties?"

Diana spoke with a sharp tone to her voice, "Like I said back on deck, other than mentioning a description of the Ophiotaurus, the mythology doesn't say anything else about the creature. If it has any other special abilities, you know as much about them as I do."

Toombs looked at the wound on Chimera' side, "The wound does not appear to have caused any real damage. Chimera's genes have been enhanced to help him heal as quickly as possible. That scratch should be fully healed in a few hours." Toombs slid towards Diana, "It seems that we have an extra day at sea." He attempted to place his arm around her, "I can think of a few things that we can do to pass the time."

Diana balled her hand into a fist and struck Toombs in the jaw sending him falling to the ground, "Listen to me, Toombs. If you ever try to touch me again, giant monsters attacking us will be a day in the park compared to what I will do to you."

Toombs wiped his chin, "What is your deal? Is it Davis? I see the way you look at him."

Diana leaned toward Toombs, "My deal, is that I think you are a pathetic, disgusting, little man. From this point on, you will only speak to me on events related to our mission. Is that clear, Dr. Toombs?"

Toombs didn't answer; he just looked up at her with a sneer on his face.

Diana stepped on his hand and dug her heel into his palm as she repeated her question, "Is that clear, Dr. Toombs?"

Toombs screamed, "Yes! Now get off of my hand! You …"

Toombs sentence was cut off when Chimera began to stir as a result of the noise in his holding bay.

Diana began walking out of the holding bay, "I suggest that you get up, doctor, and go tell General Parsons that Chimera will be ready for battle by tomorrow. It seems that your patient is starting to wake up."

Toombs stood up and ran out of the room. From a dark corner of the holding bay, Allison whispered to her brother, "That Doctor Toombs is a man that it may benefit us to take sooner or later."

Aiden looked at Allison with a mixed looked of confusion and revulsion, "That man is a hideous toad! Surely there are others who suit your fancy?"

Allison laughed, "Dear brother, you still have much to learn. Physical appearance is not everything. Let us see how events with this beast and the gods play out. If things continue as they are, we may look back on this Doctor Toombs and suddenly find him very desirable."

Allison grabbed her brother by the hand and in a flash they were gone.

CHAPTER 18

As the morning sun shone on the ship, Luke got up, dressed himself in a pair of loose fitting sweat clothes, and then made his way down to the stable that held Jason. Luke slowly approached the Clydesdale with a carrot in his hand, which the horse gladly accepted. Luke then picked a brush and ran it over the animal. Luke was going to be leading Chimera into a battle today against two of the most powerful creatures in Greek mythology. If they survived that battle, he was then going to instruct Chimera to scale a mountain and challenge the gods who lived on top of it. The same gods that had shut down the most powerful naval vessel in the world with a single attack. Luke laughed to himself a little when he thought about the Herculean task that lay before Chimera and him. The fact was that he would not even make it to attempt any of those feats if Jason fled at the first sign of the oncoming danger or threw Luke off of his back.

The horse had done fine around Chimera but he had the benefit of becoming acclimated to Chimera when the kaiju was half drugged. Jason had yet to be tested in a situation where malevolent creatures were attempting to kill him. Parsons had assured Luke that Jason was a war horse who had endured hours of training and that he would stay the course. Luke had faith in the horse just as he had faith in Chimera.

He loaded Jason up with the reinforcer food cubes for Chimera and his speaking horn. Luke then stuffed his pockets full of carrots. Jason nuzzled his face at Luke's pockets. Luke laughed, "Easy boy, if we succeed today you will have earned all of the carrots that you want." Luke then grabbed the reigns and led the horse to the small boat that would carry them to shore. When he entered the launching bay, he found Parsons and Diana waiting for him. Parsons stepped up beside Luke and reviewed the plan with him, "You will probably come across Echidna and Cerberus as you approach the mountain. Have Chimera engage them. If he is able to defeat them, immediately send him to the top of Mount Olympus. Honestly, we are not really sure what he will encounter up there, but have him destroy everything that he sees. If he survives and is able to come back down the mountain, we will send up a SEAL team to clean up and salvage whatever technology is left."

Parsons place his hand on Luke's shoulder, "You and Chimera can do this! I have faith in you, son, as does everyone else on board."

Luke nodded in reply as Diana walked over to him, "I am going ashore with you. Seeing the monsters in action may help me to better understand some of the other threats that we will face in the future." She looked into Luke's eyes, "Anyway, there is no way that I am letting you make your way to the mountain alone." Luke smiled at her and then he directed Jason into the boat. Once the horse was settled, Diana climbed in as well. The boat was in fact a thirty foot long canoe. The EMP that struck the Argos had disabled all of the motorized boats onboard, so like everything else they were reduced to pre-industrial methods. A team of sailors ran up alongside the boat and began pushing it into the sea. As the ship began to slide into the water, the sailors began jumping onto it and manning the oars that protruded from its sides.

The boat was about halfway to shore when the bay doors at the back Argos slowly began to open. The gargantuan form of Chimera's head began to poke out of the bay door. When the door was fully opened, Chimera leapt forward into the water. Luke and Diana both watched in awe as the majestic creature arched into the air and landed gracefully in the sea.

Diana leaned in toward Luke, "I have heard from people who have gone whale watching that it is one of the most breathtaking sights in the world. I can't imagine that it has anything on seeing Chimera enter the water."

Luke gently punched her in the arm, "And you called me a softy?"

The two of them laughed for a moment and then Luke noticed that Chimera was heading out to sea. He picked up his speaking horn and shouted, "Chimera follow me!" The kaiju slowly turned around and began swimming toward the small ship. At the sight of Chimera coming toward them, the sailors doubled their efforts and reached shore just before Chimera was upon them.

Luke led Jason out of the boat as Chimera waded onto the beach. While the local population had been ordered to evacuate the area days ago, a few people had stayed in their homes. When they heard the crashing of Chimera's footfalls as he walked ashore, the few stragglers who had refused to leave their homes came running out to the beach.

Luke was expecting them to scream and flee in terror at the sight of the kaiju but something Luke never would have imagined occurred. The people began cheering. He turned his head to Diana with a puzzled look on it. She smiled at him, "The government has told the public about the threat that we are facing and Chimera's role in stopping it. He is not a monster anymore. He is hero. He is the hope of every of person living on this planet."

Luke had been so focused on Chimera's ability to save the planet by battling gods and monsters that he had never considered the kaiju's ability to inspire people. A smile crept across Luke's face as he thought that it was time to try something new that he had been working on Chimera with. He yelled into his horn, 'Chimera, let them know we are coming!"

Chimera looked down at Luke and then he placed his front paws on the ground. The beast lowered his head and then it shot up into the air as he unleashed a roar that shook the countryside. The crowd fell silent for a second then answered with a chorus of cheers. Luke waved at them and then jumped onto Jason. He was about to take off when Diana climbed up behind him. She whispered into his ear, "I told you that I was not going to let you do this alone. What kind of friend would I be if did?"

Luke simply nodded at her and then directed Chimera to follow him. He then gave Jason a nudge and began the trek to Mount Olympus.

CHAPTER 19

The waves crashed onto the packed beaches of Malibu as Allison and Aiden watched the beach goers from the top of a sand dune. They were both dressed for the beach. Aiden wore his white swim trunks as low on his hips as he possibly could without having them fall off. Allison wore a wire thin bikini with a thong bottom that left just enough of her covered to tantalize the imagination.

Aiden surveyed the beach and shook his head, "Their world is ending and yet here they are enjoying themselves. Dear sister, I swear to the Fates that I will never understand how the human mind works."

Allison giggled, "Aiden, what else would you have them do? They are powerless to stop the events which are unfolding around them. How would you suggest that they spend their final days of life on this planet? By hiding in their homes and praying to their God who will not come to their aid? Is not enjoying their last few days of life the most logical way to spend the final moments of their already brief lives?"

She began walking down the sand dune toward the beach, "Come with me brother, let us stop judging them and instead allow a select few of them enjoy pleasures which their species have never thought possible."

Allison walked onto the beach and she made sure that every movement of her striking body was perfectly timed and balanced. The heads of everyone on the beach were slowly drawn to her as she made her way to the water. She saw a young couple wading out into the surf. The man was well built and handsome and the female was young and beautiful in her own right. Allison decided that it was time to entertain herself a little as she continued to gather breeding partners for the gods. She walked up next the young man and placed her hand in his. She titled her head slightly and smiled both at the man and his girlfriend. "Hey there stud, how about you leave this homely little tramp here and take a swim with me?" She then wrapped her arms around the man and kissed him.

SCOURGE OF THE GODS

His girlfriend screamed, "Hank, what the hell do you think that you are doing? Allison pulled away from the kiss and then laughed at the woman, "Forget about him, princess. He is mine now." Allison took Hank's hand and began to lead him further out into the water. His girlfriend first yelled curses at him as he followed Allison like a mindless slave. When they had reached waist deep water, Allison turned around so that the girlfriend could see her as she kissed Hank again. Allison looked over to see the girlfriend break down in tears. She maintained the kiss with Hank as a wave rolled over them. When they were submerged, a bright light surrounded them and when the wave had passed over them they were gone. The girlfriend eyes were still too filled with tears to see that her lover had disappeared.

Aiden shook his head and laughed at his sister's cruelty. He began walking along the beach himself until he saw a young woman with the body of supermodel lying on her stomach and sunbathing near the shoreline. He approached the woman from an angle that would assure his body would block her sun. As his shadow fell across her, she rolled over and her mouth fell open and the sight of him. He reached out to the girl, "Can I interest you in a quick swim?"

CHAPTER 20

Dark storm clouds started to form overhead as Luke and Diana rode Jason at a fast trot in order to keep pace with Chimera. Luke was unsure if the storm clouds were just a natural weather pattern or the work of the Olympians preparing for the coming of Chimera. He and Diana rode in virtual silence for roughly half an hour until they were less than two miles from the base of Olympus. Luke pulled Jason to a halt and when the horse stopped, Chimera sat down for a moment as well.

Luke turned to Diana, "This is your stop."

Diana's scowled at him, "I told you that I was not going to let you do this alone!"

Luke smiled at her, "You haven't. Having you this far has been a huge help to me but there is something else that you can do for me that would be a greater help to me than anything."

Diana's voice softened, "Just name it and I will do it."

Luke reached into his pocket and pulled out a picture with a woman and two girls on it that he handed to Diana, "This is my family. I talked to them before we left and every day since then but I have not spoken to them since the EMP took out all of the ships electrical systems." He paused for a moment, obviously fighting back tears, "If things go bad, if I don't make it back. Promise me that you will go back to the compound in Virginia and find them. Promise me that you will tell them that I did all of this to protect them. That I love them more than anything, and that my last thoughts were of them as I rode into the unknown."

Diana was crying herself as she took the photo from him, "I promise that I will find them and tell them everything. I will tell them how lucky they were to have had you as a husband and a father." She quickly hugged Luke and then jumped off of the horse. She pulled a pair of binoculars from her coat and pointed to the top of a nearby hill, "I am going to watch what happens from there, so that I can report back to Parsons no matter what happens."

Luke nodded and then shouted to Chimera through his speaking horn, "Chimera, follow me!" Luke then prompted Jason forward and Chimera followed in kind.

At the pace that Luke was riding Jason, he was within a mile of Olympus within twenty minutes. A light rain was falling on the open field that he was in and the clouds had turned so dark that despite being the middle of the day it looked as though night had fallen. When Luke looked up into the clouds and saw that they were swirling around Mount Olympus, he surmised that this was no natural weather pattern.

His eyes were drawn away from the top of the mountain when he heard a chorus of high-pitched howls coming from the base of the mountain. He looked toward the bottom of Olympus to see three huge wolf-like creatures coming from around the southern side of the mountain. Each of the wolves was about thirty feet high, making them far larger than any normal wolf but nowhere near the size of Chimera. The three beasts growled and then began running toward Chimera. As they were running, the wolves on either side of the wolf in middle swerved so that they ran into the middle wolf. The middle wolf's body bulged and twisted as he absorbed the other two beasts into himself. The result was far more than the sum of their parts. The three creatures had merged into the massive three headed monstrosity known as Cerberus, the guardian of the underworld. The combined height of the merged creature was about two thirds that of Chimera himself and much more than the mass of the three wolves were individually.

Luke decided that now was not the time to ponder the physics of the situation. He quickly lifted up his speaking horn, pointed at the three headed monster, and screamed for Chimera to attack. Chimera lifted himself onto his back legs, beat his chest, and roared before dropping his front hands back onto the earth and charging Cerberus.

Luke sat on top of Jason and watched as the two kaiju met in the middle of the field. It was Chimera that struck first by delivering a vicious back hand to the middle of Cerberus's three heads. The blow struck with such force that the entire front half of Cerberus's body was spun one hundred and eighty degrees. With the beast's three heads directed away from him, Chimera pressed his attack by slamming his shoulder into Cerberus's side. The impact sent the hell hound rolling across the open field. When Cerberus had finally stopped rolling, he was lying on his side and facing away from Chimera.

Chimera was running toward the three headed horror to end its existence when the ground in front of him erupted, spewing forth Echidna. The giant snake women quickly wrapped her long and powerful serpentine body around Chimera's legs. The move tripped up the kaiju and sent him crashing into the ground. Before Chimera could even attempt to lift his body off of the ground, Echidna moved like lightning and wrapped her body around Chimera's arms and torso as well. The pressure that her snake like body was able to generate was unimaginable. Even Chimera's muscles were useless against it. Chimera's chest sank as Echidna's ever tightening grip forced the air from his lungs. With Chimera's arms pinned at his side, the mother of all monsters lifted her claw above her head and slashed Chimera across his face. Chimera was in mid roar from the pain the attack had caused when Cerberus jumped onto his chest. The monster's middle head bit into Chimera's lower jaw while the two outside heads were tearing into Chimera's shoulders.

Chimera struggled in vain to free himself from Echidna's grip, but he quickly found that even his strength was unable to break her hold. Cerberus's center head tore a huge chunk of flesh from Chimera's jaw and then quickly swallowed it. In act of desperation, Chimera unleashed a narrow sonar blast on the two monsters. The effect was devastating. Cerberus's ultra-sensitive hearing was overwhelmed by the attack. Blood gushed out of his ears and nose as he shook his heads and then fell off of Chimera's body. Echidna also had blood coming from her ears, eyes, and nose. Her nervous system was in disarray and as her muscles went limp her grip loosened enough for Chimera to break free from it.

The two mythical beasts were still reeling from the attack as Chimera regained his footing. Chimera leapt toward Echidna and brought his right fist crashing down into her head. Chimera followed up the blow by landing an uppercut to her jaw with his left fist. The attack sent the snake woman's head and torso crashing into the ground. Chimera then spun and used his thick tail as club to slam into Cerberus's shoulder, knocking the foul creature onto its side. Seeing Echidna as the greater threat, Chimera leapt onto her chest and then began reigning down blows into her face. Echidna's head was slowly being driven into the ground until Cerberus jumped onto Chimera's back and began tearing into his shoulder blades. Chimera roared, reached back, grabbed Cerberus, and then he threw the three headed dog over his head and into a nearby hill.

Chimera went to resume his pounding of Echidna but was stopped short when her tail came up behind him and wrapped around his neck. She pulled backwards slowly forcing Chimera off of her body. Chimera was still standing as she once again wrapped the lower half of her body around his arms pinning them to his sides. She then leaned into Chimera's face and hissed, revealing her long fangs. She was about to sink them into Chimera's neck when the kaiju smashed his whale-like face into her nose. The blow rocked Echidna causing her to release her grip and fall to the ground. She was barely conscious as Chimera loomed over her and prepared to begin pounding her once more. As Chimera was lifting his arms above his head, he was engulfed in a wall of flames.

The kaiju staggered back from Echidna as all three of Cerberus's heads poured fire onto him. Chimera could feel his flesh burning and blistering as hellfire continued to scorch him. He forced his head to turn in the direction of Cerberus and once again he attacked the canine like beast with a narrow burst of his sonar call. Cerberus's body convulsed and his heads stopped spewing fire as his sensory organs were once again overloaded causing the beast to have a seizure.

Echidna wrapped around Chimera's left leg and then shot in front of him, preparing to once more pin Chimera's arms to his side in an attempt to crush him. This time, however, Chimera was ready for the attack. His left arm shot out and grabbed Echidna by the throat and held her in front of him. Cerberus had recovered from his seizure and quickly lunged at Chimera. The hell hound was viciously mauling Chimera's right leg and hip. Chimera ignored the pain of Cerberus's attack and continued to focus on Echidna. The kaiju held out his hand, unsheathed his lion claws, and then slashed the snake woman across her midsection where the two halves of her body connected. Her intestines spilled out of her body as the demon screeched in pain. Chimera slashed her across the mid-section a second time and the blow nearly sliced the she-beast in two. Chimera dropped the dying snake woman from his grasp and then brought his fist crashing down into the center of Cerberus's back causing the creature's legs to give way underneath him and driving his stomach into the ground. Cerberus was attempting to right himself when each of Chimera's hands clamped down on Cerberus's two outer heads. Chimera pulled the outer heads in opposite directions and tore them off of the hell hounds body. The center head howled in pain as the blood poured out of its body. When the painful howl ended, the monster's dead body fell to the ground.

Echidna was attempting to hold her intestines in her body and crawl away from the battle when Chimera brought his foot down on the middle of her tail. He then reached down with his powerful arms and grabbed Echidna's human upper half under her armpits. Chimera roared at the demon and then he began to pull her body up while simultaneously pressing down on her tail. Echidna's already ravaged stomach was unable to withstand the force being exhorted on it and her body was ripped in two. Chimera held the screaming human half of Echidna in front of him while the snake like bottom portion of her body squirmed under his foot. After ten agonizing seconds, Echidna finally stopped screaming. Chimera threw the lifeless torso to the ground. The kaiju then beat his chest and roared triumphantly.

Luke could not believe what he just witnessed. Chimera was bleeding from several serious wounds and most of his body was covered in burns, but the kaiju continued to battle on as if he were more or less unharmed. Looking at Chimera, Luke was sure that monster had to be exhausted and in dire need of whatever medical attention that Toombs could provide to him, but Luke also was sure that they would not have a better chance to directly attack Olympus. Diana had mentioned that there were literally dozens of monsters in Greek mythology. If Chimera returned to the ship now, would Zeus have ten monsters guarding his palace next time? Luke did not want to take that chance. He directed Jason to gallop over to Chimera. Once they reached the beast, Luke tossed him one of the reinforcer food bars that he had loaded up on Jason. Chimera was chewing on the bar when Luke yelled, "Good work, Chimera!" through his speaking horn.

The light rain that had been falling around Mount Olympus suddenly turned into deluge as the clouds opened up above them. Luke did not know much about mythology but he did know about behaviors and if Zeus was causing this increased rainfall after his monsters had been slain it meant that he was scared. Luke looked at Chimera and then he shifted his gaze to the top of Mount Olympus. He yelled at the top of the mountain, "That's right, you should be scared!" He then placed the speaking to his mouth and pointed to the top of Mount Olympus and screamed, "Chimera, Attack!"

Chimera lifted his head into the pouring rain and roared. He then placed his hand onto Mount Olympus and began scaling the legendary formation. Luke watched in awe through the storm as the kaiju slowly scaled the Mountain of the Gods. A few short weeks ago, Luke feared the gods of Olympus, but as he saw Chimera digging his claws into the mountain and pulling himself to toward its summit, he pitied them. Luke had no doubt that when Chimera reached the top of mount Olympus that he would leave the Olympian stronghold in ruins.

CHAPTER 21

Despite the pouring rain making the mountain extremely slippery, Chimera continued to scale the side it. The kaiju looked up into rain to see where the summit of the mountain was but the rain clouds continued to shroud the top of Olympus. The rain and wind increased their fury as he neared the top of the mountain. Chimera had finally climbed high enough to reach the clouds when the first bolt of lightning struck him. The kaiju's entire body lit up with white energy as the electricity from the bolt surged through his body. Chimera roared at the clouds that dared to attack him and then he dug his claws into the rocky cliff above his head. With his grip secure, Chimera pulled his massive body up once more and out of the storm clouds.

Chimera stood still for a moment when he realized that he was standing in bright sunlight in front of a huge structure comprised of white stone columns. The structure's height was nearly equal to Chimera and it had no roof on top of it. Chimera walked toward the structure and lifted his head over the top of it to see inside. When Chimera looked over the structure, he saw roughly twenty people standing inside of a courtyard. The gods of Olympus each stood about twenty feet tall. They were dressed in togas and gowns. Each of them brandished a weapon of some manner that varied from swords, to spears and bows and arrows. Chimera looked down at the gods and he could see the fear in their eyes as they slowly backed away from him. Chimera looked to the back of the courtyard where he could see a god that was easily twice the size of the other gods sitting on a colossal throne between two large stone pillars. While the other gods looked at Chimera in fear, Zeus the king of the Olympians, glared at Chimera with disdain.

Zeus stood up from his throne and screamed at Chimera, "This is the monster that would dare to scale Olympus and challenge the will of the gods!" He pointed at Chimera and electricity started to swirl around the pillars on either side of his throne. The electricity from the pillars arched onto Zeus. The god king took on a bright white glow for a moment and then a bolt of lightning shot from his finger and struck Chimera across the face. Once more a surge of pain wracked Chimera's body as the electricity ran through him. Chimera roared in anger. He then bent down and used his body to smash through the pillars at the front of the courtyard. Chimera stepped into the courtyard, roared, and beat his chest in answer to Zeus's challenge. The other Olympians continued to back away from the kaiju until they heard Zeus's voice booming behind them, "You are gods of Olympus! Cowardice is beneath you! Attack this monster! With the power of your king behind you, we shall defeat this beast just as we did the Titans centuries ago." When Zeus finished speaking, the pillars on the sides of his throne began to charge with electricity again. Once more the power arched onto Zeus and once more he unleashed that power onto Chimera.

The entire courtyard light up with energy when the lightning bolt struck Chimera's body, causing the hair from his mane to stand up straight. When the other gods saw that Zeus's power could indeed injure the monster, they regained their confidence. The sun god Apollo suddenly flew over the gathered gods in his flaming chariot. He lifted his spear above his head and screamed, "Gods of Olympus, follow me to victory!" Apollo drove his chariot at Chimera and threw his flaming spear into Chimera's shin. A barrage of spears and arrows followed. Within seconds, Chimera had the projectiles sticking out of various points on his body, but the attack did not slow Chimera's advance in the least. He walked through the spears and arrows as if they meant less to him than the rain which had pelted his body on his way up the mountain. Apollo turned his chariot around and charged at Chimera once again. He flew in close to Chimera and buried another flaming spear in the kaiju's chest. The sun god was pulling his flaming chariot away from the beast when Chimera's hand shot out and swatted Apollo to the ground. Before Apollo could right his chariot, Chimera backhanded the transport, sending both chariot and god flying into the pillars at the sides of the courtyard.

The other gods continued to throw spears at Chimera as he lumbered toward them. He had reached the amassed gods and he raised hand to strike at them when Zeus sent another bolt of lightning to strike Chimera. Chimera's body froze in place as it was jolted with the electrical charge. The wounds from his battle with Cerberus and Echidna were overwhelmed by pain when the electricity scorched them. After the shock from the bolt had passed, Chimera roared in defiance at the gods who continued to stab him and shoot arrows into his body. The kaiju stepped forward and brought his hand in a backward swing connecting with three of the gods at the front of the group. The blow sent the gods flying into the pillars that lined the sides of the courtyard. Another god stepped forward and drove his sword into Chimera's foot. Chimera winced and then unsheathed his claws and slashed the god across the face and torso. What was left of the god fell to the floor in a bloody mess.

Chimera directed his eyes to the back of the courtyard to see the pillars around Zeus charging up for another blast of electricity. As Chimera was staring at Zeus, two more gods stepped forward and threw spears into Chimera's chest. The massive golden weapons were still impaled in Chimera's chest when Zeus's lightning bolt struck the monster again. The spears embedded in his chest acted as conductors and sent the charge coursing deep into Chimera's body. While the other blasts had been painful, this attack had caused damage. Chimera's heart skipped a beat causing the kaiju to fall to the ground face first. The Olympians cheered as Chimera crashed into the ground. From his throne, Zeus yelled to his subjects, "Now is our opportunity! The creature has fallen! Quickly pounce upon the monster and slay it!"

The Olympians cheered in response to their king and as one they fell upon Chimera. The Olympians stabbed at Chimera and dug their weapons deep into his flesh. The pain reinvigorated Chimera and a burst of adrenaline steadied his heart. The monster roared and then stood up shaking the attacking gods from his body. When Chimera reached his feet, he went into a rage using his claws to slash at any god within his reach. The Olympian's bodies were ripped to shreds as they were sent flying to every corner of the courtyard. Zeus watched the carnage and for moment even he was in awe at the kaiju's strength and fury. Zeus began to charge up the pillars which provided him with his power when he saw Chimera lift up his massive foot and bring it in crashing down onto the last of his subjects that was still standing.

Chimera looked to the sky, beat his chest, and roared. The beast then turned his attention to Zeus. Chimera began walking toward

Zeus when the pillars around him again danced with electricity before sending it Zeus. Zeus quickly redirected that energy at Chimera but the kaiju kept walking forward as if the electricity had no effect on him.

Chimera was only a few steps from the throne as the pillars were once more charging up for another blast. The monster was directly above Zeus when he sent his last bolt of lightning coursing into Chimera's body. Chimera ignored the blast and reached down to grab Zeus. Chimera stared at Zeus as he struggled against the monster's grip and yelled defiantly at the beast, "You cannot kill us, monster! We are immortal! You have only temporarily delayed our victory! Our brother pantheons will still exterminate the blight that is humanity! The Olympians ..." Before Zeus could finish his thought, Chimera brought the god king up to his jaws and bit into him. Zeus screamed in pain as the upper part of his body was ravaged by Chimera's lion like teeth while his legs hung out of Chimera's mouth. Chimera shook his head from side to side and then he released his grip and sent the defeated god hurling into the corner of the courtyard. Zeus rolled over as the blood poured out of his broken body to see Chimera once more beating his chest and proclaiming his victory.

Zeus reached out to his pillars and once again electricity began to swirl around the stone constructs. He called the energy to himself and for a second the electricity danced around his body. As the energy was washing over Zeus, he lifted up his hand and the power shot out of his hands and began to cascade over his fellow Olympians. The Olympians' bodies began to rise into the air and then the electricity carried them back to the throne between the two pillars. The energy kept the gathered Olympians suspended above Zeus's throne. Chimera watched as the electricity around Zeus began to lift him into the air as well. Zeus stared at Chimera with hatred in his eyes as the electrical current carried him to his throne as well. When Zeus joined his fellow gods in the space above the throne, there was a bright flash and then the Olympians were gone.

Chimera roared in anger at the now vanished gods. He was unsure of what had just occurred before him but what he did know was that he was robbed of the ability to slay his enemies. Chimera stared at the two pillars. His limited intelligence was able to comprehend that the pillars both had caused him pain and had helped his enemies to escape his clutches. He roared once more then he lumbered over to the pillars. Chimera stepped on Zeus's throne and crushed it into dust. He then placed his hands against the two pillars and began to push on them. The power from the pillars coursed through his body. The hair on his mane stood straight up as electricity ran through him. Every nerve in the kaiju's body screamed with pain but Chimera refused to let the pillars defeat him. He fought through the pain and he continued to push on the pillars of Zeus's power. The pillars slowly began to bend from their original positions and a moment later two loud cracking sounds echoed through the empty courtyard when the pillars snapped in half and fell to the ground. When the pillars broke apart they lost their power and the electricity which was assaulting Chimera finally ended.

Chimera looked around the courtyard to see that his enemies were defeated and that the source of their power was crushed beneath him. Chimera roared but he lacked the energy to beat his chest. The exhausted kaiju lie down on the former throne of Zeus and shut his eyes.

CHAPTER 22

Luke and Diana had been waiting at the base of the mountain for two hours. They could hear the horrible sounds of the battle above them and when the raging storm finally halted they thought that it may have signaled the end of the battle. The question was who had won? Had Chimera defeated the Olympians or had they slain the mighty kaiju?

Diana finally placed her hand on Luke's shoulder, "It has been a while. Maybe we should go back and see what Parsons wants to do next." Luke nodded but he kept his eyes fixed on the clouds that covered the top of Mount Olympus. He jumped up and screamed triumphantly when he saw a gargantuan foot reach down from the clouds. A second later, the rest of Chimera's body began to emerge from the clouds.

Luke grabbed Diana by the waist, picked her up, and spun her around as he shouted, "He did it. That big beast did it! He kicked the Olympians' asses!"

Luke let Diana dropped to the ground and she hugged him in jubilation. Chimera soon reached the base of the mountain and Luke yelled through his speaking horn, "Good work, Chimera! Come and get your reward!" Luke tossed Chimera one of his food reinforcers and the monster fell onto top of the cube and he began to devour it.

Luke could see from the cuts and burns that were spread all over Chimera's body that the kaiju had sustained significant injuries during his battle with the Olympians. Luke lifted Diana on top of Jason then he climbed onto the horse himself. He once more looked toward Chimera, "He is in pretty bad shape. We need to get him back to the ship so that he can rest and have Toombs look at him." Luke waited until Chimera finished eating his food bar then he gave him instructions through his speaking horn, "Chimera, follow me." As the trio walked away from the Mount Olympus, for the first time in weeks the clouds over the area began to dissipate. Jason and Chimera were roughly a mile from the shoreline when Luke noticed that there was a crowd gathering around them. The people who were following them were cheering and calling

Chimera's name. They were obviously aware that Chimera had driven the gods away who had been threatening them.

Diana looked behind them and said to Luke, "I can't believe how well Chimera is reacting to having all of these people follow us."

Luke shrugged, "Chimera's entire training program has been designed to ensure that all of his interactions with humans are positive and therefore reinforcing. Chimera should not only tolerate people being around him but he probably enjoys it."

Diana was amazed, "So far all that I have learned about monsters and mythology has held true, except where Chimera is concerned. Everything from ancient stories to Saturday night on the Syfy channel suggests that when people and monsters interact, the monsters end up attacking the people. Keeping Chimera away from people and having him attack other monsters and gods is one thing, but with all of these people around him aren't you worried that he could turn on them if he gets spooked?"

Luke shook his head, "Not at all, like I said he has been trained to see people as beneficial to him. All of his interactions with humans have been positive for him." Luke paused for a moment, "Let me explain this to you through monster stories. I may not know as much about myths and monsters as you do but let me use three famous fictional monsters to prove my point. The Frankenstein Monster, King Kong, and the Incredible Hulk. All three are monsters and yet all three can be seen as victims of their interactions with humans. All three monsters are hunted, captured, or attack by humans because they are different. To those creatures, humans are the monsters because all humans have ever done to them is hunt and hurt them. In the case of Chimera, he has only received food and positive attention from humans, because of that he not only has no reason to attack humans but more importantly he is motivated to cooperate with us."

Diana laughed, "I knew there was a comic book geek in you somewhere. I just needed the right conversation to draw him out."

Luke smiled and then he turned around to see the Argos in the distance as well as the canoe waiting to take them back to it. He urged Jason ahead and into the boat. Chimera stopped at the shoreline and waited for Luke to give his "Follow Me" command before entering the water and swimming back out to the Argos.

One hour later Luke, Diana, Parsons and Toombs were back in the briefing room where power had been partially restored. Parsons stood up from his chair and began to address the group on what his SEAL clean up team had found on Olympus, "As you know, we can confirm that Chimera was able to slay Cerberus and Echidna. The palace on top of Olympus is in ruins. There are multiple samples of blood that are not human nor are they Chimera's. We can only assume that it is the blood of the Olympians; however, we can find no trace of the Olympians or their bodies. We did however find two large pillars that seem to be able conduct electricity as well as other forms of unknown energy. It is our current assumption that Chimera injured the Olympians and that they used these pillars to escape into one of the other dimensions which they have previously occupied. These pillars, as well as a perpetually flaming chariot, are being taken back to Virginia for study where we will determine how they work and if we can use them to prevent the Olympians from returning."

He turned Toombs, "Doctor Toombs, if you could please fill us in on Chimera's physical status."

Toombs went to stand up but he looked in Diana's direction as he was doing so. With her icy gaze locked on him, Toombs lost track of what he was doing and tripped over the leg of the table and fell to the floor. Parsons sighed as Toombs picked himself up. He dusted himself off then gave his update, "Chimera suffered several deep cuts and burns to his outer skin. In addition to that, it seems that his heart rate is slightly off. Given Mr. Davis' report of multiple lightning strikes visible when Chimera had reached the top of Mount Olympus, it would seem safe to assume that several of the strikes hit Chimera, thus accounting for his irregular heartbeat. The good news is that with the enhancements made to his genetics he will recover fully including his heart in roughly about a week. However, I cannot recommend that we send him into battle prior to that." Toombs then quietly returned to his seat.

Luke raised his hand, "With the Olympians gone, where do we go from here?"

Parsons shrugged, "For now, we are heading back to Virginia. We are still faced with expressed threats from both the Asgardian gods and the Mesopotamian gods. Ms. Cain will continue to search incoming data for any threats that can be linked to either or both of these sects. In the meantime, we hope that they don't attack for at least a week. In that time, Mr. Davis you may go and spend some much needed time with your family. We shall also use that time to make repairs to the Argos's internal systems. Furthermore, we are going to attempt to cover the hull of Argos in foam rubber. This will not completely shield us from another EMP but it will lessen the effects of any future attacks."

Parsons looked over the three people before him, "I also want it to be known that you three have performed above and beyond all expectations. Your country and the very world owes you its thanks." Parsons gestured toward the door, "Lady and gentlemen, please enjoy a well-deserved rest as we head home."

The three civilians exited the briefing room and went back to their separate quarters. As Luke walked back to his cabin his thoughts were happily focused on seeing Melissa and the girls.

CHAPTER 23
KURDISTAN, IRAQ

The wind blew particles of sand through the hot desert night and directly into the windshield of the car that Omar was driving. His car was meager and it had no doors so that he could hear and feel all of the elements around him. In the distance, he could hear wild dogs howling at the moon. Omar looked up and thanked the Creator that the moon was low because it gave him plenty of extra light to see with. Despite what people who lived outside of the country might think, Iraq was still an extremely dangerous place. The danger was especially high if you were a Kurd as Omar was. If the wrong people found him out at night, they would kill him simply for being a Kurd. While he was aware of this danger, he felt deeply that it was worth the risk in order to reach his destination.

After driving into the desert for forty some minutes, Omar could see the meager sign ahead of him indicating his destination. He pulled the car to a stop in front of a sign that simply read *Grave Site* in bright red letters. Omar exited the car and walked up to the area where the ground was clearly disturbed, indicating the edge of the mass grave. When he reached the edge of the grave he stopped, knelt down, and said a prayer for the five thousand some people who were buried there.

Omar took a deep breath and searched his thoughts for a memory. The memory was from his childhood and it was extremely vivid. He was a man and as such he fought back the tears that were forming in his eyes as he tried desperately to find the memory. Finally, in the deepest corridors of his mind, he found it. In the memory, he was a four-year-old boy and he and his father were fishing down at the river. It was the only memory that Omar had of his father. Two days after the fishing trip, Omar's father was murdered by those in power for no other reason than that he was a Kurd. Omar and his mother were only saved by neighbors of theirs who were horrified by the ethnic cleansing that was occurring. Omar's father had not been so lucky. There were five thousand other people in this mass grave but Omar had only come to it to speak to one soul. The one soul that meant more to him than any other soul in heaven. Omar had come here to speak to his father.

The grave was hundreds of meters long and Omar had no idea where his father's body was in relation to the grave itself. Omar had always felt that since his father was a great man that fate had put him in the center of the gravesite. Omar walked to the center of the mass grave and began talking aloud, "Father, I have come here today to discuss a great matter with you." Omar paused for a moment to compose himself, then continued, "I have met a woman, father. She is beautiful and caring and I mean to make her my wife. Though you are not with me in body, I know that you are still with me in spirit. I have come here to your resting place to ask for your blessing in this marriage."

Omar stopped talking for a moment when he saw a figure walking toward him from the other side of the gravesite. The figure appeared to be an older woman. While many people came to the gravesite to speak to the dead, it was odd that a woman would come out here alone at night. She was putting her life in mortal danger. Aside from the fact that she was alone, Omar also thought it strange that she was coming from the desert itself. Omar had driven forty minutes from the city and this woman was coming out of the vast desert? Omar shrugged and thought that perhaps she was part of a nomadic family of goat herders. He reminded himself that he was here to ask his father's blessing on the most important decision of his life and he quickly pushed thoughts of the woman from his mind.

He started speaking again, "She is a fine woman, father. She will honor our family and bear you many grandchildren to honor your memory and…" Omar stopped talking as he watched the form of the old woman walking directly over the disturbed ground of the massive grave. In a rage, Omar screamed at her, "Woman, how dare you walk there! Have you no respect for the dead beneath your feet?"

The old woman made no reply. She simply turned her face toward Omar and as the moon revealed her features, Omar began to scream in terror. Her flesh had a putrid yellow color and as

Omar looked at her more closely he could see that her flesh was literally rotting off of her body. The only clothing that she wore was a torn and faded brown hooded garment that ran from her head to her knees. She was turning toward Omar when she removed the hood from her head and revealed her ghastly face. The woman had long black hair that was knotted and tangled. She had only a few teeth in her mouth that stuck out from the decayed flesh of her gums. Her most horrifying aspects were the hollowed out sockets that once housed her eyes. The woman was not a goat herding nomad. She was Akhkhazu, the Mesopotamian goddess of plague and death. She looked briefly toward Omar before turning her gaze to the ground below her. She opened her mouth and a sound like the wind whipping through the desert emanated from it and Omar thought that he heard the sound say *"Rise!"*

The ground that comprised the gravesite began to move and shake. Omar watched in disbelief as a skeletal head began to pierce the ground and reach up to the night sky. Omar was frozen with fear at the sight of the dead rising before him. The thought that his father's body was among the newly raised dead drove the fear deeper into his heart than he would have ever have thought possible. The horror he was witnessing frightened Omar to the point where his body was not responding to his mind's command to run to the car, but the sight of what happened next was more than his mind could withstand.

The bodies that were rising from the grave began to walk toward each other. As they came into contact their arms, legs, fingers, toes, and hair began to weave together. Some of the bodies began to bend at angles that caused their bones to snap and break. Once a base had been formed, the bodies began to pile on top of one another as their limbs and extremities continued to intertwine. Omar watched in horror as the corpses continued to weave themselves together into a Colossus of interwoven corpses. The Colossus was hundreds of feet tall and had the outline of man but with no distinguishable facial features. While the Colossus itself had no features, Omar could make out the faces of each and every corpse that was lashed together comprising the giant's body. The sickening sound of bones cracking could be heard as the demon took a step and the faces of dozens of corpses served as his foot.

The nightmare began walking toward Omar and he tried to run, but as he stood up, he caught a glimpse of the corpses that comprised the foot of the Colossus and there staring back at Omar was the decayed face of his father.

After so many years, his father's face was little more than a skeleton but Omar saw that face every day in his memory and he knew every curve of his father's face. By the structure of the skull alone, Omar knew that he had found the father he had come out to the land of the dead to speak to. The tears that Omar had fought to hide from his father now streamed down his face as the Colossus took a step toward him bringing the mangled face of his father right in front of his son. Omar was stricken with grief when he suddenly felt his skin burning. He tore off his shirt to find boils and lesions forming across his skin. He felt a wave of vertigo and then he fell to the ground. Omar was dying from a plague as the corpse of his father watched him from the body of the Colossus of Death.

Omar's senses were failing as he beheld what happened next. Akhkhazu reached up into the night sky and waved her hand downward, beckoning something to descend from the heavens. The area around Omar went dark as the moon itself was blocked from the sky. A form far larger than the Colossus of Death landed next to the giant. Omar squinted his quickly failing eyes to focus his vision. What he saw was a massive eagle with the head of a lion. Omar briefly recalled the legend of Anzu, the ancient god of storms and wind. Omar rolled onto his back because the pain of the boils spreading across his stomach was too much to bear. He turned his head toward the horrors that were standing where the communal grave once was. Even in death, he was unable to tear himself from looking at macabre events taking place around him. Once more he heard the wind like sound of Akhkhazu speaking.

First, the goddess spoke to the Colossus, "*Marduk has sent me to deal with the humans. Go and spread my plague to them. Let nothing stop you until the last human lays dead before you. I will remain here. From this place of death, I can channel my power into you.*" The formless face of the Colossus nodded then turned to face the city from which Omar had come. Next, she looked toward Anzu. She pointed at the Colossus, "*Follow him. Protect him from the humans and their weapons. Beware the leviathan that walks. His strength is such that he was able to topple Olympus."* Anzu roared then shot up into the sky. Omar could see him circling above the Colossus. The last thing that Omar saw was Akhkhazu returning to the middle of the grave where she sat down and folded her legs as if she was meditating. Omar took one last breath and then his suffering finally ended. As the Colossus walked past Omar, one of the bodies that had comprised one of its toes finally shattered into pieces under the weight of the corpses that it was supporting. As though it was a puppet controlled by a marionette, Omar's corpse rose to its feet and walked over to the Colossus. The arms of the other bodies around the area of the toe where the previous corpse had shattered reached out for him. They grabbed Omar's body and within seconds, his body had intertwined with the rest of the bodies comprising the toe of the Colossus. Omar's body was only a few scant feet away from that of his father. Omar had come to the gravesite to ask his father's blessing in marrying the woman he loved. Now with each step that the Colossus took, both Omar and his father were heading closer to Omar's would be bride. Omar had dreamed that one day his father would meet his bride in the afterlife, but as the Colossus reached the edge of the city, Omar's dream became an all too real nightmare.

CHAPTER 24
VIRGINIA

Luke was walking down the long corridor toward Chimera's holding bay with his family. Melissa had known all along what Luke what was working with but due to security reasons she had been unable to actually see Chimera. That all changed when the general public became aware of Chimera and his role in the war against the invading gods. Luke's oldest daughter Stacy had also seen him with Chimera on television and she had questions about the monster. Luke explained to her that Chimera was Daddy's friend and that he was working with Daddy to save the world. Sally was happy that Daddy was doing well at his new job as a rescue hero. Once Chimera had been given the week of rest that he had required, Luke had managed to get approval from Parsons to take his family to see the kaiju.

When they had reached the doors at the end of the corridor, Luke bent down and put his eyes up to the retinal scanner. The light shined on them and the door opened. Stacy ran over to him, "Daddy, can the computer look at my eyes too?"

Luke hugged her, "Sorry, honey, the computer will only open the door for Daddy and a few other people. If I put your eyes up to it the computer would shut down and not let us in."

Stacy replied with a dramatic sigh, "Okay, Daddy."

The door opened and they were immediately hit by the smell of Chimera. Luke winced a little while Melissa began to gag, and Stacy screamed, "Daddy, it smells like a huge fart" and the eighteen-month-old Sally repeated her sister with, "Stinky fart."

Melissa looked toward Luke, "My god that smell is awful! How do you work with it every day?"

Luke shrugged, "You become a little more desensitized to it each day. The smell is always there but it becomes a little more tolerable each day that you are exposed it."

Melissa was coughing as she replied, "Well I don't know that I will want to come down here often enough to become used to the smell."

Luke reached over and kissed his wife then he switched on the lights to the corridor. He then picked up both girls in his arms. Luke was grinning from ear to ear as he walked with his family down the foul smelling corridor. After the affair in Greece and the journey home, he had been able to enjoy three full days with his family. He had filled Melissa in on most of the details of his adventures with Chimera, although he purposely left out the most dangerous parts to him and the gory details of Chimera's battles. After the three days, he had spent the next week working with Chimera a few hours a day then returning home to his family.

As they were completing the long journey down the corridor, they suddenly felt the entire hallway shake. Melissa gave her husband a worried look. Luke smiled, "I have been conducting a preference assessment with Chimera. Basically, it means introducing new things to him to find out what he enjoys interacting with. Given that he is composed of part of gorilla and lion, a ball seemed like a good place to start. I had the largest rubber ball in existence constructed for him. It allows him to get some exercise and adds more to his life than simply fighting and earning food."

Melissa smiled and hugged Luke, "Only you would think about assuring that a giant government-made monster got the most that he could out of life."

Luke shrugged, "Chimera is more than a monster or a weapon; he is my student. I see working with him in the same light that I saw myself working with students with autism. In both cases, I have two goals. To teach them functional skills and to improve their quality of life. Chimera has already mastered the functional skill of protecting humanity from threats. Now I have to add the improving quality of life aspect to his curriculum." He paused for a moment and his voiced softened, "The ball is at least something. I wish I could do more for him to help him enjoy his life."

Melissa placed her hand on his shoulder, "Don't worry. I have faith that you will find something else he will enjoy."

The ground shook again and Luke and his family bounced up and down a little. They took a few steps forward to where they could see Chimera running back and forth across the massive area that held him. Stacy screamed, "Daddy, I see him!" she jumped down from his arms and went sprinting to the observation deck. Melissa looked a little scared but Luke reassured her, "She can only make it to the observation deck. She will be perfectly safe there, and even if she were to run into the pen, Chimera is perfectly safe around humans. I have even been working with him on putting his ball down when humans are around."

Stacy ran up to the observation deck and simply said, "Wow!" The toddler Sally asked to be put down. She hit the ground and immediately ran after her sister to the observation deck where she gave a "Wow!"

Melissa and Luke quickly followed them and Melissa fought the urge to say, "Wow" when she saw Chimera for the first time in person. Chimera pushed the ball away from him and then did a summersault as he pursued it. The monster was making the excited sounds that a gorilla would make if he were playing with a favorite toy. Toombs was quietly sitting at his desk in the observation room reviewing some of Chimera's vital signs. This was the first time that he had seen Luke with his family. Toombs shook his head as he thought, wasn't it enough that Luke was tall and athletic? That he had the admiration and respect of Diana? That he was the one seen on the news leading Chimera into battle and the new hero of millions? All he did was train the monster? Didn't the man who created the creature deserve at least some of the credit? Toombs stood up and stormed out of the room. Luke turned around to introduce his family to Toombs when he saw the doctor walking out of the room. Luke called out to him but Toombs either didn't hear him or he chose to ignore him.

Melissa kept her eyes on Chimera even though she was talking to Luke, "I saw him on TV but to see him in person gives you a different perspective." She shook her head as Chimera picked up the massive ball and studied it for a moment before throwing it across the compound and then bounding after it. She whispered, "Look at the way that he examines the ball. You can see that he is studying it." She looked to Luke, "I know that you said it but from the pictures I saw on TV I could only think of him as a monster, but you are right, he is more than that, isn't he?"

Luke nodded, "He is roughly about as intelligent as a two-year-old human."

Melissa gestured to her youngest daughter, "Are you telling me that Chimera is as smart as Sally?"

Luke nodded, 'Well, in an overall sense, yes. Obviously, he does not have the communication skills that Sally has, but if we were to test the two of them on various types of intelligence, their overall scores would come out to be roughly the same."

Stacy grabbed her dad's leg, "Daddy, I don't want to see this stinky monster anymore. Can we go and see that pony I saw you riding on TV?"

Luke laughed, "I don't think Jason would like being referred to as a pony! Yes, we can go see him. You know that if you give him a carrot he will be your friend for life!"

Stacy jumped for joy. "Daddy please, please, please. Let me give him a carrot!"

Luke picked up Stacy, "I might know where we can find a carrot or two." The floor shook again as Chimera went tumbling after his ball once more. Luke pointed to the kaiju, "Say goodbye to Chimera, girls."

Stacy said a quick goodbye and Sally followed with "Bye, monster. Bye," and then she blew him a kiss. Luke then led his family down to the stables where they met Jason. The girls and Melissa were all enthralled with the majestic warhorse. Stacy once more referred to him as a pony to which Luke suggested that he was a noble steed. Luke and his family enjoyed their day together. The time with his family not only refreshed Luke, but it helped remind him what he was fighting for. They were preparing to leave the stable and head home when Luke's phone rang.

The caller ID flashed the name of Parsons across the screen. He looked to Melissa, "Duty calls." He answered the phone, listened to what Parsons had to say, then he ended with the military style, "Yes, sir." He turned to Melissa, "There is something going in the Middle East that looks like it will require Chimera's attention."

Melissa's face lost its color, "The Middle East! What happened to the no active combat zone part of this job?"

Luke hugged his wife, "Believe me, the world as a whole is starting to see that fighting each other is something we can longer afford to do. If the gods are attacking the Middle East, the various groups of people there will soon find themselves faced with a common enemy. The only threat will come from the gods and their monsters and I have Chimera to deal with them. I will be fine." He looked into his wife's eyes, "I will miss you and the kids though. Hopefully with the rubber covering added to the Argos we won't lose contact with you again for so long." He gave his wife a hug and kiss then reached down and hugged his kids before running off to join Parsons and the rest of the team onboard the Argos.

Through a portal beyond the abilities of human senses to perceive, a single eye watched the interactions with Luke and his family. A massive hand reached up to scratch a chin buried under long white beard as the wisest of all of the gods studied his enemy.

CHAPTER 25
BAGHDAD, IRAQ

Aiden stood in the shadows of one of many alleyways of the streets of Baghdad. He was watching as a platoon of tanks and soldiers composed of collation forces as well as the Iraqi army marched down one of the main streets of the city. The soldiers thought that they were marching to meet the Colossus and stop him from spreading his plague across the country. Aiden was keenly aware, however, that the soldiers were marching to their deaths. Even if the military believed that they stood a chance against the Colossus in direct combat, they had no idea what was circling in the air above them at an altitude far too high for any human to see it.

Aiden watched as the Colossus turned the corner and began marching toward the military. With each step, the Colossus of Death covered an entire city block and as he passed each block any human within one hundred feet of him immediately develop lesions and boils on their skin. As if the Colossus itself was not disturbing enough, there was also the parade of newly deceased corpses that followed him and were constantly being absorbed into his body to replace the corpses that fell apart as a result of being part of the gargantuan horror.

Even for Aiden, it was difficult to look at the Colossus. The grotesque creature's body was constantly in motion as some corpses fell off of it and others either jumped onto its foot or scaled the creature to be interwoven into the mass of the dead.

The sun was high in the air and the temperature was sweltering, causing the smell of the rotting giant to permeate throughout the city. Aiden watched as several of the hardened soldiers vomited at the combined sight and smell of the Colossus. Still Aiden had to admit that the men and women of the military were brave. They continued to march toward the Colossus even though they must have known by now that doing so would expose them to the plague that the giant carried with it. In a way, Aiden knew that most of the soldiers would be rewarded for their bravery as they would not suffer from the sickness of the Colossus and that their deaths would be quick.

There were at least twenty tanks lined in rows of two with the soldiers intermixed within them and behind them. The tanks rolled to a stop roughly ten blocks from the Colossus and took aim. The tanks were about to fire when a huge shadow fell over the city. Aiden found the shack that he was looking for and stepped inside the doorway. He saw the family that was cowering in the corner looking at him in disbelief. Aiden typically dealt with humans with an arrogant demeanor but in the shadow of the Colossus he actually pitied them. He spoke to the family in their native language, "Don't worry, I am here to offer my assistance." The father of the family simply shook his head at Aiden. Aiden could see that the man was clearly terrified beyond belief at what was happening around him.

Aiden looked back out of the door to see the shadow over the city growing larger by the second. The soldiers looked skyward to see the massive Anzu swooping down at them. The creature opened its eagle-like wings as its lion's head emitted an ear-shattering roar. The roar was followed by multiple crashes of thunder and flashes of lightening. The tanks and all of their electronics were rendered inert. The soldiers began to fire their useless rifles at Anzu as he continued to flap his wings unleashing hurricane force winds in conjunction with continued bursts of lighting. In under a minute, the entire defense force had been slain by Anzu. The lion-headed eagle roared then took back to the sky. When the Colossus walked over the fallen soldiers their corpses rose off of the ground and they began to follow the walking horror. Aiden turned around to face the family huddled in the corner awaiting their deaths as the Colossus approached their home. The family consisted of a father, mother, two sons and two daughters. Aiden kept his eyes fixed on the oldest daughter. She was a beautiful girl of nineteen years old. He approached the family and addressed the father and the daughter, "That creature will be here in a minute and you will all die from the plague it is spreading." Aiden paused for a moment to let the words sink in. He knew full well that he could have simply taken the girl and there would have been nothing the rest of the family could do about it. While he truly did not care if any human lived or died, he did understand that to die as a result of being exposed to the Colossus was an experience that he would not wish on any creature. With that in mind, he used the family's beliefs to give them some small measure of comfort in their final moments. He spoke in a very sincere tone, "Your oldest daughter has been chosen by Allah to be saved from the horror that is coming. I will take her and spare her the suffering which accompanies the giant."

The mother burst into tears and wrapped her arms around her remaining children as the father praised Allah, kissed his daughter, then handed her over to Aiden. Aiden took the girl in his arms as she looked at her family and whispered that she loved them. The ground shook as the Colossus took another step closer to the family's house. Aiden placed his hand on the girls chin and turned her head to face him, "Time to go." Aiden then kissed the girl and in a flash they disappeared. Aiden and the girl had no sooner vanished than lesions began to appear on the skin of the huddled family. Several minutes later, the corpses of the family were part of the ever growing walking dead that followed the Colossus waiting until they were called to become part of the nightmare.

CHAPTER 26

Two hours after alerting General Parsons to the horror that was currently taking place in Iraq, Diana found herself aboard the Argos and once more in the briefing room. She was sitting with her laptop and putting together the final aspects of her presentation on the threat that they were going to intercept. Given the location of the activity, she was pretty much certain that the Mesopotamian gods were making their play. From the reports that she was receiving, she was able to identify at least one of the kaiju that was currently attacking the Middle East. The lion-headed eagle was almost assuredly Anzu. She laughed to herself that only a few short weeks ago she was telling her college class that myths about giant birds were actually reports of Teratorns. She could just hear some of the students jumping at the chance to tell her how wrong she was now that Anzu himself was flying around Iraq.

While she knew who Anzu was, the other creature was more of a mystery. There was nothing in Mesopotamian mythology or any other mythology about a plague-spreading giant composed of hundreds of corpses. Her best guess was that the creature was an avatar of one of the Mesopotamian' goddess.

Diana was also starting to gather numerous reports from all over the world about abductions that were taking place involving a blond haired man and woman who seemingly abducted people in a flash of light. She suspected that the abductions may be related to the god's declaration that they were going to take numerous attractive people as breeders for a new race of hybrids. She did not yet have enough information to present the situation to Parsons. She was unable to identify who or what these two blonde people were and without identifying them she would not be able to start researching various mythologies on how to stop them.

She had just typed the last few lines of her report when Parsons, Toombs, and Luke walked into the room. When she saw that the men remained standing, so she too stood up, knowing that Parsons was about to turn on the monitor that was linked to the President's situation room.

The monitor came on showing the face of the president. Parsons saluted and immediately began to fill the president in on the situation in Iraq, "Good morning, Mr. President. Yesterday we received information that a giant composed of corpses appeared outside of Kurdistan. We suspect that it may have originally been formed from the corpses buried in the mass gravesite outside of the city. It seems that giant carried a plague into Kurdistan that wiped out the entire population of the city. The giant is currently making its way across Iraq and spreading the plague, killing thousands of people per day. We also have unconfirmed reports that bodies of the plague victims are following the giant. When armed forces attempted to confront the giant, they were attacked and wiped out by a massive winged creature. The good news is that this plague burns itself out quickly in that is only being spread by the giant. So far everything that we know indicates that if we are able to stop the giant, then we will be able to stop the plague without having a pandemic on our hands." Parsons motioned to Diana, "I will now allow Ms. Cain to review with us what we are up against."

Diana stood up and brought her report onto the screen showing an artist's rendition of Anzu, "This creature is Anzu. He is a giant bird with the head of a lion and he is the Mesopotamian god of storms. He had wiped out the platoon that encountered him, but given our experience with Zeus, it is likely that he also possess the power to generate EMPs and therefore shut down much of our technology."

She clicked to another slide showing a decrepit corpse of a woman, "There is really nothing in Mesopotamian mythology that describes a giant composed of corpses. We have heard that some people in the area are referring to the giant as the Colossus of Death." She then highlighted the woman on the screen, "Given that we know the giant is spreading a plague, I suspect that he may be an avatar or representative of the Mesopotamian goddess of death and plague known as Akhkhazu. It seems that the Colossus and Anzu are operating in the same fashion that the Charybdis and the Scylla served for the Olympians. With the Colossus spreading the means of mankind's demise, and Anzu acting as his guardian."

The President addressed the entire team with his next line of questioning, "Okay then. How are we going to deal with the current threat and how do we put an end to this sect of gods permanently?"

Parsons handled the first part of the question, "In regards to the Colossus and Anzu, the Argos should arrive in the Middle East in the next twenty four hours. The current path of the Colossus has him headed directly for Saudi Arabia. At the speed he is moving, we should be able to have Chimera intercept the Colossus and presumably Anzu shortly after they cross the border into Saudi Arabia. The good news is that much like the Charybdis, this plague seems to only be affecting humans so Chimera should be able to engage the Colossus directly. Mr. Davis and the strike team that will support him will be placed in hazmat suits as protection against the plague. I will defer to Ms. Cain for the final solution to this sect of gods."

Diana sighed as she offered her explanation on how to end the threat of the Mesopotamian gods, "These gods did not have definitive base of operations in the way that the Olympians used Mount Olympus. In Mesopotamian mythology, their supreme god Marduk lived on the banks of the Euphrates River in Babylon or what is current day Hillah. Mythology also suggests the Marduk is in possession of the Tablets of Destiny. These tablets are said to be the source of all knowledge and understanding. If we are able to find and defeat Marduk, these tablets should contain the information on how to force the Mesopotamian gods to leave Earth for good." Diana took a deep breath, "I cannot guarantee that these tablets exists or even if they do that we will be able to use them, but given what he have seen the past few weeks, the possibility that they are real seems plausible." She could see from the look on the President's face that he was not overly pleased with all of the unknowns in this course of action. She shrugged her shoulders, "At the very least if we march Chimera directly into Babylon it should be enough to get Marduk's attention."

The President nodded, "It seems that this is our best course of action." He looked toward Parsons, "General, get every ounce of speed that you can out that expensive ship. I want Chimera engaging these creatures before the oil supply is put into jeopardy."

Parson's responded with a simple, "Yes, sir." He then dismissed the group.

Luke walked over to Diana, "Can I assume that you are also being fitted with a hazmat suit so that you can ride with me and Jason again."

She smiled at him, "You got it, cowboy. How many times do I have to tell you that I won't let you face these things alone?"

Luke smiled, "Hopefully this is the last time you have to tell me that but I am afraid I may here it quite a few more times before this all said and done."

He held his arm out to Diana, "Well then, Milady, once more into the unknown?"

She looped her arm through his, "After you, my brave and gallant knight." The two of them strolled out of the briefing room arm and arm joking with each other and laughing.

Toombs sat fuming in his chair. His mind was awash in frustration and jealousy. Did anyone even notice that he was in the room? They didn't even acknowledge him in the meeting. Had he been reduced to simply giving medical reports on Chimera and then going back to his room to sit by himself while Luke was friends with everyone on the ship? He stormed out of the room. He was well aware that Parsons either did not notice or did not care that he had left in such a fashion. He began talking to himself as he walked back to his cabin, "I created the monster. They should be worshipping me. Without me, every human on the planet would already be dead." Toombs mumbled to himself, "I'll find a way to show them how much I am worth. Then they will all see who the hero of this operation is." Toombs turned a corner to find two sailors standing in the corridor to his cabin. One was a tall blond male and the other was a gorgeous blonde woman. The homely little doctor took notice of how the woman arched her back and thrust her firm breasts forward as he was walking toward her. He slowed his pace to stare at the woman for a moment longer before rushing off to his cabin.

Allison turned to Aiden, "You see, brother. The gods we are slaves to and the humans they are fighting are playing a game of checkers while we are playing chess. Should the gods be defeated by simply standing here and making a subtle motion, I have laid the foundation for our rise to power." She looked down toward Toombs' cabin for moment before addressing her brother again, "Speaking of the gods, we still need to harvest a few more breeders for them. Should they prevail in this war, we will want to make sure that we stay in their good graces until such a point that the means to overthrow them presents itself." She closed her eyes and leaned back against the hull of the ship. A second later her eyes snapped open and she was smiling, "It seems that I am due at a wedding." She turned to her brother and winked at him then she disappeared in flash of bright light. Aiden started walking down the corridor to make sure that when he teleported he was unseen. In a world where gods and monsters battled for supremacy of the planet, the creature that he feared the most was his sister. He knew that both her cunning and ruthlessness reached depths of which neither god nor monster could conceive.

CHAPTER 27

Allison appeared outside of church in Boston. Her clothing had switched from the military fatigues she was wearing on the Argos to a skimpy dress that most women would find far to risqué for a wedding. She adjusted herself properly so that her dress was barely managing to hold in her body in certain places that were sure to draw attention to her.

She entered into the church and immediately drew the attention of the friends of the groom serving as ushers. All three of the young men quickly rushed whoever they were escorting to their pew to the closest seat and then rushed back to meet Allison. She smiled at the first young man to come meet her. He immediately tried to hit on her, "You must be on the bride's side, because you are far too hot to be connected to Mike in anyway."

The playfully vindictive Allison jumped at the opportunity to sit on the bride's side of the church. As the young man was escorting her, she could hear all of the women in the church quietly commenting on how she was dressed. Allison reveled in being the target of their jealousy. As she was being escorted through the church, she could see the eyes of her target lock onto her. The groom was staring at her and she could already see him reconsidering his decision to spend the rest of his brief life with only one woman. Allison smiled realizing that she could make her move now if she wanted to and take this young man to the gods, but she would enjoy herself more if she waited a little to make her move all the more dramatic.

The music changed and the bridesmaids began to make their way toward the altar. Each of them took a moment to look at Allison as they walked by. She could see in their eyes a mixture of confusion as to who she could be along with disgust at the way that she was dressed. The music changed once more, signaling the traditional bridal entrance. The bride entered the church and while most of the eyes were fixed on the bride, the eyes of the groom were still fixed on Allison.

She laughed to herself. This poor human bride didn't stand a chance of holding the attention of the men in the church when there was a nymph-like Allison nearby. In a way, Allison thought that she was doing this young woman a favor by taking her would be husband from her and sparing her a life of monogamy. As a nymph, Allison's life revolved around pleasure and sex. The disappointing part of her existence was that she was only in control of one aspect of the pleasurable part of existence. Nymphs were free to have sex with anyone that they pleased. To a human male, a nymph-like Allison was almost irresistible. This was a fact that she relished in flaunting to human females as she had done at the beach and was going to do here on a grander scale in a few moments.

The downside to her existence was that she and the other nymphs served as little more than glorified sex slaves to the gods. If a god wished for her to have sex with him, she was required to be there at his request. She didn't mind if a god like Zeus or Apollo called for her but when a hideous deity like Hades called for her, it was nothing short of torture. In addition to those duties, the nymphs were also the conduits through which the gods and goddess engaged in their escapades with mortals. The gods could rarely be bothered to gather their mortal desires themselves. Her brother Aiden had been sent by Zeus to gather Alcmene when his liaisons with her had created the demi-god Hercules.

Allison smiled as she considered the fact that gods had neglected to check in on the humans for too long of a time. Even the gods did not yet want to admit that the humans had evolved to the point where they represented a threat to overthrowing them. The Chimera monster was proof of their power. The behemoth had already overthrown the proud Olympians and now he was going to challenge the Mesopotamian gods. In the end, it did not matter if the humans and their monster or the gods won this war. All that mattered is that as a result of the war both sides would be significantly weaker, allowing her and her fellow nymphs to rise to power. She laughed to herself; monsters, swords, cannons… these are things that the gods and humans thought were powerful weapons. The fools didn't realize that the oldest and most powerful weapon in existence was sex. Allison was all too aware of this fact. She knew what a powerful force sex was and she was a master of that particular weapon.

The priest had almost reached the pivotal point in the ceremony. Allison still had to play her part for the gods and gather the breeders that they required but soon she knew that she would be in position to rule over this world and any other that she chose. The priest turned to the gathered friends and family, "If anyone has anyone has a reason that this man and this woman should not be joined in holy matrimony let them speak now or..."

Allison raised her hand and stood up, "I have a reason!"

A collective gasp echoed throughout the church as she was walking toward the altar. Everyone in the church turned to look at her. When the videographer saw her, he focused his camera on her, thinking that he could edit her out of the video later and keep the footage of her for himself.

The priest was clearly forgetting his vows of chastity as he looked at Allison and stammered, "Yes, my child, what reason is this?"

Allison laughed, "Isn't it obvious? This gentlemen would much rather be with me than this sad excuse for a woman."

The bride screamed, 'Excuse me, but who the hell are you?"

Allison smiled, "Silly girl. I am the woman who is going to take your husband from you." She looked into the groom's eyes, "Isn't that right, lover?"

The groom didn't say a word. He was helplessly trapped in Allison's stare. He simply walked away from his bride and into Allison's embrace. Allison kissed him once and then she looked at the bride with sly smile and mouthed the words "Sorry." She then went to kiss the groom again and with her trademark flash of light she teleported him away. Throughout the entire ordeal the videographer had kept his camera focused on Allison.

CHAPTER 28

Luke and Diana were wearing hazmat suits as they rode on top of Jason through the Saudi Arabian desert toward the border with Iraq. Chimera was walking at a slow pace behind them and he was followed by SEAL Team Beta who were also wearing hazmat suits. Luke was moving Jason at a slow walk due to the heat of the desert. With the team wearing the bulky hazmat suits, dehydration was a legitimate concern in the desert. Everyone had made sure that they were as hydrated as possible prior to leaving the ship. Jason and Chimera were both given plenty of water as well.

Luke looked back over his shoulder at the kaiju. Chimera appeared to be weathering the desert sun and heat well so far. Chimera had yet to be tested in extreme heat and the team was unsure of how quickly dehydration would hit him. To look at Chimera's whale-like skin Luke was concerned that he would roast in the desert sun, but Toombs assured him that he did better work than that when he had created the beast. Toombs explained that while Chimera's skin appeared to mainly be comprised of the part of him that was derived from the sperm whale, in actuality his skin was composed of equal parts lion and gorilla as well. Toombs also felt that he would function as well in the heat as a lion would. He further suggested that with a generous supply of water prior to leaving the ship that Chimera would be capable of withstanding the desert heat for several hours even under battle conditions before he succumbed to the heat.

Luke and Diana remained relatively quiet as they rode atop Jason. Aside from the heat and bulky hazmat suits, their thoughts were focused on the task at hand. Finally, Diana was unable to hold her feelings in any longer. She spoke at a level barely above a whisper, "Luke, I ah... I am not sure that I am going to be able to handle what's coming. I mean a giant snake woman and a three headed dog are terrifying enough but this thing. This Colossus of Death. It's made up of dead people. Dead people who all died under the most horrifying conditions. In one way or another, they were killed simply for being who they were. They were executed for being a Kurd, for being someone who spoke up against the state, or for simply being human. Isn't it enough that they died under such circumstances? Does their torture have to be continued in death as they become part of that giant of death?"

Luke sighed, "I don't know what to tell you. Those people have suffered more than anyone ever should suffer in life or in death. I am not a theologian. I don't know if there is any part of those people trapped in that creature. The only thing that I do know is that if there some part of them trapped in that monster, then it is all the more reason for us to destroy the Colossus and free those poor souls from that hell."

Jason suddenly stopped walking. The horse took a step backward and then shook his head. At the same time, Chimera stopped walking and shook his head as well. He looked into the distance and roared, but this roar was different from the roar that he unleashed when he was challenging an opponent. This roar sounded almost as if it was sympathetic.

Diana whispered, "What's wrong with them?"

Luke responded in a solemn voice, "Their sense of smell is far better than ours. They can smell it. They are picking up on the scent of thousands of corpses rotting in the desert sun on the horizon. They can smell death itself coming for us."

Luke steadied Jason and then urged him on. The mighty horse was reluctant but he obeyed his master's command. As Jason started moving forward so did Chimera and the SEALS who were following a good distance behind the kaiju.

The duo rode on in silence for ten minutes until they saw it walking across the desert sand. The Colossus was directly ahead of them and the site of the monstrosity was far worse than they ever could have imagined. Even from the distance they were at, they could see the corpses writhing and moving as they either fell off of the Colossus or joined its horrible mass. Behind the Colossus, they could see the army of the dead that was following it and waiting to be called to become part of the nightmare.

Diana almost screamed at Luke, "Quickly, take off your helmet and direct Chimera to attack that thing. We don't know how close it has to get before we are risking exposure to the plague!" Luke ripped his helmet off of his face, lifted his speaking horn, pointed at the Colossus, and shouted, "Chimera, attack!"

Chimera lifted his front hands off of the ground, beat his chest, roared, and then charged at the Colossus. The Colossus maintained its steady pace. Chimera had covered almost half of the distance between Jason and the Colossus when a huge shadow fell over him. Chimera looked skyward to see the winged form of Anzu above him.

Luke and Diana watched as Anzu swooped down toward Chimera. As massive as Chimera was, Anzu was nearly twice the size of the kaiju. They looked on in disbelief as Anzu wrapped his claws around Chimera and lifted him off of the ground. Anzu flew one large circle over the area then he began streaking off into the desert with Chimera.

Luke and Diana suddenly found themselves with nothing but a few hundred feet of desert between them and the Colossus of Death with his seemingly endless following of zombies.

Chimera roared in defiance at the creature that had lifted him off of the ground. The kaiju unsheathed his claws and began swiping at the winged god but he was unable to reach the monstrous bird. He then tried to shake his body free but he could not break Anzu's grasp. Finally, Chimera lifted his head up and fired a sonar blast directly into Anzu's face. Anzu's lion-like face contorted in pain causing him to lose control of his flight pattern sending both monsters crashing into the desert below. The impact of the crash jarred Chimera loose from the god's grip. Chimera found his face buried in the sand. He stood and up and shook the sand out of his eyes.

Chimera looked around to find Anzu still trying to recover from the effects of having his sensory organs overloaded from the sonar blast. Anzu was shaking his head and flapping his wings when Chimera charged him and then leapt onto his back. Chimera sank his claws into the god's back and then he opened his jaws and bit deep into Anzu's neck. Anzu roared in pain and shook his body violently sending Chimera flying off of his back and crashing into the sand once more.

Anzu roared at Chimera and began to flap his wings causing him to rise into the air. Anzu circled around Chimera twice before hovering directly over the kaiju. Anzu's wings began to shimmer and a second later Chimera was hammered with a barrage of thunder and lightning. In addition to having his body racked with pain from electricity, Anzu's wings generated a windstorm that sent the desert sand whipping into Chimera. The sand was traveling at a velocity of well over two hundred miles per hour. The effect was similar to having millions of automatic rifles firing at the kaiju in unison. Chimera was staggering backward from the attack when he bent down and dug his claws into the sand to steady himself.

Chimera immediately recalled his battle with Zeus and he knew that this attack would wear him down in time. The wind and sand had disoriented the kaiju. He had no idea where he was in relation to his enemy. The monster sent out a low level sonar wave just as a whale would do when hunting in the dark depths of the ocean. The sonar wave bounced off of Anzu and came back to Chimera giving the kaiju the location of his enemy. Chimera forced his head to look in the direction of Anzu then he unleashed one of his focused sonar blasts. When the invisible blast hit Anzu, it caused him to convulse and fall to the ground in agony.

For a moment, the two kaiju stood in the desert panting and not moving as each beast recovered from the other's attack. It was Chimera that recovered first. The monster ran toward Anzu and stretched his head out in front of his body. Using his sperm whale head as a battering ram, Chimera crashed into Anzu's midsection. The collision sent the winged god tumbling onto his back. Chimera sprang on top of Anzu then he brought his fists crashing down into Anzu's lion like face. Chimera lifted his hands up to strike the god again when Anzu's gargantuan jaws shot up and clamped down on Chimera's arm.

Chimera roared in pain as the larger Anzu stood up and lifted Chimera off of the ground. Chimera hung helpless in the god's grip. Seeing that the monster was at his mercy, Anzu extended his massive wings then brought them crashing into Chimera's ribs. Anzu repeated the move as Chimera used his free hand to claw at Anzu's face but the kaiju's efforts were in vain as the god refused to yield his grip. Anzu brought his wings crashing into Chimera twice more before Chimera was able to time the attack. When Anzu brought his wings forward for the fourth time, Chimera turned his head and sent his face crashing into the joint that connected Anzu's wing to his body. Chimera could feel the bone underneath Anzu's feathers snap in half as his reinforced head smashed into the wing.

Anzu released Chimera and stepped backward as he roared in pain. Anzu began to flap his good wing but the broken wing hung helplessly at his side. Seeing that Anzu was unable to fly and that he was defenseless on his left side, the lion hunting instincts buried in Chimera's mind snapped into action. The kaiju dropped down to all fours and he began to circle towards Anzu's left side.

Anzu attempted to turn with Chimera to protect his injured left side but his avian body was not nearly as mobile on the ground as Chimera's body was. When Chimera had circled around Anzu, he leapt toward the injured wing. Chimera latched his claws and teeth into the crippled appendage. The kaiju then began pulling on the wing and tearing at it. Anzu tried in vain to strike Chimera with his right wing but the hybrid was well out of range. Anzu shirked in pain and fear. In an attempt to free himself from the kaiju's grip, Anzu generated a lightning strike from his good wing and sent it streaming into Chimera. Chimera once again felt the pain of electricity but instead of forcing him to release his grip it only caused the kaiju to double his efforts. Chimera bit down even harder into Anzu's wing then the monster began to pull his body away from the god. The struggle continued for several minutes before Chimera finally tore Anzu's wing from his body.

A waterfall of blood poured out of Anzu's body and into the sand. The god-monster shrieked in pain as he spun around in helpless circles. Seizing his opportunity, Chimera leapt onto Anzu's chest and knocked him down. With Anzu trapped beneath him, Chimera bit into the god's throat. Chimera did not attempt to tear out Anzu's throat. He simply used his weight to pin Anzu to ground and he used his canines to pierce Anzu's trachea and inhibit the god's ability to breath. Unable to breath and bleeding profusely, Anzu struggled to push Chimera off of his chest. Chimera pressed down on Anzu and buried his claws into the body of the winged god. With his grip secure, Chimera continued to apply pressure to Anzu's throat. Anzu's struggles grew weaker by degree until the combination of lack of oxygen and blood loss caused the god-monster to expire.

Chimera maintained his grip for a few moments after Anzu had ceased struggling to make sure that the beast had perished. When Chimera released his grip he did not beat his chest and roar in triumph. He simply sniffed the air. His face contorted in revulsion when he had located the odor of the thousands of rotting corpses that comprised the Colossus of Death. He roared and began walking in the direction that the odor was coming from. The kaiju's mind was fixed on carrying out the last order that his caretaker had given him. Chimera was going to destroy the Colossus of Death.

CHAPTER 29

Luke and Diana watched Anzu carry Chimera over the desert until the two beasts faded over the horizon. Once they were out of view, a cold shiver ran down Diana's spine when she saw how quickly that the Colossus of Death and his zombie followers were approaching them. She screamed at Luke, "Turn the horse around! Run back to the SEALS!"

Luke did not hesitate. He threw his face mask back onto his head and ordered Jason to turn around and run. The horse was galloping at a speed that Luke had yet to experience. The former teacher was still attempting to master the craft of horsemanship. Up until this point, he had only ridden at a fast trot so that he was able to keep pace with Chimera. Now Jason was running as if he were trying to hold the lead position at the end of the Kentucky Derby.

Diana wrapped her arms around Luke as the two of them were jostled from side to side from the power of the sprinting horse below them. Diana was nearly thrown off of the animal but Luke's quick reflexes were able to grab her arm and rewrap it around his waist. In a matter of a few minutes, they had reached SEAL Team Beta.

The captain of the squadron looked to Luke, "Without Chimera, what should we do sir?"

Luke gazed down at the man as if he was crazy, "I don't know! I am not military officer! Try to shoot the dammed thing!"

The captain replied with a "Sir, yes sir!"

The captain spun around to see the Colossus and his zombie horde just over two hundred yards from where they were standing. The horrible smell of decaying bodies wafted through desert. The odor was almost enough to make the hardened captain vomit. Aside from the disturbing smell, there was also the eerie buzzing sound that was coming from the Colossus. No one had noticed from a distance but millions and millions of flies were surrounding the Colossus and feeding off of the corpses that made up its putrid body.

The members of SEAL Team Beta winced in disgust at the sight of the abomination. The captain lifted his rifle and yelled to his men, "Open fire!" The roar of automatic rifle ripped through the desert as thousands of bullets tore into the bodies of the Colossus of Death. The rotting and mangled deceased that held together the body of the giant began to fall apart under the assault causing the Colossus itself to stumble. For a brief moment, Diana though that SEAL Team Beta might actually slay the beast. Then she watched in disbelief as the walking dead that followed the Colossus were absorbed into the giant itself. The new corpses were interwoven into areas where the damaged corpses had fallen from. When the new bodies merge with Colossus, the giant righted itself and began to walk toward SEAL Team Beta once again.

When the Colossus reached the SEALS, he stepped on those directly in his path, crushing them instantly, but for the most part he ignored the humans below him. Once he had stepped over the SEALS, he continued his march into Saudi Arabia. The SEALS looked at the beast in bewilderment for a second until the zombies that followed the Colossus fell upon them.

The first zombie to reach one of the SEALS pulled off his hazmat mask. The moment that the man was exposed to the air the plague that followed the Colossus infected him. The SEALS's face quickly became covered in boils as he rolled in the sand and screamed in pain. The scene repeated itself over and over again as the SEALS emptied their clips into the attacking zombies. The barrage of gunfire was able to render some of the corpses unable to move but for every one corpse that the SEALS destroyed there were a hundred more behind it. One by one, the members of SEAL Team Beta had their hoods ripped off exposing them to the deadly plague.

Luke and Diana watched in horror as the bodies of the dead SEALS rose from the ground and joined the zombie horde. Seeing that the SEALS had fallen, Luke forced his mind to break away from the horror. He directed Jason to turn around in an attempt to escape the dead only to find himself surrounded by deceased plague victims. The zombies slowly began to move in closer to Jason. One of the deceased SEALS had gotten close enough to the horse to grab Diana by the leg. Never one to be a damsel in distress, Diana grabbed the rifle off of the dead SEAL and then leaning on every zombie movie she had ever seen she fired a shot into the corpse's head.

To her dismay, the zombie ignored the bullet and continued to pull at her. She pointed the gun down and fired at the undead creature until its body fell to pieces. The disembodied hands and mouth of the zombie continued to reach for Jason even as they lay on the ground disconnected from the rest of the body.

Luke was on the verge of panic. The zombies were trying to pull him off of Jason and the cloud of flies that followed the zombies was so thick that they almost completely blocked out his vision. He was going to scream in frustration when he noticed that the zombies were only reaching for Diana and himself. For the most part, they were leaving Jason alone and free to move. Seeing his one chance, he yelled to Diana, "Hold on tight! I am going to try something!" Diana slung the rifle over her back and wrapped her arms around her best friend. When he could feel that Diana had a hold of him, Luke yanked up on Jason's reigns causing the horse to buck up and lift his front legs into the air. With his legs out in front of him, Jason began to use them like clubs to knock zombies to the ground. When Jason's front hooves fell back to the ground, Luke dug his heels into Jason's side and made silent promise to give the horse a basket full of apples and carrots if he could get them out of this alive. As soon as Luke's heels slammed into Jason's sides, the horse kicked out with his back legs, knocking down several of the zombies behind him. With some space to operate, Luke urged the horse to move forward. Jason trampled over several zombies then broke free of the horde as Luke and Diana kicked away the corpses that had gotten a hold of them.

Luke quickly urged Jason to start running into the desert. Diana turned around to see that the zombie horde had forgotten about them and had started following the Colossus who was making its way deeper into Saudi Arabia.

She screamed to Luke, "They are peeling away from us and following the giant again." She paused for a second, "What's the plan?"

Luke yelled, "We are going to find Chimera. Last that I saw of him that lion-bird was carrying him off in this direction."

Diana shook her head, "Anzu was like twice the size of Chimera. What makes you think that Chimera is even still alive?"

Luke answered bluntly, "Because he is Chimera! Besides, do you have a better plan about how the two of us are going to stop that thing after it just mowed down a team of Navy SEALS?"

Diana shrugged, "No, I don't. Let's hope that Chimera is as tough as we think he is."

Luke nodded, "Trust me, he is more than tough enough to have killed that big bird and still have enough to stop that walking nightmare." Luke urged Jason to pick up his pace. Luke knew that he had to find Chimera and catch up to the Colossus before it reached another populated area causing the deaths of countless more innocent people.

CHAPTER 30

Ashik and his family had been nomadic goat herders for generations. Currently Ashik's family consisted of about two dozen people. He and his wife had four children and each of his six brothers also had wives and multiple children. Their herd of goats numbered around two hundred animals. These creatures provided the family with all of the meat, milk, and clothing that they needed. In addition to that, the family would often sell either the goats or their milk for a profit.

Today, Ashik and his family had led their goats deep into the desert to graze on the meager grasses that grew in thin patches in the harsh climate. The goats had been walking and grazing under the hot sun for nearly an hour when a terrible stench caught Ashik's attention. Ashik knew the scent well; it was the smell of a rotting corpse of some kind. When one spent most of his life in the desert, one occasionally found the body of dead animal or even a human that had wandered off too far into the desert unprepared and had perished.

Ashik's first concern was that his goats may accidentally eat something that they should not. Goats were not carnivorous but they may opt to eat the clothes of a dead man if they came across one. If that happened, the goat would have to be put to death as her meat and milk would have been soiled. Not wanting to have to kill a goat for no reason, Ashik began to scan his herd. He was looking over his herd when a fly landed on his nose. Ashik brushed the insect away then continued to scan his sheep. A moment later, several more flies landed on Ashik. He brushed them away as well. In addition to the flies, the odor of death was growing stronger. Ashik began to wonder if perhaps the dead creature was behind him and that somehow they had missed it when his herd went over the area. Ashik mused that perhaps it was a body which was only buried in a shallow grave. A shallow grave would account for the smell and the flies.

Ashik turned around and shrieked when he saw the Colossus of Death approaching him. He screamed for his family to leave the goats and run. Ashik ran to his youngest son and picked him up.

He then began sprinting through the herd. As the rest of his family saw the approaching horror, they too began to run in terror. Ashik had run for nearly a minute when he suddenly felt as if his skin was on fire. He looked down to see horrible lesions forming on his hand. His young son then screamed in pain and fear. Ashik lifted up the boy to see lesions forming on his son's face and neck. More screams echoed over the sounds of the bleating goats and Ashik watched in disbelief as his family members fell to the ground screaming. A moment later the pain spread from Ashik's hands to his chest. He and his son fell to ground in the middle of the herd screaming in pain. Through the bodies of several sheep, Ashik watched as the Colossus of Death stepped over him. Ashik saw the hundreds of bodies woven together that made up the giant's foot. By the time the Colossus had passed over him, Ashik and his son had died. A few seconds after their deaths, Ashik and his son rose up from the ground. They stood amongst the herd for moment. Then the corpses of Ashik and his family began walking through the goats that they had been running through while they still lived. In life, Ashik and his family had run from the Colossus in fear of it, now in death they slowly walked after the monster waiting until they called to join with it.

CHAPTER 31

Luke had ridden Jason deeper into the desert for about twenty minutes when he saw a walking mountain coming toward them. Luke stopped, pulled off his hazmat helmet, and began to cheer. Diana finally loosened her grip on Luke and looked past him to see Chimera lumbering toward them. She also pulled off her helmet and began cheering. As Chimera came closer to them, Luke could see the scars that the kaiju had incurred during his battle with Anzu.

Luke climbed down off of Jason and pulled one of Chimera's food bars from the carriers on Jason's sides. When Chimera was close enough, Luke tossed the heavy block to the monster. Chimera scooped up the bar and hungrily swallowed it down whole. Luke pulled his speaking horn off of his back and yelled, "Chimera, follow me!"

Luke then climbed back onto Jason and turned the horse around. Luke urged Jason forward at a fast trot. He turned back to Diana, "We have to be fast but we can't push ourselves, Chimera, or Jason too hard in this heat. If we catch up to the Colossus and Chimera is dehydrated or exhausted, he won't be able to battle the Colossus." Diana nodded in reply then the two of them were silent as they rode after the incarnation of death itself.

After pushing themselves for nearly an hour, Luke and Diana came across a herd of wandering goats with no one to tend to them. Diana suggested that this was a sure sign that the Colossus had recently been through here, as a herd this large would never have been left unattended. The goats quickly ran away when they saw Chimera. Shortly after passing the goats, Luke and Diana rode to the top of a sand dune where they could see the Colossus and its disciples of the dead wandering into an oil pumping field.

Luke turned to look at Chimera. He could see that the kaiju was both hot and exhausted, but much like the battle that had taken place at the top of Mount Olympus, Luke knew that he had to push the monster or risks millions of more people dying. Luke pointed at the Colossus and through his speaking horn screamed, "Attack!"

Chimera roared and then charged through the desert toward the rotting giant. Unlike other beasts that Chimera had challenged, the Colossus gave no attention to the charging kaiju. The mindless abomination simply continued to walk forward determined to spread its plague.

Chimera crushed the bodies of hundreds of the zombies that were following the Colossus as he made his way to the giant. When he reached the Colossus, Chimera unsheathed his claws and swiped at its back. The blow sent dozens of broken body parts flying into the desert. The Colossus turned and wrapped his grizzly hand around Chimera's throat. The kaiju ignored the hold and slashed at the giant twice more tearing out its midsection and causing the giant's torso to fall to the ground. With the Colossus laying in the sand ripped into two pieces, Chimera began to pound on the fallen horror using his hands and feet to crush the bodies that had once made up the terrible creature.

With the Colossus crushed beneath him, Chimera raised his body to its full height and beat his chest. He was about roar when he saw the zombies that had been following the Colossus converging into a single point. The bodies continued to pile onto each other and intertwine themselves while Chimera watched in confusion as the enemy he had just destroyed rebuilt itself before his eyes.

Chimera roared in anger at the undead horror that refused to die. Chimera sent one of his focused sonar blasts at the Colossus but, as the giant had no central nervous system, the blast had no effect on it. The Colossus stepped up to Chimera and attempted to grapple with the kaiju. Chimera was far more powerful than the Colossus and he quickly broke the hold by bringing his fists down onto the arms of the Colossus and breaking them in half. The armless Colossus was standing in front of Chimera when the kaiju smashed his head into the chest of the giant causing the bodies that composed the torso of the walking monstrosity to fall apart. Chimera quickly pounded the still standing lower half of the Colossus's body into paste. He backed away from the grizzly scene only to watch as the zombie minions of the Colossus once again converged to reform the horrible creature. Chimera's shoulders slumped for a second. The kaiju took a deep breath, roared, and then engaged the Colossus once again.

Luke shook his head, "Chimera is wearing down. The battle with Anzu, the trek through the desert, the fight with Colossus, and the heat. It's all finally starting to get to him." Luke looked over the countless zombies that were still following the Colossus. "The Colossus doesn't seem to be able to hurt Chimera. The problem is that it does not have to hurt him. All it has to do is out last him and with all of those corpses following the Colossus, Chimera will pass out from heat exhaustion before the Colossus runs out of zombies."

Diana looked down upon the battle. Her eyes perked up as a plan formed in her head, "Luke, you said that you had taught Chimera how to pick a ball and throw it right?"

Luke nodded, "Yes but how is that going to help?"

Diana pointed at one of the oil wells that was pumping hundreds of gallons of oil out of the ground per minute, "If you can get Chimera to pick up the Colossus and throw it into one of the oil pumps, I still have a couple of rounds left in this rifle."

Luke nodded, "So all we have to do is ride in between two kaiju engaged in a death struggle. Convince one of them to pick up the other one and toss into an oil well. Then use your rifle to ignite the one monster without being crushed by the monsters and managing to avoid the army of zombies that want to expose us to a lethal plague."

Diana smirked, "Do you have a better plan?"

Luke shrugged and then directed Jason to charge into the madness taking place in the oil field.

Chimera sent a backhand fist crashing into the featureless face of the Colossus once more sending bodies flying across the desert. Instead of pressing his attack, Chimera took a step back and inhaled another deep breath as more of the walking dead climbed the body of the decapitated Colossus to reform its head.

Jason rode up beside Chimera and Luke quickly lifted his hazmat hood off of his head and screamed through his speaking horn, "Chimera, pick it up."

Chimera looked down at Luke for a brief minute and then the kaiju reached out, grabbed the Colossus, and lifted it over his head.

The zombie horde was closing in on Luke and Diana when Luke pointed at the closest oil pump and screamed, "Chimera, throw!"

Chimera turned toward the oil pump and threw the Colossus at it. The Colossus flew through the air and crashed into the pump sending a geyser of oil shooting into the air. Luke urged Jason to back away from the oil field and called for Chimera to follow him. The exhausted Chimera turned and began to lumber after Jason. From the back of the horse, Diana turned around to see the oil drenched Colossus rising from the debris of the oil pump. She took aim with her rifle and fired at the abomination. The first shot failed to ignite the creature. Diana was not used to firing a rifle let alone doing it while riding a horse. She steadied her aim and focused her mind. When she felt that the Colossus was in her sights, she fired three more shots at the giant. One of the shots ignited the oil that the Colossus was soaked in, causing the giant to explode. The shockwave from the explosion knocked Jason to the ground and sent Luke and Diana crashing into the sand.

Luke dug himself out of the sand to see a fireball with the vague frame of the Colossus staggering after them. The burning giant took a few steps before it collapsed again. The giant no sooner hit the ground then dozens of the zombies that had been following it threw themselves into the fire in an attempt to reconstruct the Colossus. The Colossus tried to stand again and once more it fell to the ground as the flames consumed the new corpses that were trying to reform it. After another attempt to stand, the Colossus fell to the ground for the final time. Luke and Diana watched from a distance as the zombies that had been following the Colossus continued to throw their bodies into the inferno. After an hour of walking into the fire, the last of zombies had been reduce to ash and cinders.

Luke looked at the exhausted Chimera and said to Diana, "Let's get Chimera back to the ship. I think we could all use a rest."

Diana sighed, "Rest maybe, but I don't know that I will ever be able to sleep again without having nightmares about that thing."

Luke joked, "Just picture Toombs in the shower and all the thoughts of the Colossus will be forced out of your mind."

Diana laughed, "And that is now an image that will be ingrained in my mind forever. Thanks a lot, Luke."

Luke smiled, "Whatever it takes to help you out, my dear." They both laughed, then Luke tossed Chimera another reward cube and directed the kaiju to follow him. A long and exhausting hour later, they had returned to the Argos.

Kurdistan

Akhkhazu's eyes snapped open as she came out of the trance like state that she was in while she was controlling the Colossus. She looked down at the mass grave below her and lifted her arm in an upward motion. As her arm rose into the air, hundreds of more bodies began to pull themselves out of the ground. The bodies began to converge and weave their limbs together. Within seconds, the Colossus of Death had been reformed!

Akhkhazu opened her mouth and a hollow voice commanded the giant, "Follow me. We are going to Babylon. The time to seek Marduk has come." Akhkhazu began to float over the sand and the Colossus of Death followed her spreading its plague to any human that they encountered.

CHAPTER 32
EUPHRATES RIVER: THE ARGOS

Toombs walked through the line in the cafeteria absent mindedly placing food onto his tray. He was grabbing his usual diet of burgers and fries with a donut and a few candy bars. One of the servers jokingly offered Toombs a salad. The portly scientist gave a sarcastic laugh to the man then moved on. He scanned the tables in the cafeteria to see where he could sit. He saw both Luke and Diana sitting by a window. As usual, they were surrounded by a large group of sailors eager to hear about their exploits from the previous day. Diana was telling the story about how Chimera was carried off by Anzu only to slay the beast. She went on to describe how she and Luke escaped an army of zombies to find Chimera and lead him back to the Colossus where she and Luke developed the plan that destroyed the undead giant.

Toombs found one of the many empty tables at the far side of the cafeteria from Luke and Diana where he sat down by himself. He took a bite of his burger and anger welled up inside of him as he saw how enthralled everyone was by Diana's story. She and Luke were treated like they were Hulk Hogan at Wrestlemania. Why were they so damned important? Luke did nothing more than point his creation in the right direction and sic him on a monster from far away. Diana didn't even do that! She just rode along for fun. Toombs didn't buy their friend act for a minute. He was sure that they were screwing each other on the side and just keeping it quiet so Luke's wife wouldn't find out.

Toombs was still staring at the two when the most perfect pair of breasts that he had ever beheld suddenly filled his view. He looked up to see the gorgeous blonde he had come across in the hallway a few days ago. He was still staring at her chest when she began talking to him, "It's Dr. Toombs, isn't it?"

Toombs smiled widely as he finally looked at the woman's face, "Indeed it is, my dear."

The woman slid into the seat next to him and Toombs immediately became aroused when her leg brushed up against his under the table. He smiled at her as he was sure that the casual contact was intentional on her part. She leaned forward and smiled slightly allowing her cleavage to show, "My name is Allison. Do you mind if I sit with you?"

Toombs shifted his plump leg so that it rubbed against hers. When she didn't pull away, his heart began to race. He shrugged, "It's pretty lonely on this side of the cafeteria and I am always willing to dine with a beautiful woman."

Allison giggled and brushed her hand against his when she reached for her soda. She looked into Toombs' eyes and immediately his eyes were locked with hers as she continued the conversation, "Word around the ship is that you created Chimera?"

Toombs sighed and pointed to Luke and Diana, "If you are looking to hear about his adventures you should join the unwashed masses over at that table."

Allison pursed her lips and leaned in closer to Toombs, "A racecar driver may get the fame for winning a race but it's really the man who designed the car that deserves the credit. " She shrugged, "Anyone can drive a car," she looked in the direction of Luke, "or ride a horse and point, but how many men can design and create one of the fastest cars in the world? There are not many of them." She rubbed her hand on Toombs' arm, "There is only one man in the world who can make a monster that can kill gods." She whispered into Toombs' ear, "Any man that is one of kind in the world is a man I that want to get know better."

Toombs put his hand on top of Allison's hand. He tried to sound cool as he spoke with a chunk of hamburger sticking out from between his teeth, "Exactly how well would you like to like to get to know me?"

Allison let her tongue touch the tip of his ear as she whispered into it, "Well, I bet someone who can make a giant monster knows all sorts of fun things about topics like chemistry, biology, and anatomy."

Toombs felt a rush of heat surge through his body. He squeezed Allison's hand, "If you would like to stop by my executive cabin when you are off duty, I can show you all kinds of things about anatomy."

Allison was sweating when she suddenly stood up from the table. Toombs was surprised at how quickly she had pulled away until he realized that the heat he thought was his body's reaction to Allison was actually affecting the entire ship. Everyone in the cafeteria was sweating and the windows around the room were quickly fogging up from steam. The ship's alarm went off, calling all hands to their battle stations. Allison and all of the other sailors took off for their stations. Toombs, Luke, and Diana ran onto the deck to see steam rising out of the river itself. Toombs jogged over to the edge of the ship and looked down the side to see the river itself boiling. Dead fish were floating in the water as they were cooked alive in the river that had given them life.

Toombs looked back at the deck to see Luke and Diana sprinting across the ship toward the briefing room. He cursed his luck. The hottest woman on deck was coming onto him and some stupid god had to go and attack the Argos. Toombs ran as fast as his stubby legs could carry him to the briefing room. He was still trying to catch his breath as Diana was rushing to bring up a website and the face of the president was coming onto the screen at the head of the table.

Parsons quickly addressed the president, "Good morning, Mr. President. To make you aware of the situation, the Argos is making its way up the Euphrates River. We are heading to what was once the city of Babylon and is current day Hillah. Ms. Cain believes that the monarch of the Mesopotamian gods, Marduk, may be operating out of the city." Parson's paused for moment and brought up the camera feed from the river outside onto the President's screen, "The Euphrates itself is currently boiling beneath us. Ms. Cain believes that this may be an attack from another of the Mesopotamian gods in an attempt to stop us from reaching Babylon." Parson's looked over to Diana to see her still typing frantically at her laptop. He looked back to the President, "Ms. Cain has a theory on the god who is behind this attack. She will have her data on the screen momentarily."

Parsons sat down and a second later Diana finished typing. She hit the key that linked her laptop to the main screen. She didn't bother with the proper protocol of addressing the President by name. She simply started filling everyone in on her thoughts,

"Mesopotamian mythology has a shark god called Asag. According to legend, his presence will cause any body of water that he inhabits to boil." She hit the page down button on her laptop and the image of a massive shark filled the screen, "There is very little information regarding Asag's appearance. He is typically said to have the shape of a giant shark similar to that of the ancient megalodon." She moved her presentation onto the next page showing the Thing from the Fantastic Four comic book. Diana sighed as she spoke, "I apologize, for the comic book character, but Asag is said to be accompanied by an army of rock monsters and this is the first image of one that I could find." When no one commented on the image, she continued her presentation, "Asag is closely tied to Marduk in several mythological stories. So I would suggest that his appearance means that we are on the right track by heading to Babylon."

Diana sat back allowing everyone to process the information that she had given them. The president looked to Parsons to answer the rest of his questions, "General, what is the plan when you reach Hillah?"

Parsons stood at attention, "The good news is that since Chimera has already slain their god of thunder, we should be able to take the Argos directly into the port of Hillah without fear of an EMP attack. At our current speed, we should enter the port in just under two hours. We will dispatch SEAL Team Sigma to search the area for Marduk. We will also monitor the river for any signs of Asag and his rock monsters." Parsons voice became even more serious when he reviewed his contingency plan, "Mr. President, if Seal Team Sigma should fail to find Marduk, I would like to request permission to evacuate the city and then turn Chimera loose on it. Ms. Cain believes that Marduk is tied to Babylon and that a direct attack on the city may force him reveal himself."

The president's face lit up with surprise, "General, you want me to green light our kaiju to attack a foreign city in order to draw out an ancient god? Do you have an evacuation plan for Hillah before I send in Chimera to destroy it?"

Parsons was about to respond when an alert came up on his laptop. A look of fear flashed into Parson's eyes, "I am sorry Mr. President, it seems that there will be no needed to evacuate Hillah.

I have just received an alert that the Colossus of Death has returned and it has entered the city of Hillah. Our analyst project that entire population of the city will be deceased within the hour." The president shook his head in disbelief, "To make sure that I understand the situation correctly, we currently have a walking giant made up of dead people spreading a deadly plague, a giant shark that can make the river boil, a group of rock monsters, and Marduk the king of this sect of gods all converging in Hillah?"

Parsons nodded, "Yes Mr. President. That is correct."

The president took a deep breath, "Very well then. General, you have the most powerful ship in the US Navy as well as a kaiju at your disposal. Let me make this perfectly clear. I want you to use those resources to put an end to this threat even if you have to raze Hillah to the ground. Do I make myself clear?"

Parsons saluted, "Yes, sir!" The president shut off his feed and Parsons immediately addressed his team. "Ms. Cain, I want everything you know about Asag and Marduk on my computer in a half an hour. Luke, join SEAL Team Sigma and outfit yourself in another hazmat suit. With the Colossus back, you are going to needed it." Finally, he turned his attention to Toombs, "Doctor, I need you prepared to treat Chimera. I fear at the conclusion of this battle he may need serious medical attention."

Toombs nodded and ran out of the briefing room to double check his inventory of medical supplies for Chimera. While his goal was to prepare to perform a medical examination on Chimera, his mind was focused on the examination that he was going to give Allison if they survived Babylon.

CHAPTER 33

Luke was dressed in his hazmat suit when he brought Jason up onto the deck as the Argos was closing in on the city that was once known as Babylon. Luke's mind and his senses were overwhelmed by the circumstances that he currently found himself in. The rubber coating added to the Argos to protect it from EMPS was melting away in the boiling river that it floated on, resulting in the acrid smell of burning rubber wafting through the air. Luke could hear the water bubbling and boiling beneath him and as unsettling as that sound was, he glad to hear it because it covered the other sound that Luke knew was coming from the shoreline.

When Luke looked at the riverbank and the desert behind it, he could see the newly formed army of the dead who were following the Colossus of Death. He was well aware from previous experience that zombie disciples of the giant would be uttering a harrowing moaning sound from their dead lips. The fact that he could see the army but not the Colossus itself made Luke all too aware of how many corpses were following the giant. Each zombie was another life that the Colossus had taken, another soul that he had made his own. Luke shivered as the thought of facing the Colossus again crossed his mind. The cold shiver quickly faded in the brutal heat that was crushing Luke and everyone else on board. The desert itself was over one hundred and fifteen degrees and with the additional heat from the boiling river the temperature on deck was well over two hundred degrees.

Luke took in the environment in its entirety. A barren wasteland, sweltering heat, boiling rivers, the foul smell of things burning, and the bodies of the damned following after a demon. If someone had simply described this place to him and then asked him where it was Luke knew exactly what his answer would be: Hell. Everything around Luke fit the description of eternal suffering that he learned about in Sunday school as a kid. Hell itself had literally come to Earth and it was up to Luke and Chimera to send the demons that were causing this back to the pit from where they had come. Luke feared what have happened to his family if the vortex generated by the Charybdis had reached them. Then their deaths would have been painful but at least it would have been quick. Luke almost cried as the thought crossed his mind again of the bodies of Melissa and the girls joining the ever growing parade of the dead waiting to become part of the Colossus. He knew that Virginia was a good distance away from their current position but Luke was determined to stop this insanity here and now. Luke had no shame in admitting that he was afraid to face the Colossus again but that fear was overridden by the sense of responsibility that he felt as a husband and a father. Luke spoke aloud to himself, "Yes I am afraid, but my family will give me the strength to overcome this fear and stop this monster."

Jason whinnied in reply. Luke laughed, patted the horse on the head, then he gave Jason a carrot. Jason was just finishing up the carrot when, in the distance, Luke could see the outline of the city of Hillah. The buildings were relatively small and the low skyline allowed Luke to see the Colossus standing in the center of the city streets. The last time that Luke had seen the Colossus it was wandering around trying to spread its plague as quickly as it could. Luke and Chimera had to chase it down in order to engage it. This time however, the giant was waiting for them. It was looking for a fight. In Luke's mind, the actions of the Colossus confirmed Diana's theory. Why else would the Colossus remain stationary unless if he was looking to protect something? Luke reasoned that the only thing that the Colossus would protect was Marduk and his Tablets of Destiny. Luke stared out at the Colossus and felt his blood run cold. He was sure that the eyeless sockets of the ever shifting face of the Colossus were staring right back at him. Luke clenched his fists and gnashed his teeth, "All right you son of a bitch, time for round two."

Luke looked to his left to see SEAL Team Sigma checking their hazmat suits. Luke led Jason over to them. The leader of the team introduced himself as Commander Ardan then he handed Luke a rifle, "I understand that you have recently taken basic fire arms training?" Luke nodded in reply. Ardan smiled, "Good. In about sixty seconds, the Argos is going to unleash hell on that army of zombies in an attempt to clear us a path to the city. The Argos should be able to take out the zombies walking toward Hillah but the ship won't be able to target zombies in the city without fear of hitting us. Hillah is overrun with the dead. We are going to enter the city and make for a high building that you can direct Chimera from. We want you to get him to bring the Colossus as close to us as possible." Ardan pointed to the men behind him, "We have flamethrowers and accelerant. We are going to try and replicate what you did in the desert. Soak the Colossus in accelerant and then cook his ass. Once the Colossus is destroyed, we are going to start searching the city for Marduk. If we find him or if he finds us, you send Chimera in to kick his ass too." Commander Ardan looked at the horse, "We do not believe that EMPs are a threat. We are going to use Hummers to enter the city. Are you sure that still want to ride the horse?"

Luke patted Jason on the side of his neck, "Commander, this horse has stood by me through several battles already. There is no way that I am leaving him behind. Plus Chimera is used to taking orders from either me on foot or from the horse. I don't think that now is the time to start introducing him to new venues of instruction."

The Commander nodded, "Okay, then let's get on the launch vessel." Luke led Jason onto the long boat connected to the side of the Argos. The launch reminded Luke of the types of boats that took Tom Hanks ashore in Saving Private Ryan. It looked like a long metal box with no top that was loaded with three Hummers and Horse. Luke smiled to himself when he thought that those things were a great opening to a joke. The launch was being lowered to the boiling water when the siren sounded on the Argos. Luke looked up to see to the massive turret guns on deck turning toward the riverbank. A second later, hundreds of sailors appeared on deck with rifles aimed at the shoreline as well. When the siren stopped, the turret guns and the sailors opened fire on the army of the dead.

The sound was deafening! Luke felt the urge to reach up and cover his ears from the sounds of the guns and rifles firing non-stop above him. He peered over the side of the launch to see body parts flying as explosions ripped into the seemingly endless horde of the dead. The zombies seemed oblivious to the fact that they were being attacked. Their rotted minds had only two driving thoughts: to spread the plague to anyone that they encountered and to join the Colossus when they were called to do so.

The launch came to a rest on the boiling water and the heat inside of the vessel quickly grew unbearable. Jason was bucking and lifting his hooves off of the scalding hot bottom of the launch. Luke felt as if he was literally being cooked alive. Ardan gave the order for the launch to head to shore and Luke was thankful that the trip only took a few seconds. When they hit the riverbank, Luke quickly pulled the suffering Jason ashore to allow his hooves to cool down. As Luke stood on the riverbank with Jason, a hand from the one of zombies that had been blown apart grabbed his foot. Luke grimaced at the appendage and then kicked it into the boiling water.

Luke looked at the Argos to see the bay door opening to reveal Chimera. The blitzkrieg from the Argos stopped for a second so that Chimera could hear Luke's commands. The kaiju roared at the boiling in front of him. Luke felt for the monster but from the battles that he had already been through, Luke knew that Chimera would be able to survive a quick swim through the scalding water. He lifted up his speaking horn and shouted, "Chimera, follow me!" Chimera looked to Luke then down into the bubbling water. The beast hesitated for a brief moment then he waded into the river. The water came up to Chimera's shoulders and the kaiju roared in pain as the top layer of skin was boiled off of his body. Chimera came ashore and looked to Luke who quickly threw the beast a reinforcer cube.

When the monster was eating the cube, the gun fire from the Argos erupted again cutting down more of the thousands of zombies that were still between Luke and the city. The Argos was only firing for a few seconds when the water alongside the ship exploded, revealing a massive shark like creature with long thin arms at its sides and a row of spikes running down its back. Luke thought that the megalodon that Diana had shown on the screen was terrifying enough but Asag was far more terrifying than any prehistoric shark. The monster's long arms reached up onto the ship and he pulled himself up so that the top half of his body was slumped across the deck. Asag's bulk caused the ship to list toward him, sending dozens of sailors sliding into his snapping jaws. Luke was about to direct Chimera to attack Asag when Commander Ardan grabbed him by the shoulder, "No! We have our own mission and our own problems!" Ardan pointed to the city and Luke saw the army of zombies heading toward them. At the back of the army, the Colossus of Death of was making his way out of the city and directly for Chimera.

The turret guns aboard the Argos began to fire at Asag at near point blank range. Even the shark god was unable to withstand the barrage at close range. He released his grip on the ship and slid back into the river. Asag continued to swim alongside the Argos for a moment then he took a quick turn and slammed his body into the hull of the ship. The blow prompted the sailors to run to that the side of ship and fire at the monster. While all of the attention on one side of the ship was focused on Asag, a stone hand came out of the water on the opposite side of the ship. An eight foot tall rock monster dug his hands into the hull of the Argos and it began to climb up the side of the ship. The rock monster was halfway up the side of the ship when two more sets of stone hands emerged from the water and grabbed the hull of the ship as well.

Ardan screamed to his team, "Open fire with your rifles! Save the flamethrowers for the Colossus!" The members of SEAL Team Sigma began firing into the mass of corpses approaching them. The first twenty or so zombies were cut to shreds but without the additional firepower of the Argos, the team was only delaying the inevitable. Seeing the futility of their approach, Luke yelled, "Stop firing!" into his speaking horn so that the SEALS would hear him over the gunfire. The SEALS stopped firing and looked at Luke. He pointed to Chimera and shouted, "We have the world's largest living bulldozer! Let's use him!"

Luke grabbed his speaking horn and the pointed over the massed zombies at the quickly approaching Colossus, "Chimera, attack!"

Chimera roared and beat his chest at the foul creature that he had battled once already. Chimera fell to all fours then began walking through the approaching zombies. Hundreds of the recently deceased were crushed as Chimera's tremendous weight came crashing down on them. The Colossus itself began walking through the zombies, crushing many of its followers and causing more to cease following it and to join its horrible mass. When the two creatures met in the middle of the amassed zombies, the number of the walking dead that was between them had been reduced to less than half of what it was only moments before. The two kaiju came together and began grappling atop of the zombies. Luke watched as Chimera lifted the Colossus off of the ground and slammed him on top of his followers. Luke almost laughed at the fact that the Colossus was nowhere near capable of matching Chimera in terms of strength when Chimera was dehydrated, exhausted, and injured. What chance did the horror have against a rested and healed Chimera? Luke's thoughts returned to what was happening around him when the gunfire erupted again. Even though Chimera had greatly reduced the amount of zombies attacking them, there were still literally hundreds of corpses that were trying to peel the men out of their hazmat suits and expose them to the plague. A zombie had grabbed Luke and he quickly swung his rifle like a club and knocked the foul creature's head off. The arms of the corpse continued to reach for him and he was forced to have Jason buck up and use his front legs to crush the zombie's body into paste. He looked up to see more zombies coming toward him and at the back of the zombie horde he could see Chimera stomping on a half reformed Colossus. Just behind the battle, he could see what looked like the corpse of a woman sitting with her legs crossed and floating in the air. Luke assumed that she had to be the death goddess who Diana thought might be using the Colossus as an avatar. It was at that moment, that Luke realized the true threat the Colossus posed to Chimera and his team. The Colossus could be reduced to nothing over and over again by Chimera but the creature would continue to reform until Chimera was either exhausted or until there were no bodies left to reconstruct the abomination. Even if there were no bodies, the death goddess would simply recreate the Colossus somewhere else and send it into the world again. Luke now understood that to stop the Colossus they needed to stop the goddess who was pulling his strings.

There were at least fifty zombies between Luke and Commander Ardan. Luke galloped closer to the horde of zombies that were overwhelming SEAL Team Sigma. When he reached the horde, he briefly looked up to see the reformed Colossus and Chimera grappling once again. This time Chimera pushed the Colossus to the ground. It crashed into the desert hard, crushing many of the corpses that made up its legs and backside. Before the Colossus could even attempt to stand up, Chimera stepped forward and with claws extended he slashed at the horror tearing off its face and a large part of its chest. The blow sent the torn up remains of zombies raining down on Luke. As Luke was dodging the falling body parts, he looked over to see a large contingent of zombies walking over to reform the damaged part of the Colossus. In an attempt to dissuade them from reforming the giant, he began to fire his rifle into the horde and to scream. A large portion of the zombies turned away from the partially destroyed Colossus and toward Luke. With several hundred zombies facing him, Luke dug deep inside himself to find the courage to do what he needed to do next. Luke completed his soul searching exercise and he opened his eyes to see that the zombies had almost reached him. With the corpses almost upon him, Luke attempted to summon his courage, then he turned Jason around and directed the horse to run away from the horde.

Parsons and Diana were watching from the bridge of the Argos as the sailors continued to fire down on Asag who maintained his position alongside the ship. Parsons's keen eyes saw something on the opposite side of the ship from where the sailors were positioned. He snapped his head around to see three ten foot tall bipedal humanoids composed of rock lumbering across the deck of the ship. A second later Diana saw them as well, "The sailors can't hear them coming over the gunfire; we have to help them. The rock monsters will crush those men in an instant!"

Parsons removed the safety from his sidearm, "I am going to help them. You stay here." Parsons ran out of the bridge and headed for the deck. Diana watched him go then said, "The hell I am going to stay here." Diana looked around to see if there were any weapons nearby and she was discouraged not to find any. She shrugged and said to herself, "I guess that I will just have to improvise something." A second later, Diana was running out of the bridge and toward the deck.

Parsons ran onto the deck to see the rock monsters tearing apart the turret guns that were one of the main offensive weapons of the Argos. Parsons aimed his gun at the nearest monster and unload the ineffectual weapon on the creature. The rock monster ignored the bullets and proceeded to smash the turret into scrap metal. Once the turrets were destroyed, the rock monsters began heading for the sailors who were still firing at Asag. Diana dashed out onto the deck with a fire extinguisher in her hands. She ran in front of two of the rock monsters and emptied the canister on the creatures. The foaming mist didn't slow down the creatures at all but as the wind blew the mist onto the sailors, it caught their attention and several of them turned around to see the rock monsters closing in on them. The sailors who saw the coming danger began firing on the rock monsters. Diana threw herself flat on the deck as a spray of shards of rock and bullet fragments began to fall on her. She rolled to her side to see the horrifying form of Asag jump out of the water and throw the upper half of his body back onto the deck. His massive weight crushed over a dozen sailors. The men who were crushed were the lucky ones as many of the sailors were being snapped up by Asag's jaws where they were shredded to death. Diana rolled the other way to see the rock monsters tearing apart sailors two and three at a time with their massive hands. The few remaining sailors gathered around Diana. The sailors were firing frantically in both directions as Diana found herself trapped between the crushing fists of the rock monsters and the gnashing jaws of the gigantic shark god!

Luke was racing back to the riverbank where he could see the shark-like Asag thrashing around the deck and swallowing sailors whole. He looked behind him to see a group of over fifty zombies following him. Luke began to turn Jason in a wide arc. He arced back around the zombies to see Chimera once again stomping the remains of the Colossus into the Earth. He also saw another horde of zombies heading toward the Colossus to reconstruct it. The good news was that between the zombies that were chasing him and the zombies going to reconstruct the Colossus, Ardan and his remaining men only had few zombies to contend with. Luke switched on the radio inside of his hazmat hood, "Ardan, this is Luke. Take a look to your left! Do you see the zombie woman floating in the air? I am guessing that she is actually the goddess who is controlling the Colossus. You and your men need to attack her! I have an idea to get rid of the Colossus and the zombies, but the Colossus may just come back as long as the goddess is around! You guys need to take her out for good!"

Ardan replied, "We are on the goddess. I hope you have good plan. Chimera keeps trashing that thing but it just keeps reforming."

Luke shouted, "Don't worry, I've got this!" Luke pulled Jason to a stop in front of Chimera and the Colossus. The Colossus had reformed again and it was once more trying to strangle Chimera. Luke pulled off his hazmat hood and prayed that he would be spared the effects of the plague while at the same time accepting that if had to die to stop this horror then he was willing to do so. Luke put his speaking horn to his mouth and pointed at the Colossus, "Chimera, pick up!" The kaiju reached out, grabbed the Colossus, and lifted the writhing creature over his head. Luke yelled again, "Good work! Now follow me!" Luke turned and road Jason toward the horde of zombies that was still following him after he had made the wide arc by the riverbank. Luke rode Jason as close to the zombies as he could without going directly through them. The horde began to turn around at the same time that Chimera began walking through them crushing scores of zombies with each step. Luke smiled, so far his plan was working. Chimera was crushing zombies and he had the Colossus lifted over his head. It was at that point that Luke felt a burning sensation on his face. He didn't need to pull off his hazmat mask to know that lesions were forming across skin. He took deep breath; if he was going to die he only needed a few more minutes. He just had to make it to the riverbank and give Chimera one more command. From there, nature would take its course.

Ardan and his men closed in on Akhkhazu. Ardan and two other men positioned themselves directly in front of her and fell to one knee with their rifles pointed at the goddess. Ardan began to fire on her and the other two men on either side of him did the same. As they were firing hundreds of bullets at the death goddess, the other two men with flamethrowers quickly ran up alongside Akhkhazu. When they were in range of Akhkhazu, their flamethrowers jumped to life enveloping Akhkhazu in flames. The barrage continued until Akhkhazu floated out of the flames and looked directly at Ardan. She spoke to him in her hollow voice, "You dare to challenge a goddess of death? You shall suffer!" Akhkhazu moved with speed beyond comprehension from one man to the next tearing off their hazmat suits. A moment later, Ardan and his men fell to the ground covered in lesions. Akhkhazu floated past the men and headed for the riverbank.

Luke had finally made it to the riverbank with Chimera carrying the Colossus right behind him. There were still some zombies near Luke that Chimera had not crushed and they were reaching to pull Luke off of Jason. Luke knew that it didn't matter. All that they would do is pull off his hazmat suit and expose him to a plague that he already had. Luke looked at the Argos to see Asag still thrashing about on the boat. Blood was pouring off of the deck on either side of the god from the men and woman that he had chewed to death. Luke was a teacher. He didn't know much about ancient gods, but he was required to teach earth science and each year he taught a lesson on sharks. Luke had taught his students how sharks could smell blood in the water from a mile away, how they were opportunistic feeders, and how anything that bumped into them they would bite to see if it was food. Luke's vision was getting dim when he saw Chimera looming over him with the struggling Colossus still above his head. Luke pointed at Asag and hoped that the creature was as much shark as it was god when he gave Chimera the order to throw.

Diana saw the sailor standing in front of her, smashed into a pile of blood and bones by a massive rock fist. She rolled to her left as the same rock fist came crashing down where she was laying only a second before. She looked at Asag and realized that she could only roll one more time before rolling into the jaws of the shark god. Tears were streaming from her eyes when she saw Chimera standing at the edge of the river holding the Colossus of Death over his head. She watched in disbelief as Chimera threw the Colossus at Asag. When the Colossus crashed into Asag's back, the shark god began thrashing wildly. The Colossus slid off of the back of Asag and into the boiling water of the river. Asag flopped off of the deck and attacked the readily available source of food that was the Colossus. Diana stood up and ran to the side of the ship, putting as much distance between herself and the rock monsters as possible. She peered over the edge to see the Colossus struggling in vain against Asag. The shark god was tearing the Colossus to shreds as it pulled the giant of intertwined corpses under the boiling water. On the shore, she could see hundreds of zombies throwing themselves into the boiling water of the river. They were attempting to reach the Colossus but the river boiled the flesh off of their bones before they reached the giant. Diana spun around to see a rock monster standing in front of her. She closed her eyes expecting to die when she heard a loud explosion and was nearly knocked into the river as chunks or rock flew around her. She opened her eyes to see Parsons holding a smoking bazooka over his shoulder. She also saw several other sailors aiming bazookas at the remaining two rock monsters. She screamed with joy when they explode as well when shells connected with their rigid bodies.

Luke was gasping for breath when he saw the necrotic form of Akhkhazu floating next to him. He could hear her harrowing voice shouting at the shark monster, "Asag, you dim-witted fool! You are destroying my Avatar!" Chimera was looking down at Luke. He could tell the kaiju was concerned for him and Luke was touched that the creature cared for him. Luke knew that he was only few seconds away from dying but he was determined to make those seconds count. He put his speaking horn to his mouth and pointed at Akhkhazu, "Chimera, smash!" Luke closed his eyes and his last thought was that it was a shame Diana missed that one; she would have loved the Hulk reference.

Chimera roared lifted his hand above his head then brought it down on Akhkhazu with such force that it simultaneously crushed the death goddess's body and drove her remains into the ground. The second that Akhkhazu died, Luke snapped back to life and the zombies that were throwing themselves into the river reverted back to unanimated corpses. Asag finished chewing on the remains of the Colossus and then it began swimming through the boiling water and devouring the bodies of the former zombies.

Luke stood up to see Asag swimming back and forth alongside the Argos. He guessed that once the shark beast finished with the corpses that he would turn his attention back to the Argos. Luke pointed at the shark god and screamed, "Chimera, attack!" The Kaiju roared, beat his chest, and then waded into the boiling water.

Chimera was waist deep in the water when Asag swam up to him and bit into the kaiju's thigh. Chimera roared, and unsheathed his claws which he used to rake Asag along his streamlined body. The aquatic deity released his grip and swam a long circle around the Argos prior to attacking Chimera again. Asag was swimming straight at Chimera when the shark god leapt out of the water and crashed into Chimera. Asag wrapped his arms around Chimera's shoulders to hold himself up and then he bit into Chimera's neck. Blood poured down Chimera's neck as Asag's saw-like teeth tore into the kaiju's flesh. Chimera used his long jaws to latch his teeth onto Asag's thin arm. With his grip secure, Chimera pulled back with his mouth and used his powerful arms to push Asag's body in the opposite direction. Asag's thin arm quickly succumbed to the tremendous strength of Chimera as it was ripped out of its socket.

Asag wailed in pain, released his grip on Chimera's neck, and fell back into the boiling river. Asag's body no sooner hit the water than the fish beast surfaced again and latched onto Chimera's left arm. The kaiju lifted his arm out of the water, pulling the upper half of Asag's body with it. The tenacious shark god held his grip on Chimera's left arm until the kaiju brought his right fist crashing into Asag's mid-section. Asag released his grip once more and swam another circle below the surface of the river. Even the dim-witted shark god was starting to realize that he was no match for the powerful kaiju. Asag circled Chimera under the water looking for a point of attack. He finally settled on Chimera's fluke like tail. Asag swam at Chimera's tail like a torpedo streaking through the water and then he bit into Chimera's fluke. Asag once more began thrashing wildly as he tried to tear a chunk of the tail off. Chimera roared, looked down into the water behind him, then he fired a concentrated sonar blast at Asag. The shark god's central nervous system immediately shut down leaving him helpless in the water. Chimera reached down and grabbed Asag by his tail with both hands. The kaiju then dragged the disoriented shark god out of the river and onto the shore. When Chimera was on land, he yanked on Asag's tail, lifting the creature over his head. Chimera then brought the shark god crashing to the ground as if his body was a giant sledge hammer. Chimera repeated the move several more times in rapid succession. From the deck of the Argos, Luke heard Diana cheering and yelling, "Puny god!"

After slamming Asag to the ground several times, Chimera released his hold on the creature. Chimera was looking down to see if he had killed the beast when Asag's jaws flashed open and quickly closed on Chimera's left hand. Chimera roared in pain then dug the claws of his right hand into Asag's lower jaw. With one hand trapped in Asag's mouth and the other impaled in his lower jaw, Chimera pulled his hands in opposite directions. Luke, Diana, Parsons, and the sailors on the Argos watched in awe as Chimera tore Asag's face completely in half. The blood of the god pooled around Chimera's feet as the humans watching the spectacle stared on in stunned silence. Chimera looked down at his defeated foe and then he beat his chest loudly and roared. As Chimera's roar echoed through the desert, the Euphrates River ceased boiling and the remaining crew of the Argos cheered in celebration!

CHAPTER 34

Doctor Toombs had made his way out to the deck as Parsons and Diana were on a small boat headed to the shore to rendezvous with Luke and Chimera. He was standing at the edge of the ship and staring out at the carnage on land when he was shocked to feel something bump into him from behind. He looked down to see a pair of slender feminine arms wrapped around him. He felt warm breath on his neck as he heard an angelic voice, "Doctor Toombs, thank god you made it through that attack unharmed!"

Toombs spun around to see Allison dressed as one of the sailors aboard the Argos. Before he could say a word, Allison leaned in and shoved her tongue into his mouth. Toombs was totally overwhelmed by her kiss. Throughout his entire life, women had rejected and scorned him. He could hardly believe that he was kissing a woman who was attractive enough to be a supermodel.

Allison pulled away from Toombs and she could tell that she already had him hooked. The only thing left for her do was to reel Toombs in like the disgusting fish man that he was. Centuries of performing sexual acts with some of the most disgusting gods in existence had prepared her for this moment. She steeled her nerves and prepared to separate her mind from her body to the greatest extent possible. She whispered into Toombs ear, "All of this excitement has me fired up. I was thinking that we could go back to your cabin and find some productive way to work off all of this energy."

Toombs grinned from ear to ear. He took one look at the shoreline. Despite his battle with the Colossus and Asag, Chimera seemed relatively unscathed. Parsons would have him searching for Marduk and his Tablets of Destiny. Toombs's sex drive quickly deduced that finding a hidden god would take a good amount of time. Chimera would not need him for a while. Toombs turned off his radio, grabbed Allison by the arm, and said, "Come into my parlor said the spider to the fly."

Allison laughed. She didn't laugh at what Toombs thought was a clever application of a classic line. She was actually laughing at the fact that Toombs perceived himself as the spider in the scenario. Allison knew full well that Toombs was slowly being drawn into her web of sexual control. She also knew that once Toombs was trapped in that particular web that he would do anything that she said. As they were walking back to Toombs's cabin, she looked at the scientist and giggled. Toombs of course thought that it was a playful giggle of foreplay but Allison was really laughing at how one of the most intelligent men in world quickly turned into a fool in the hands of a beautiful woman.

Toombs opened the door to his room and then he ushered Allison into it. The nymph closed her eyes for a minute and pictured herself in Apollo's bedroom. She then focused very hard to imagine the portly little scientist as the sun god himself. Toombs skipped any attempt at stimulating her. He simply grabbed her, kissed her again, and then he tossed her onto his bed. As Toombs was undressing in front of Allison, she fought the urge to vomit and reminded herself that pleasuring this man would be a key step in her finally assuming control, not only her own destiny, but of the entire world.

Luke was standing at the river's edge watching as Parsons' and Diana's boat was quickly coming toward him while Chimera and Jason stood next to him. Both of the beasts were chewing on their hard earned snacks. Luke was surprised to hear someone call his name from behind. He turned around to see that Ardan and several other members SEAL Team Sigma who had fallen victim to the plague were still alive. Luke hugged the Commander who did not seem overly enthused by the act of affection. Ardan stepped back and starting asking Luke questions about the events which had just occurred, "Mr. Davis, the last thing that I remember was being infected by the plague and watching helplessly as that death goddess floated past us. What happened after that? How are we still alive?"

Luke pointed up to Chimera, "You have him to thank, Commander. When Chimera crushed the death goddess, it seems to have put an end to both the Colossus and the plague." Luke then pointed to the remains of Asag, "Chimera destroyed the shark monster as well."

Ardan looked up at Chimera and nodded at the kaiju. The moment was interrupted as Parsons and Diana came ashore. Diana ran up to Luke, "Chimera went total Hulk on Asag with that whole slamming him from side to side thing!"

Luke hugged her and smiled, "You would have been proud of me. When I gave Chimera the command to attack the death goddess, I said 'Chimera, smash!'"

Diana laughed, "Awesome! Way to be quick witted under pressure."

Parsons interrupted the two friends, "If you two are done, we still have to find the monarch of the Mesopotamian gods. Also, in case you have not noticed, over a third of our crew was killed by the shark god and his rock monsters. So if we are going to going to find this Marduk, let's do it now before he summons more gods or monsters to protect himself with."

Diana nodded, "The mythology suggests that Marduk is closely connected with the city of Babylon." Diana looked toward the modern city of Hillah, "General, all of the inhabitants of the city of Hillah were killed by the Colossus and its plague. There are only empty buildings over there right now. I know that the president said to do whatever it takes to put an end to the threat posed by the Mesopotamian gods. May I suggest that we direct Chimera to start tearing the city apart? If Marduk is hiding in the city, then this tactic will drive him into the open. If he is protecting the city, then he may very well come to us to try and stop Chimera."

Parsons nodded in affirmation of Diana's suggestion. He turned to Luke and said, "Give him the command. Have him attack the city."

Luke lifted his speaking horn to his mouth, "Chimera!" Luke waited until Chimera was looking down at him. When he was sure that he had Chimera's attention, he pointed at the city, "Attack!" Chimera roared in reply then the kaiju began lumbering toward the city that had once been Babylon.

CHAPTER 35

The team from the Argos watched as Chimera reached the first small building on the outskirts of the city. The kaiju crushed the structure with one stomp from his foot. Chimera took several more steps and crushed several other small buildings as he made his way to the largest skyscraper in sight. He was heading for the building and roaring at it when a bright flash of light appeared between the kaiju and the building. When the light faded, it revealed the figure of a humanoid roughly thirty feet in height with several stone tablets embedded in his chest. Chimera was immediately reminded of the beings that he had fought atop Mount Olympus. Anger rushed through the mind of the monster as he recalled the battle with the Olympians.

Marduk reached down into the sand and lifted a scorpion from beneath the ground. He held the scorpion in his hand as he addressed the monster, "Beast, you have slain my brothers and my sister and now you attack my city! You do this in order to protect the virus of the humans that infects this planet and is killing it!" Marduk removed one of the stone tablets from his chest. The god gazed down at the tablet and then he extend the hand in which he held the scorpion, "Now creature you will pay for the lives of my brothers and sister! You shall pay for protecting the humans!" Marduk began to recite an ancient chant and as he did so the scorpion in his hand began to spin around in erratic circles. As Marduk continued to chant, the scorpion began to bury itself into Marduk's hand. Marduk chanted a few more lines and then he slammed the stone tablet back into his chest. Marduk wrapped his arms around his ribs and screamed in pain. He then fell to his knees and Chimera watched as the god's body began to stretch and grow. Marduk's body had doubled in size when one of his hands was torn apart and the pincer-like claw of scorpion emerged from his forearm. Marduk looked at Chimera with a mixed visage of pain and anger as his other hand burst open to reveal a second pincer claw.

Marduk's body continued to enlarge as a grotesque stinger and scorpion tale shot out of the base of his spine. The tail was swinging behind his head as Marduk's body continued to grow until its size matched the size of Chimera himself. Marduk let out a scream of pain that echoed over the desert as his legs tore themselves apart and the eight arachnid legs of a scorpion took their place. Marduk retained the face and torso of a man with the Tablets of Destiny still embedded in his chest. The god's lower half and extremities had taken on the form of a gigantic scorpion.

Diana walked up between Parsons and Luke, "Marduk has turned himself into a scorpion man. The scorpion men are the most feared and deadly creatures in Mesopotamian mythology." She paused for a moment then added, "The Rock turned himself into one in the second Mummy movie."

Luke shook head, "In the movie, did the Mummy beat that thing?"

Diana sighed, "No. It sent the Mummy to Hell."

Chimera charged at the scorpion man and brought his forearm crashing into its jaw. The scorpion man staggered back a few steps but its eight long legs quickly scrambled to regain his balance. The scorpion man shot out his left claw and grabbed Chimera by the throat. Chimera's thick lion main prevented the pincer from penetrating his flesh but the powerful grip was slowly crushing the kaiju's windpipe. Chimera raked his right claw across the scorpion man's chest, causing sparks to fly into the air as the kaiju's claws came into contact with the stone tablets embedded in the god's chest. The scorpion man's other pincer shot out and grabbed Chimera's claw at the wrist. Chimera struggled to free himself but even his powerful muscles were not strong enough to break the hold of the scorpion man. Chimera looked into the eyes of the scorpion man and then fired a sonar blast directly into the god's face. The scorpion man convulsed, causing him to release his grip. The scorpion man's legs scrambled to carry him backwards, but with his central nervous system disrupted, the legs of the beast became tangled, causing the god-beast to fall onto his side.

The scorpion man was lying on his side with his legs and tail flailing wildly as Chimera approached him. Chimera looked down on the god beast, roared, and then the kaiju lifted his hands above his head and brought them crashing down onto the scorpion man's chest. Once more, the attack was absorbed by the Tablets of Destiny protruding from the god-beast's chest.

As quick as lightning, the scorpion man's tail shot out from behind him and impaled itself into Chimera's shoulder. Chimera screamed in pain as the scorpion man's stinger pumped a stream of venom into the kaiju's body. Chimera reached up with both of his hands, grabbed the end of the tail, and pulled the stinger out of his arm. Chimera then kicked the scorpion man in the face, pulled on its tail, and used it to whip the god-beast into a large building. The building collapsed on top of the scorpion man, burying him in rubble.

Chimera staggered backward and Luke could see that the scorpion venom was starting to affect the kaiju. He turned to Parsons, "How will Chimera's body hold up against a monster sized dose of scorpion venom?

Parsons shook his head, "I have no idea!" He picked up his radio, "Dr. Toombs, come in." Parsons only heard static in reply. He tried to raise the doctor again, "Toombs, this is General Parsons please respond." Once again, Parsons received no reply. He cursed, "What in the hell is that man doing?" Parson switched channels, "Attention Argos. I need Dr. Toombs located now!"

The scorpion man exploded out of the rubble and scurried toward Chimera. The scorpion man brought one of his huge pincers crashing into the side of Chimera's head and the other crashing into the kaiju's ribs. Chimera shook off the blows and responded with a fist to the scorpion man's face. Chimera then spun around and used his thick tail to knock the scorpion man's legs out from under him. With the scorpion man knocked down before him, Chimera's shoulders sagged forward and he maintained his position instead of pressing the attack on his downed foe.

Luke grabbed Diana by her shoulders, "That venom hurt him and he is cautious of engaging the scorpion man because he is afraid of being stung again."

Ardan shook his head, "That scorpion man is a walking tank. The scorpion armor protects its arm and legs and those tablets protect its chest. Only its head, face, and back are vulnerable but for Chimera to get to them he has to get in range of that tail!"

Luke looked into Diana's eyes, "The tablets! They gave Marduk the power to become the scorpion man! How do the tablets figure into Marduk's mythology again?"

Diana closed her eyes to focus her thoughts, "Marduk was a relatively minor god until he gained possession of the tablets. They gave him the power to overthrow the previous god king and take his position."

Luke looked over in the direction of the battling monsters as he shouted out his idea, "Ardan, I need you and your men to keep that scorpion man distracted for about one minute. Diana, I need you to come with me. We are going to teach Chimera how to beat that thing." No one argued or asked questions. They all trusted Luke, especially when it came to Chimera. Ardan and the remaining members of SEAL Team Sigma jumped into their vehicle and Luke and Diana rode Jason into the city and toward the two monsters.

The scorpion man stood up and Chimera immediately charged and used his battering ram like face to smash into the tablets in the god-beasts chest. The blow sent the scorpion man sliding backward but the creature maintained its balance. The scorpion man moved back toward Chimera with his tail swinging back and forth behind him. Chimera took a half step back and he staggered as he did so. The shot of venom that was coursing through his veins continued to sap the kaiju's strength. Chimera shook his head in an attempt to shake off the effects of the poison. The kaiju's reflexes were inhibited and he was unable to react quickly when the scorpion man moved in on him and used his pincers to grab both of Chimera's wrists. Chimera saw the stinger at the end of the scorpion man's tail coming at him and, out of desperation, the kaiju unleashed another sonar blast into the scorpion man's face. Once again the scorpion man convulsed and fell to his side. As the scorpion man convulsed on the ground, Chimera dropped to all fours as he continued to fight the effects of the venom.

Luke and Diana rode up next to Chimera. Luke quickly tore the rough shape of a rectangle from his hazmat suit. Then he jammed the scrap piece into Diana's chest, "Hold it there until I try to take it away, then fall down when I do." He quickly looked at the scorpion man to see Ardan and SEAL Team Sigma surrounding the god-beast and hitting him with a barrage of bullets and flames. Luke then turned his attention to Chimera who was swaying from side to side. Luke thought that the monster looked as if he had eaten two tons worth of horse tranquilizer. He lifted his speaking his horn and yelled, "Chimera, look at me!" The drowsy kaiju slowly turned his head to Luke. Luke pointed at Diana and screamed, "Tear off!" he then moved to Diana, grabbed the rectangle that she was holding on her chest, and pulled it off. When he pulled the rectangle off of Diana, she fell to the ground. Luke looked back at the scorpion man who had regained control of his senses. The god-beast paid no attention to the efforts of SEAL Team Sigma. He simply waded through their barrage and made his way to Chimera. Luke pointed at the scorpion man and yelled through his speaking horn, "Chimera, tear off!"

Chimera let out a tired roar and began walking toward the scorpion man. Seeing Chimera coming at him, the scorpion man dashed forward and lashed out with his tail sticking the stinger in Chimera's stomach. The pain of the attack sent a surge of adrenaline through the monster's body. Chimera roared, took a step forward, unsheathed his claws, and then he buried them in the scorpion man's chest just above the Tablets of Destiny. Chimera pulled down with all of his might and in a single motion he ripped the giant stone tablets out of the scorpion man's chest. The scorpion man screamed as his body began to shrink and revert back to the natural form of Marduk. The stinger of the god-beast pulled itself out of the kaiju's stomach as it shrank in size and quickly disappeared. Marduk was standing in the center of the city and looking up at Chimera who was still holding the Tablets of Destiny in his claws. Chimera tossed the tablets to the ground as he swayed from side to side. The kaiju then let out a moan and collapsed directly on top of Marduk, crushing the god king.

Diana ran over to the tablets while Luke ran toward Chimera. When Diana touched the tablets, they immediately shrank to a size that could fit into her hands. She looked at the first tablet and she was surprised to see that the writing on front of it was in English. It read *Simply ask the question and the secrets of the universe shall be revealed to you*. Diana looked at the tablet for a moment then she said, "How do I prevent the Mesopotamian gods from coming to Earth again?" The writing on the tablet began to shift and it read *Destroy the Temple of Light*. Diana asked the obvious follow up question, "Where is the Temple of Light?" Once more the writing on the tablet began to shift until it read *The Alberes Ruins*. Diana scooped up the tablets for later study and yelled out to Parsons, "General, call in an air strike on the Alberes Ruins. It's the portal the Mesopotamians are using to access our world!"

Luke was standing next to unconscious form of Chimera and he could hear the kaiju's heartbeat slowing down. He also yelled to Parsons, "We need Toombs out here now!"

Parsons grabbed his radio, "Argos, come in. This is General Parsons. I am calling in an air strike on the Alberes Ruins roughly 15 miles south of here and has anyone found Dr. Toombs?"

CHAPTER 36

Allison was supporting herself on her hands and knees and Toombs was positioned behind her. She could feel his bulbous stomach pressed up against her ass. His hands were moving over her perfect body as if they were a catfish carefully probing every inch of a lake bed for food.

Like others that she had sex with who she found repulsive, she found that the act was much more tolerable if she was not looking at her partner. Toombs was grunting like the pig and that he was when someone starting pounding on his door. Toombs ignored the knocking and he continued to thrust himself into Allison. A sailor began yelling through the door that Toombs was urgently needed by General Parsons. Allison was well aware that the toady little man was far too focused on her to let any outside stimuli distract him. The sailor began shouting to Toombs that they had orders to find him by any means necessary and that they would break into the room if he did not answer the door immediately. Toombs continued to have his way with Allison as if there was no one else in the world let alone just outside the door. Allison thought that as unsatisfying as her current experience was that she would at least have the pleasure of seeing the looks on the sailors' faces when they found her with Toombs.

She smiled as she prepared to give the sailors a show. She arched her back and dug her fingers into the sheets as if she was in ecstasy. She was set to let out a moan when she realized that she was being summoned. The god who was summoning her was not to be trifled with. She would miss out on her fun but at least she had assured that Toombs would be her willing servant for the rest of his miserable life. A second before the sailor kicked in the door, Allison said to Toombs, "Sorry doctor, but I am needed somewhere else right now." In a bright flash, she disappeared at the same moment that the sailor kicked in the door to Toombs's cabin. The sailor looked at Toombs kneeling naked on his bed with a look of total confusion on his face.

The sailor picked up his radio, "This is Sergeant Duggan. Tell General Parsons that we have found Dr. Toombs. It seems that he was busy occupying himself." Duggan looked at Toombs in disgust, "Get dressed, doctor. Chimera has been hit with two large doses of Scorpion venom. The General needs you ashore to assess the kaiju's medical status.

Toombs looked around the room for Allison as he was still trying to understand what had just happened. He looked at the sailor and nodded his head. He then climbed off of his bed and starting getting dressed.

Fifteen minutes later, Dr. Toombs was on shore and approaching the unmoving form of Chimera. Parsons stopped him before he reached the monster, "Doctor, what you do in your free time is your own concern. From this point on however, you are to keep your radio on at all times in case that we need your help with Chimera's medical status. Do I make myself clear?"

Toombs nodded and continued to walk to Chimera. He could see Luke and Diana glaring at him. He knew what they were thinking, that he was busy pleasuring himself while they were out here fighting to save the world. Toombs was sure that even if he knew what had happened to Allison himself that none of them would believe that he had a woman in his room, especially a woman the caliber of Allison. Toombs was sure that he could hear Diana giggle as he walked by. No doubt the cold-hearted bitch was laughing because she was so vain that in her mind Toombs was pleasuring himself on her account.

Toombs tried to push the thought from his mind in order to focus on Chimera. No matter what they thought of him, they still needed him. Their little clique was useless without his expertise. He checked the wounds on Chimera's shoulder and took samples from the wound to verify if it was scorpion venom that was affecting the monster. Once he had run a quick test and assured himself that it was scorpion venom, he checked the monster's vitals. Due to the fact that Chimera had fallen on his face, he was unable to examine the wound on the kaiju's stomach.

After he had finished his examination, he returned to Parsons, Luke, and Diana. He looked down at the ground when he was talking to them as he was unable to look them in the eyes, "He will heal from the wound in his shoulder and I would suspect from the wound in his chest as well. I took a few samples from the wound in the shoulder and I can say for sure that the venom in him is scorpion venom. The good news is that, while painful, scorpion venom is only a temporary paralytic. Chimera will recover in time. The effects of scorpion venom can be partially offset by the application of pain killers. It will take virtually every pain killer we have aboard the Argos, but I can have a dose prepared and put into the syringe that we were using to tranquilize him prior to Luke training him."

Parsons nodded, "Very well doctor, make it so."

Toombs began the long walk back to the boat that would return him to the Argos. He was determined to mix this syringe up as quickly as possible and then to find out exactly what had happened to Allison. Toombs knew that the gods were taking attractive people from around the world and given how hot she was, Allison certainly fit that description. Toombs looked to the sky; if the gods had taken her then he would get her back. He needed to see her again no matter what the cost and if the gods had taken her, then heaven help them, because he had created the most powerful creature on the planet and he would use it to destroy any god that stood between him and Allison.

CHAPTER 37
ASGARD

Allison opened her eyes to find herself in the great hall of Asgard. Of all three sects of gods, she feared the Asgardians the most and of all the gods, she feared Odin more than any other. Unlike the other sects of gods who often feuded within themselves, the Asgardian society operated under a very strict hierarchy. Odin was their king and his word was unquestioned. His son Thor was their most powerful warrior and military leader. He enforced his father's commands. All of the other gods followed the roles that they were assigned as well. This strict code extended to all aspects of the Asgardians lives, including their sexual proclivities. In Asgard, a man only mated with his wife and the main purpose of love making was to bear children. These children, both males and females, were sired for the sole purpose of one day being warriors in the service of Asgard.

This is the aspect of the Asgardians that most frightened Allison. Through sex, she was able to, in small ways, manipulate or influence the Olympians and the Mesopotamians. Allison was literally thousands of years old and in that time not once had she been called upon to enter the bedroom of any Asgardian god. The Asgardians were far too focused on their military goals to be distracted by the pleasures of a nymph. They did not even use the nymphs as conduits through which to engage in sexual interactions with humans.

Odin was the only Asgardian to ever call upon the nymphs and when he did so, it was never with pleasure in mind. He would only call upon the nymphs if he could in some way use them to attack or undermine an adversary. This is why Allison feared Odin and the Asgardians, because before them she was totally powerless. Her charms and sexual vitality were as useless against the Asgardians as sheet of paper was at stopping a charging bull.

She entered the throne room to see her brother already kneeling before Odin and Thor. Thor was standing and his father was seated in his throne. Even when sitting in his throne, Odin wore his battle armor. The Asgardian king believed that his kingdom should always be prepared for war, and by always wearing his battle armor, he exhibited to his subjects that he expected them to adhere to this belief. The only part of Odin's attire that identified him as a king was his crown, and even this symbol served a functional purpose. Unlike the crowns of other god-kings, Odin's crown had a sheet of leather that extended down from it and covered his left eye. Long ago when the earth was first formed, Odin traded his left eye for the gift of wisdom. It was this exchange that made Odin the most powerful and dangerous of the god kings. Zeus was often more concerned with his next sexual escapade than he was with ruling his kingdom. Odin, on the other hand, was focused on expanding the rule of Asgard and increasing their resources. Odin was an intelligent warrior and he was not to be trifled with.

With a wave of fear overwhelming her mind, Allison dashed forward and knelt down at the throne of the god king as well. Odin often chose his words carefully so that his commands were understood and followed to the greatest extent possible. Realizing that Odin would take a few minutes to gather his thoughts, her eyes drifted to Thor. In all of her years of existence, she had never seen Thor in person and as such she knew that his presence meant that Odin was preparing to make war on the humans. She took the unique opportunity presented to her to examine the Asgardian god of thunder. She was disappointed that the god himself was far the image portrayed by comic books and movies. The human who portrayed Thor in the movies Allison would have loved to have spent the night with but the actual god did not appear nearly as inviting.

Thor was massive and well built. He had long red hair and a shaggy red beard that extended all the way to the center of his chest. Unlike his father, he did not wear armor but rather the skins of animals that he had slain. What looked like a bear skin covered his chest and legs. His legendary hammer hung at his side but, as opposed to being the refined weapon Allison had imagined it to be, the hammer looked more like a large flat stone tied to a log. Allison was well aware that the primitive appearance of the weapon did nothing to diminish its actual power. To Allison, the most noticeable difference between Thor and his fictional counterpart was his eyes. In the movies, Thor was always shown to have a kind and caring demeanor. The actual god however had the hardened look of warrior who had been in thousands of battles and slain countless enemies. As those eyes shifted toward Allison, she quickly looked to the floor knowing that she would find neither mercy nor desire in their gaze.

The twins knelt staring at the floor for nearly fifteen minutes before Odin finally spoke. Allison could hear his voice boom throughout the throne room as he gave them a command, "Rise! I have decided how to best utilize your skills."

The twins stood up and both of them made sure that their body language and facial expressions conveyed to Odin that he had their complete attention. The giant god stood up from his throne as he described his course of action to the twins, "The Olympians and the Mesopotamians are arrogant fools. Their lack of foresight and desire to breed with the mortals has been their downfall." Odin paused for a moment and looked to Aiden, "Boy, have you carried out my commands and brought the impregnated females you abducted for the other sects to Asgard?"

Aiden replied, "Yes, my lord."

Odin nodded, "Good. They shall remain with us in Asgard. While their offspring may have the blood of the other gods and mortals in them, they shall be raised as warriors of Asgard. With the defeat of their fathers, we shall need their strength at the coming of Ragnarok." He then turned his attention to Allison, "Girl, the mortal men that you have gathered, they are to be slain as soon as you leave this chamber. No warrior woman of Asgard would mate with a mortal man."

Allison nodded, "Yes, my lord."

Odin then informed the twins of their part in his war against humanity, "With the fall of the other sects of gods, the coming of Ragnarok is likely at hand. We must destroy these humans and save what is left of the Earth before the humans destroy the planet and accomplish the goals of the Dark Ones for them. The other sects of gods simply sought to unleash their power on the humans without any focus. We Asgardians are warriors and we shall attack with purpose, and by doing so we shall be victorious. We shall attack what the humans covet most and then when their attention is focused on their petty treasures, we shall destroy that which they have come to rely on to live."

Odin turned his head so that his single eye was focused on Allison, "Girl, you are to go to the cave of the foul dragon Fafnir. Inform him of the vast treasure that is located in the land known as Kentucky. The dragon is infatuated with gold and he will claim this treasure for himself. The humans are as greedy as the dragon and they will attempt to drive Fafnir from their treasure at all costs."

Allison bowed, "Yes, my lord."

The god king then directed his attention to Aiden, "Boy, you have a simpler and yet much more vital task to complete. In order to crush the humans, we must first defeat their behemoth. Engaging this creature in direct battle is unwise as he has overthrown the Olympians and the Mesopotamians. Though powerful, the creature is dimwitted. He relies on the human Luke Davis to guide him. To defeat the behemoth, we must incapacitate Mr. Davis."

Thor knelt down before Odin, "Father, simply give the word and I shall crush this Luke Davis like the insect he is."

Odin shook his head, "No, my son. I have watched the beast carefully and he cares for this human. To slay this human may cause the beast to go a mindless rampage. In such a state, the beast may be even more dangerous to us than he is now. We do not need to slay Luke Davis. We simply need him to lose his desire to engage in battle."

Odin's eye shifted its focus onto Aiden, "Boy, this Luke Davis is unlike most humans. He values something far more precious than gold. You are to take that which he holds most dear and return here with it. Go to Virginia, abduct the woman known as Melissa Davis, and bring her here. Once we have possession of his wife, Luke Davis will lose focus and his beast shall be rendered inert."

Aiden bowed and then in a flash of light both he and Allison disappeared to complete their tasks. Odin placed his hand on Thor's shoulder, "Now my son, take the Rainbow Bridge to Earth. Use the power that I have bestowed within your hammer to alter the world so that the universe can destroy the humans for us. These humans are not as resourceful as those who we left behind all of those centuries ago. We shall plunge them into darkness and then we shall listen to the sounds of their anguish as they call out to their god in vain."

Thor stood up and replied, "I shall make you proud, Father." The legendary warrior bowed then exited the throne room. When his son had left, Odin sat back down in his chair. He closed his eye so that he could focus his mind on observing his plan as it went into action.

CHAPTER 38

Luke was sitting in his cabin and he was using his Skype feed to talk to Melissa and the kids back at home. Stacy was showing him all of the new dances that she had learned and the dozens of art projects which she had completed in the two weeks since he had left for the Middle East. When she was finished, Melissa sent her out into the other room to play. She then turned to the screen with a look of concern, "What's wrong? I can tell by the look on your face that something is bothering you. There was no news feed on what happened over there. What kind of monsters did you run into?"

Luke shook his head as the horrible image of the Colossus of Death and his zombie army ran through his mind, "There was no news feed because anyone who came across the things we encountered is dead." Luke closed his eyes and he was silent for a moment. Melissa had known him long enough not pressure to him to continue. After taking a second to stead himself, Luke opened his eyes, "I saw horrors over here that deeply disturbed me, but in the end with the help of Chimera we were able to put an end to the threat." Luke took another deep breath, "Honey, I am not really ready to talk about what I saw here yet. Maybe when I get home and we can talk face to face, but right now I just can't talk about it."

Melissa nodded, "That's okay. When you are ready to talk about it I am here for you." The doorbell rang and Luke could here Stacy yelling that someone was at the door. Melissa smiled, "Well maybe I am not here for you right this second. Let me go see who that is before Stacy goes nuts."

Through the Skype feed, Luke watched as Melissa walked over to the door and opened it. He could see a tall, well built, man with long blond hair at the door in a UPS uniform. Luke sighed; it was just his luck that a guy who posed for romance novels would be at his wife's door when he was Skyping with her. He trusted Melissa of course, but he could see from the way she perked up that she found the guy attractive. That didn't bother Luke. After all, it wasn't like he never noticed an attractive woman. He was already thinking about how he was going to playfully give her a hard time about the delivery guy when he saw the delivery guy grab Melissa and kiss her. Anger rushed through Luke but it was quickly replaced with fear when a bright flash of light filled the screen causing him to close his eyes. When he opened his eyes again, he could see that both the delivery man and Melissa were gone. The sound of Stacy screaming came pouring through the Skype feed.

Luke's thoughts immediately shifted to his daughters. He felt helpless as he started yelling at the screen to get Stacy's attention. Finally, the five year old came running over to the computer, "Daddy, Daddy, that man took mommy in the light!"

Luke did his best to project a sense of calmness to his daughter, "It's okay, Stacy. Mommy will be back soon. Where is your sister?"

Stacy was crying, "She is upstairs sleeping in her room."

Luke nodded, "Okay Stacy, listen carefully. I want you to take the computer, keep it on so that I can see you, then go into your sister's room and the lock the door. I am going to send over some of the soldiers on the base to come get you and keep you safe. We are going to make a secret word and I don't want you to open the door unless the people who knock on the door say the secret word. Do you understand?"

Stacy was still crying hysterically but she nodded that she did. Luke spoke in a calm voice, "Okay honey, Ariel is your favorite Disney Princess, right?"

Stacy nodded, "Yes, Daddy. I love Ariel."

Luke smiled at his daughter, "Okay honey, once you close the door don't open it unless the man on the other side of the door say's that your favorite princess is Ariel and keep the computer with you so that I can see you until help comes."

Luke picked up his laptop and grabbed his radio, "Parsons, Diana, I have an emergency! I need your help! Meet me in the briefing room now!"

Parson's replied, "Copy that Luke, I am heading to the briefing room now."

Diana was running as she spoke, "I'll be there in a second! What's wrong?"

Luke was fighting with every fiber of his being to stay calm for his daughter who was still watching him through the Skype feed, "It's my wife. They have taken Melissa. Parson's, my kids are in the house by themselves, I need you to get a security team over there ASAP! My kids are locked in the toddler's room. I have them on Skype feed. Tell the security team that the safe word is Princess Ariel."

Parsons came back, "Copy that Luke. I will have a team there in less than five minutes."

Luke sprinted into the briefing room and placed his laptop on the table. Through the Skype feed he could see Stacy slamming the door closed and locking it. The slamming door had woken up her little sister who started crying. Stacy ran over, hugged her, and said, "It's okay, Sissy. Daddy is on the computer and Mommy will be back soon."

Luke was overwhelmed with emotions as he watched the scene on his laptop. He had never been so terrified in his entire life and at the same time he had never been so proud. Diana ran into the room and Luke made a motion with his hand indicating to Diana to remain calm. He then pointed at the laptop. Diana quickly understood the gesture and quietly took a seat at the conference table.

Parsons entered the room talking on his radio, "I want those men in that house now!" Luke could hear a voice reply that the team was currently entering the house. Luke kept talking to his daughter, "Stacy, some of Daddy's friends are coming to help you. Remember to not open the door unless they say your favorite princess." Stacy nodded in reply as she kept hugging her crying sister. Luke heard a knock on the door through the feed and he heard a voice say, "This is Sergeant Stone, your favorite Princess is Ariel. We are friends of your dad's. Please open the door, Stacy."

Stacy looked at her laptop, "Can I open the door, Daddy?"

Luke nodded as tears welled up in his eyes, "Yes, honey. Stacy, I am so proud of how well you did with following my directions and protecting your sister. I love you, honey and I will be home soon. I have to go now. I will call Grandma and have her come down and stay with you girls until I can get home."

One of the security team members came into the room and Stacy looked toward her computer, "Okay Daddy, I have to stay with sissy or she will be scared, bye-bye."

Luke whimpered, "Bye, bye, honey." He then switched off his computer and immediately broke down in tears. Diana ran over and hugged him. She held him in her arms. She didn't say a word. She knew that there was nothing that she could say that would comfort her friend. All that she could do was be there for him. Parsons was silent as well. He knew that Luke needed a minute to deal with what had just happened to his family.

After several minutes, Luke stopped crying. He wiped his eyes and quietly whispered, "Thank you," to Diana who nodded in reply. He looked to Parsons who answered his question before he could even ask it, "The girls have been taken to my house to stay with my wife. I have a team of guards stationed at the house as well. I have also radioed Maguire Air Force base in New Jersey. They are sending out a team to pick up your mother. They will fill her in on the situation and have her on military plane to Virginia ASAP. She should be with your kids by the end of the day." Parsons walked over and put his hand on Luke's shoulder, "Luke, I am so—"

Luke cut him off, "Don't say it, Parsons. There is no time to be sorry. It's time for action. I am getting my wife back!"

Parsons nodded, "Of course we are. Did you see anything through the feed that might help us identify who took her?"

Luke nodded then he replayed the Skype feed. The three of them watched as Aiden knocked on the door, talked to Melissa for a minute, and then kissed her, causing them to disappear in a flash.

Diana cleared her throat, "I, ah… I think that I know who took Melissa." She pulled out her laptop and connected it the main monitor. Dozens of reports filled the screen, all of them detailing instances where people went missing in a flash of light when they were approached by either an attractive blond man or woman. The reports suggest that all of the people who were taken were both young and attractive themselves." She paused for a second and turned to Luke, "I am sorry Luke, but I think that these people may have been abducted so that they can serve as the breeding partners for the gods in their quest to create a species of demi-gods."

Luke shook his head, "Melissa had her tubes tied after our second child. She couldn't be used as one of their breeders."

Parsons interrupted, "Then it's clear that she was kidnapped to be used as leverage against Luke and Chimera. We will probably be contacted soon in some fashion with a threat against Melissa unless Luke and Chimera stand down."

Luke clenched his hands and gritted his teeth, "That's not going to happen. I love Melissa and I know her. With our kids in danger, she would tell me to press on no matter the danger to her. These bastards think that they have crippled me but all they have done is piss me off. Chimera and I are going to destroy everything that even looks like it's remotely related to the gods."

Luke walked out of the conference room and onto the deck of the Argos. He stared out over the ocean and silently said a prayer that Melissa would be safe. He thought back to when he had talked to her about accepting this position. He told Melissa that he needed her by his side because every challenge that they had faced in their adult life they had done so together. Now this new challenge Luke accepted has put Melissa in grave danger. He thought of his wife and looked to her for strength. As he had said to his friends, she would tell him to press on. He cleared his eyes and made a promise to his wife, "Melissa, I swear to god that I will do everything possible to get you back and to make these so-called gods pay for taking you." He began to cry as he finished the last part of his promise, "If they hurt you in any way, I promise that you will be the last person that they ever hurt because Chimera and I will destroy them and everything that they hold dear!"

Luke turned around to see Diana standing behind him. He looked at her with a grim determination, "We have work to do."

She held out her hand to him, "Let's get to it then." Luke took her hand and they walked back to the conference room together.

CHAPTER 39
GERMANY

The smell coming from the entrance to the cave was horrid and overwhelming. The odor was the stench of thousands of years of decay. Allison stood in front of the cave for a moment and thought to herself that this is another reason that she hated the Asgardians. The Olympians and the Mesopotamians had her finding the most attractive men on Earth for them. The Asgardians sent her to retrieve a dragon that had been wallowing in his own filth and self-pity for countless centuries. She took a cautious first step into the dark cave. She walked over the remains of deer, bears, horses, and cows. Long ago, the dragon had nearly been slain by the hero Siegfried. Siegfried also succeeded in taking Fafnir's treasure. It took Fafnir several centuries to recover from his physical wounds but the beast had never recovered emotionally from the loss of his coveted treasure. The presence of the animal remains showed that Fafnir was eating just enough to sustain himself in between his long slumbers. If a cow went missing every twenty years or so no one asked any questions. Fafnir was able to eat quickly and return to his cave where he would hibernate until his body forced him to wake again and feed.

As Allison walked deeper into the cave, she was forced to form a ball of light in the palm of her hand so that she could see where she was going. She walked into the darkness for several more minutes and then suddenly she found that the cave was filled with a thick white mist. Unlike most dragons that had the ability to breathe fire, Fafnir was capable of emanating poison gas from his mouth. Had Allison been a mortal, she would have begun choking and died in under minute. Allison walked through the gasses and continued down further into the cave.

A deep a guttural voice came from the darkness ahead of her, "Even an immortal shall not disturb my sleep and leave my cave unharmed. Be warned intruder, if you tread any further you shall incur the wrath of Fafnir!"

A chill ran down Allison's spine, as she was more than aware of what a dragon like Fafnir was capable of doing to her. She stopped walking then shouted down into the darkness, "I come with word from Lord Odin! He feels that you have suffered long enough. He has a new treasure that is yours for the taking if you are willing to fight for it!"

The grim voice rose an octave at the suggestions of acquiring a treasure, "A new treasure? I warn you, if this is a ploy you shall pay dearly!"

Allison shook her head, "It's no ploy. The treasure is across the ocean in the land of Kentucky at the Fort of Knox. The humans have this treasure and they guard it with their guns, planes, and tanks."

Fafnir was silent for a moment then he replied with renewed vigor in his voice, "I have slept for a long time, but in my dreams I have seen many of the treasures amassed by the humans. Often have I dreamt of the treasure at the Fort of Knox. I have also dreamt of the pitiful defense that the humans have placed around the treasure. Long have I wished to obtain a new treasure and yet I have not done so for fear of retaliation from the gods and yet you claim that Odin himself has decreed that I may have this treasure?"

Allison smiled, "Lord Odin stated that if you can take the treasure from the humans that it will be yours as long as you can defend it."

Fafnir laughed, "I shall crush the humans who horde this treasure! Then I welcome any challenger who seeks to take my treasure from me!"

The ground beneath Allison's feet started to shake as Fafnir began making his way out the cave. She quickly teleported herself to the mouth of the cave. When she was outside of the cave, she ran to a nearby tree and crouched behind it. She watched as a long snake-like body slithered out of the cave. First Fafnir extended his four powerful legs, then used them to lift his massive body off of the ground. With his legs beneath him, the dragon spread his wings, covering Allison beneath their shadow. Fafnir roared and began flapping his wings. Allison was knocked to the ground by the force of the wind generated by the flapping wings. She was lying on the ground as she watched the dragon streak off in the direction of the Atlantic Ocean. She was considering the dragon's boast of welcoming any challenger in regards to Chimera. She watched as Fafnir flew out of sight then she whispered, "Be careful what you wish for, dragon."

Fafnir flew out over the ocean where he broke the sound barrier causing as sonic boom, then flew straight up into the stratosphere. When he was far above the planet, he accelerated to speeds beyond human comprehension. He could detect a piece of gold as small as a gram from across the planet. Fafnir could sense the store of gold in Fort Knox as easily as a shark could smell a gallon of blood in a tank of water. He zeroed in on the treasure and calculated that at his current speed he would reach his destination in just under two hours. A smile formed across Fafnir's reptilian face as the thought of possessing a treasure crossed his mind. For centuries, he had stayed in his cave and tried to sleep off his desire to obtain a new mound of gold for fear of angering the gods, but now that Odin had directed him to take this Fort for his own, he finally had a purpose in life again. Fafnir shifted his course slightly to the south as he could sense the gold of Fort Knox growing closer by the second.

Norway

Two large stone pillars stood roughly twenty feet apart in the vast forest region of northern Norway. The pillars were so deep in the woods that they had not been seen by human eyes for hundreds of years. The runic inscriptions on the pillars were long grown over with moss and lichens. As the sun slowly rose on the forest, the light pierced the trees and shone through the pillars and, for the first time in nearly thirteen hundred years, when the light passed between the two pillars it began to refract and form a rainbow. The rainbow started out as a small band of light between the ancient structures. The band of light slowly grew until the rainbow filled the entire space between the two pillars. The rainbow was shining brilliantly until the form of a large Viking warrior suddenly stepped through it. The thunder god Thor breathed the air of Earth for first time since he and his father had left this planet in the hands of the humans many centuries ago. Simply by taking a breath of the air, Thor could feel the changes that men had brought upon the planet through their actions. Even in this untouched forest, Thor could sense that the air was filled with particles of smog and smoke that tainted the atmosphere. While it was cold in the early morning, Thor could sense that it was much warmer out than it should be in an area so far north. Thor shook his head in disappointment; he and the other gods had left the precious gift of this planet in the hands of the humans and they were destroying it for no other purpose than to serve their own greed. Thor looked to the heavens and realized that his cause was just, that he needed to eliminate the humans from the planet if there was to be anything left worth defending at the coming of Ragnarok when the Dark Ones retuned.

Thor began heading even further north through the dense forest. After walking for a few minutes, he had reached the appropriate area of the Arctic Circle. When he was in deep enough into the Arctic Circle, he reached into his garments and pulled out the Belt of Strength given to him by his father. Thor snapped the belt around his waist and his body began to grow until he towered over the trees at a height of over three hundred feet tall. With his strength at its peak, he placed the iron gloves on his hands, which he required in order to use his hammer, to control the elements. After placing the gloves over his hands, Thor removed his hammer from his belt. Holding the hammer by its handle, he began to swing the weapon over his head, causing a massive storm the magnitude of a class five hurricane to form above him. The trees in the forest were bent and broke as the wind from the storm tore through the ancient woodland. Thor focused his thoughts and bent the storm to his will. He caused a bolt of lightning to shoot up from the clouds and into the outreaches of Earth striking the magnetosphere. Once the first bolt of lightning struck the magnetosphere, he could feel the shield around the planet condense slightly. Even with his powers, Thor could sense that in order to condense Earth's magnetic shield to the point that he required would take time and most of his energy. Thor closed his eyes and then focused his energy on lessening Earth's defense from the sun itself.

East Coast US

Fafnir exited the stratosphere over the Atlantic Ocean off the coast of Massachusetts. The dragon shifted his course slightly to the south then continued in his westward direction. Fafnir was crossing over New York State, when he saw seven small gray shapes flying directly at him. The dragon had previously caught only glimpses of the machines that the humans had used to fly through the air in this modern world. Fafnir fixed his eyes on the US Air Force as jets they were closing in on him. The dragon smiled. It had been a long time since he had the opportunity to engage in an aerial battle. Fafnir relished the thought of proving to the humans who was truly the master of the skies. The six Lockheed Martin F-22 Raptors entered a V formation as they came within range of Fafnir. The dragon saw bright flashes of light coming off of the jets as they unloaded their machine guns on him. Fafnir could feel the bullets as they struck his thick hide but the large caliber bullets did little more than annoy the beast.

Fafnir roared and flew straight into the apex of the V formation. The dragon closed his jaws on the lead jet crushing it while simultaneously using his wings to destroy two more jets. The remaining four jets continued to fire on Fafnir as they streaked passed him. The dragon knew that he could easily out distance the remaining three jets but the beast was enjoying the battle. Fafnir turned in a wide arc to see that the jets were circling around to take another run at him. Fafnir watched with curiosity as two long thin streaks of white smoke shot out from each of the planes. A series of projectiles struck the dragon, causing multiple explosions to occur across his body. Fafnir was engulfed in flames but once more the weapons of the humans were not able to pierce the dragon's thick scales. Fafnir emerged from flames and he could see the look of disbelief on the eyes of the pilots inside the jets as he streaked toward them. This time Fafnir did not even bother to open his mouth; he simply used his body to plow through the remaining four jets. Prior to crashing into the planes, the dragon saw the tops of two of the machines pop off and shoot the chairs that the pilots were sitting on into the air. Fafnir flew around again to see two large white mushroom shapes open up above the pilots slowing their descent to the ground. The dragon smiled to himself. He had not eaten in many years and the two men dangling beneath the mushrooms offered a tempting snack. The two pilots screamed and kicked in vain beneath their parachutes when they saw Fafnir open his mouth as he flew toward them. A moment later, the pilots saw nothing but darkness as Fafnir closed his jaws and swallowed them whole. With the battle complete, the dragon once more adjusted his course and continued on toward Fort Knox.

Twenty minutes later, Fafnir saw a large gray building enclosed by a fence ahead of him. The aroma of the gold coming off of the Fort sent Fafnir into a frenzy. Like a drug addict in need of a fix, Fafnir felt an obsessive need to control the gold in Fort Knox overwhelm him. The dragon made a large circle around the building as security alarms around the complex blared at him. Fafnir stared at the building with lust in his eyes. He could tell that the treasure stored at this place was buried in a large vault deep underground. The beast realized that once he had claimed the Fort as his own that all he would need to do was sit atop of the ruins of the building and his new treasure would be safely stored in the vault beneath him until the end of time. Fafnir altered his course and dove straight at the building, bringing all of his weight down on top of it. The building itself was not half as large as the dragon so that when Fafnir landed on top of it, all four walls were crushed into rubble. Fafnir did not care about the building. It was the gold beneath it that the beast coveted.

Fafnir adjusted the rubble beneath him until it was crushed flat. He was then satisfied that he had formed a liar were he could spend the rest of his days with his new treasure. The dragon looked around to see vehicles and men running toward him. Fafnir roared in defiance at the first creatures to challenge him for the right to own his treasure. The soldiers who were charging at Fafnir opened fire but their rifles and high-powered guns and no effect on the dragon. Fafnir bent his long serpentine head down toward the soldiers. He then opened his jaws and a white mist poured out of them blanketing the attacking soldiers in a thick cloud. The soldiers who were in the mist began to cough and gag. One by one they fell to the ground and died an agonizing death in the poisonous breath of the great serpent.

The dragon had no sooner slain the attacking soldiers than he felt an impact and explosion on his back. While uninjured from the attack, Fafnir was annoyed by it. He spun around to see more than a dozen tanks coming right at him. Fafnir heard several loud booming sounds and felt a multitude of explosion occur across his body as the tanks fired their shells at him.

The dragon slithered out of his new nest in the direction of the advancing tank brigade. Fafnir reared up and spread his wings in front of the tanks. Even at close range, the weapons of man were unable to harm the ancient dragon. The shells simply continued to explode harmlessly against his thick scales. Fafnir's neck stretched out and his jaws closed on the nearest tank. He lifted the machine off of the ground and he shook it from side to side before letting go of the tank and sending it crashing into the ground.

Several more tanks fired on Fafnir but the dragon ignored the blasts as he used his front claws to swipe at a tank, tearing it to pieces. Fafnir quickly grew tired of the human's feeble attempts at driving him away from his treasure. The beast roared, then tore into the tanks, crushing them with his claws, teeth and tail. The massacre lasted only a few minutes before Fafnir had destroyed the last of the bothersome machines. Fafnir looked over his new liar to see destroyed tanks, dead bodies, and a crushed fortress all atop his treasure of gold. For the first time in over a thousand years, Fafnir finally felt satisfied. He crawled over the remains of the tanks and then he rested his body in the rubble that was once Fort Knox. Beneath him, Fafnir could sense the treasure that was now his. The dragon that slept for so many centuries was now wide awake. Once more he had a treasure to defend and Fafnir was prepared to fight off all challengers to his fortune.

CHAPTER 40

Melissa found herself in a cold and dark room that smelled like a barn. As she further surveyed her surroundings, she could only guess that she was in some sort of cell or a dungeon. The walls were made of thick steel and the stone floor was covered in a thin layer of straw. She was shocked at the lack of any other furniture in the room because there were roughly two dozen other women in the cell with her, all sitting on the cold hard floor. The women all appeared to be very young either in their late teens or early twenties. Melissa quickly realized that the most disturbing aspect of the other women in the cell was that they all appeared to be in the third trimester of a pregnancy.

The last thing that Melissa remembered was right out of a late night Cinemax movie. She was talking to Luke on the Skype feed when the attractive delivery man came to the door. She had no sooner moved her daughter out of the way to answer the door when the stranger reached down and kissed her. She remembered seeing a bright flash of light and then finding herself here. That was when it hit her. Her kids were still in the house either alone with the stranger or totally by themselves! Melissa's mind was racing. She felt the immediate need to find out what had happened to her children. She began screaming at the bars, "Help! I need help! My kids have been left alone with a dangerous man!" Tears began to stream down her face, "Please, won't someone help me? Won't someone tell me what's going on?"

None of the women that she shared her cell with bothered to react to her. They all appeared to be severely depressed and in pain as they shifted their pregnant bodies from side to side, trying to find some small measure of comfort from the thin coating of straw on the floor.

Melissa shifted her attention to the long and dark hallway outside of her cell. She could see the outline of what appeared to be a tall man walking toward the cell. When the form walked past the flickering light of a torch mounted to the wall, she could see the face of the delivery man who had kissed her a minute ago.

The young mother's fear was quickly replaced with anger, "You bastard! Where have you taken me! What have you done to my children?"

Aiden casually sauntered over to the cell and smiled, "Relax, beautiful. Your kids are fine. The last that I saw of them they were still talking to their father over the computer. He was sending someone to watch over them. By now they are probably protected by an entire division of soldiers."

Despite the situation that she found herself in, a profound wave of relief came over her. Her children were safe. Somehow even from the middle of the ocean, Luke had found a way to protect them. With the knowledge that her children were not in danger, her mind shifted to her own well-being. She began to question Aiden, "Who are you? Where have you taken me? Why I am I here?"

Aiden grinned, "One thing at a time love. My name is Aiden. I am a nymph who serves the gods. You are currently in the dungeon of Asgard beneath the palace of Odin." Aiden paused for a moment, "The why you are here is a much more complex question. I can tell you that part of the reason that you are here but the rest of that answer is up to you and your husband."

Melissa stammered, "Wh... What are you going to do to Luke?"

Aiden shrugged, "I don't do anything to anyone. I am just a messenger. In fact, I am going to take a message to Luke concerning you. The question is, what are you going to have me tell him in my message?"

Melissa shook her head, "What message? What are you talking about?"

Aiden backed away from the cage, "Odin is the king of Asgard. He is also the wisest and most powerful of all of the gods. He wants me to deliver an offer to your husband. If he and his monster stand aside and let what needs to be done to the humans occur, he will offer your husband and your children asylum here in the realm of Asgard. The monster your husband controls will have to come as well. The beast has proven himself to be a juggernaut. Odin feels that with the other sects of gods destroyed, the beast may prove an invaluable weapon in the defense of Earth at the coming of Ragnarok." Aiden turned and smiled at Melissa, "So can I tell your husband to accept this generous offer from Odin?"

Melissa was silent for a moment. She began to cry and then her cries quickly turned into hysterical laughter. She pressed her face against the bars of her cage, "You say that Odin is wise? Well let me tell you that he is a fool. He may know a lot things that I will never understand, but there is no way that he knows my husband as well as I know him, or as he knows me." Tears were still streaming down from her face as her emotions changed from jovial to angry, "I have known Luke for a long time. I can tell you that he does not respond well when he is threated or challenged. He responds even worse when someone threatens his family. Does Odin really think that Luke would sacrifice the rest of the human race to save me? Does Odin think that I would want to be spared at the expense of every other person on Earth?"

Melissa almost snarled, "He and Chimera are going to destroy everything that you and Odin send at him on Earth, and if I am not returned home safely to him, Luke will find a way to bring to Chimera here and together they will tear this kingdom to rubble. He will do all of this because he knows that is exactly what I would want him to do." She glared at Aiden, "Don't worry about taking a message from me to Luke, instead take a message to Odin. Tell him to release me or see his people and his kingdom laid to waste!"

Aiden stood there a moment staring at Melissa. She screamed at the nymph, "You said that you're nothing but a lowly servant. A messenger? You have been given a message. Do the only thing that your sorry ass is able to do and deliver my message!" Melissa waited for second then added, "Or are you waiting for a tip?" She reached into her pocket pulled out a nickel and tossed to Aiden. The nymph let the coin fall at his feet as he glared at Melissa in anger. In the thousands of years that he had existed, no human had ever spoken to him in such a way. With a few words, this woman had reduced him to a being who was beneath her. Aiden swallowed his pride. As much as it hurt him, he could not touch this woman without Odin's permission. He spun around on his heels and walked out of the dungeon.

Melissa heard a voice from behind her, "That was great! It's about time that someone put that bastard in his place." Melissa turned around to see a young blonde woman who, like all of the other woman, was clearly pregnant. The young woman was using the wall to help in lifting her body off of the floor. When she was standing, she looked at Melissa and pled, "Please tell me that it is true? That your husband has monster that is fighting those things?"

Melissa walked over to the young woman, "Yes, it's true. In fact, they have already defeated two sects of gods!"

The blonde nodded, "That would explain why we were taken here so quickly."

Melissa placed her hand on the girl's shoulder, "What happened to you and all of these other women?"

The girl sighed, "My name is Felecia and all of the women here have the same story. That bastard you just told off seduced us and then when he kissed us there was a flash of light and we found ourselves in something that looked like it was ancient Rome or something. We were trapped inside of a palace. It was much nicer than this but it was still a prison. There were young men there too who had been seduced and trapped by a blonde woman." Felecia began to cry as she told her tale, "When we were in the palace, there were men dressed in long white togas. I guess that they were gods but whatever they were, they came and had sex with us as they pleased." She took a deep breath, "It was horrible. We were little more than their sex slaves. Within a day or two after they had their way with us, we all began to notice that we were pregnant, but this was not a normal pregnancy; it was progressing at a rate far too quickly to be normal." She pointed to her stomach, "I have only been pregnant a couple of weeks and it looks like I am do any day now." Felecia was unable to continue her story as she broke down in tears.

Melissa comforted her for a moment and then she tried to coax the rest of the story out of the young woman. Melissa was well aware that if she ever saw Luke again, any information she could give him about these gods would be tremendously helpful. When Felecia calmed down Melissa questioned her, "What happened next? How did you come here and where are the men who were with you?"

Felecia calmed down and finished her story, "There were goddesses who had sex with the men. A few weeks ago, the gods and goddess in the togas stopped coming. We were left alone for a few days during which our pregnancies continued to progress quickly. Everyone there did what they could to help each other until these giants dressed up as Vikings came into our prison. They didn't ask questions or give orders, they just killed all of the men and then they had us women march out of the prison and onto a rainbow of all things. We took one step onto the rainbow and then we wound up in this dungeon. The guy who I guess is their king came to see us when we were first put in here. He looked like a scary version of Santa Claus dressed like a Viking with a crown and an eye patch." Felecia began to cry again, "He said that we were carrying the children of gods and that once we gave birth that we be slain like the vermin we are. He said that our children would inherit our world and succeed on it where we had failed!" Felecia was crying uncontrollably as she collapsed into Melissa's arms.

Melissa held the young girl and looked around at the other women in the cell. The thought that each of the women was carrying a demi-god both scared Melissa and at the same gave her hope. Odin had said that they were children of gods but Melissa knew that they were also the children of humans and that thought gave her hope.

She stroked Felecia's hair and whispered into her ear, "Don't worry. My husband is coming for us and he is bringing the most powerful creature on Earth with him."

CHAPTER 41
VIRGINIA

Luke said good-bye to his mother and daughters then he walked out of his house on the base. Stacy was still upset about her mother but she was sure that, "Daddy and his monster would be able to get Mommy back." Luke could not guarantee his daughters that he would bring their mother home but he could promise them that he and his monster would do everything they could to get her back.

Luke was heading to the command center on base. He was optimistic about the meeting. He knew that they had defeated two of the three sects of gods prior to the time that Melissa was taken. That made both Parsons and Diana reasonably sure that the Asgardians had abducted Melissa as opposed to killing her. If the Asgardians had Melissa and she was alive, then there was still a chance that he would be able to bring her home.

Luke entered the command center to find Toombs sitting by himself. Luke didn't say anything to the doctor he simply sat down in his chair. Toombs was staring at Luke and for the first time since they had met, the doctor felt a connection to the teacher. The gods had taken Luke's wife from him just as they had taken Allison. Toombs felt as if he shared Luke's pain. For all of the animosity that Toombs had toward Luke, he knew how bad Luke was hurting because he was hurting in the same way.

Toombs stood up and walked over to Luke, "Look Luke, about your wife..."

Luke glared at the tubby little man, "Don't go there, Toombs. Just don't go there."

Toombs quickly turned and walked away. Under his breath he muttered, "Asshole."

A moment later, Parsons and Diana entered the room. Parsons turned on the monitor to the White House and the president's face filled the screen. He greeted the group then addressed Luke directly, "Mr. Davis, I am sorry to hear about what happened to your wife. Don't worry, son. We are doing all that we can to get her back." Luke responded with a thank you. The president then quickly got to the matter at hand, "General, a dragon has not only entered the US, it has demolished Fort Knox and he is currently sitting on the gold reserves that play a large part in supporting our nation's economy. How quickly can we get Chimera to engage this creature?"

Parsons cleared his throat, "We are going to use a truck to transport Luke and his horse. Chimera will follow the truck on foot. We are currently evacuating the route that we will take to Fort Knox. Ms. Cain can inform you on the specifics of this dragon. Chimera should be able to engage the dragon within twenty four hours."

Diana stood up, "I believe that the dragon is Fafnir. In Norse mythology, he was a prince who became obsessed with keeping hold of a vast treasure of gold in his possession. According to the myth, the gods cursed the prince for his greed and turned him into a dragon. Fafnir was supposedly slain by the hero Siegfried. Obviously, Fafnir survived this encounter. In addition to his size and ability to fly, Fafnir was said to have the ability to emit a poisonous mist from his mouth. Casualties from area around Fort Knox would appear to support that Fafnir has this ability." Diana took a deep breath, "Mr. President, my team and I have come across another phenomenon that looks like it may be connected to the Asgardians and may present a more pressing threat than Fafnir." She sent her information to the president's monitor and then continued her presentation, "We came across an atmospheric anomaly originating in the forests of Norway. It seems that a massive storm is forming there, however, the odd thing is that lighting strikes from the storm seem to be going up into the atmosphere rather than down into the ground. The physicists on my team tell me that these strikes are causing the electromagnetic field around the planet to condense. It seems that this will cause Earth to be susceptible to electromagnetic bursts from the sun. These bursts can knock out electronics on a planetary scale. In effect, if the Earth's electromagnetic shield is compromised, the sun could literally knock us back into the Dark Ages." Diana moved her presentation forward, "I believe that the god Thor is responsible for this anomaly. He is the Norse god of thunder and in mythology he is nothing like the character that we see in comic books and movies. The real Thor is much more powerful and brutal. The storm he has conjured has also created an electromagnetic field roughly ten miles in diameter. This means that our only chance of attacking Thor would be with Chimera." Diana swallowed hard and then offered her final thoughts, "Mr. President, despite the fact that Fafnir is in control of our gold reserves, my team feels strongly that we should address this matter prior to using Chimera to attack Fafnir."

The president sighed, "How long does your team think it will take for Thor to alter the electromagnetic shield to the extent that Earth's technology is in danger?"

"My team figures that we have between a week and ten days. However, they caution that they are unsure of how to quantify Thor's ability so the margin for error in their calculations could be wide."

The president turned to Parsons, "General, how long will it take you to get Chimera from Fort Knox to Norway?"

"At best we could make the trip in five days."

The president nodded, "That gives us at least two days to play with. Listen up people. That dragon is not only sitting atop of our gold reserves, it has invaded US airspace and soil. Take out that dragon and then head to Norway. I have complete faith that you can accomplish both missions in time."

Despite her better judgment Diana spoke up, "Mr. President, it is hard to tell with all of the electromagnetic interference but my team has also picked up an energy signature similar to the one we have found from Zeus's pillars. They believe that this energy signature may be a portal to Asgard itself. Not only could it afford us access to the gods' stronghold, but it also may represent the best and only chance that we will have at rescuing Mrs. Davis and the other abductees."

Parsons attempted to support Diana's case, "Mr. President, if I may. Having Fafnir attack our gold supplies may be a classic misdirection. By engaging the dragon first, we may be doing exactly what the Asgardians want us to do."

The president shook his head, "We will explore the situation in Norway after we deal with the problem here. I am sorry Mr. Davis but millions of American lives are in imminent danger as long as the dragon is within our borders. We need to destroy that creature."

Luke silently nodded in reply as the president ended his transmission. Parsons looked at his team, "Alright everyone, we head out in one hour. Let's slay this dragon and head to Norway."

Diana ran over and hugged Luke, "I'm sorry. We should go to Norway first."

Luke returned the hug, "No, Melissa would want us to think of others before her. We will take out this dragon and then put an end to this war in Norway. Once we kill Thor, I will take every step necessary to get Melissa back."

The two friends walked out of the room as Toombs remained at the conference table. The scientist hated Luke more than ever. He had tried to extend his hand to Luke in friendship and that bastard spit in his face. Toombs stood up from the table. He would help them fight this dragon and then head to Norway. In Toombs mind, he saw himself charging into Asgard and freeing Allison from the gods. Finally, he would be the hero and get the girl and then Luke, his wife, Parsons and Diana could all go to hell as far as he was concerned.

Kentucky

Fafnir was sitting in his nest of rubble and looking out over the vast fields that surrounded him. His sensitive nostrils had picked up a strange odor. The odor was unlike anything that he had smelled before. It seemed to have elements of both lion and elephant in it as well as another scent Fafnir could not identify. In the distance, he could see the gargantuan shape of a bipedal creature coming toward him. Fafnir growled, "It seems as if the first true challenge to my treasure has finally made his appearance." Fafnir shifted in his nest as he prepared to defend that which was most precious to him.

Luke and Diana had exited the truck and were now riding atop of Jason as they led Chimera toward Fort Knox. They could see Fafnir in the distance. The dragon was clearly waiting for Chimera to come closer prior to engaging the kaiju.

Diana held on tightly to Luke. She somehow felt that the tighter that she wrapped her arms around Luke the more that she was able to lessen his pain. Luke was uncharacteristically quiet throughout the journey. Diana knew that the losing Melissa was hurting Luke far more than he was letting on. She was about to try and say something to comfort Luke when she saw Fafnir rise into the air and come flying toward them. Luke lifted up his speaking horn and directed Chimera to attack.

The kaiju dropped to all fours and ran like a lion chasing his prey. Fafnir flew over Chimera and opened his mouth. The dragon's poison mist cascaded over the kaiju like the fog descending on the streets of London early in the morning. Chimera's eyes, nose, and mouth burned as the poison made its way into his orifices. The kaiju shook his head and coughed while the dragon circled in the air around him. Fafnir flew directly into Chimera and the force of his attack knocked the kaiju to the ground. Fafnir stood atop of the kaiju and insulted the creature, "Foolish behemoth! Did the humans truly think that you were capable of driving me away from my treasure?" Fafnir raked his claw across Chimera's face and then he sprayed another burst of poison into Chimera's mouth. Chimera's face continued to burn but the kaiju reached up with his powerful left hand and clamped it down on Fafnir's face forcing the dragon's jaws shut. The kaiju then used his right claw to slash the dragon across his midsection. Blood poured over Chimera as the kaiju forced Fafnir off of his chest. Chimera maintained his grip on Fafnir's face as the monster regained his footing. Once the monster was standing upright, he grabbed the mid-point of Fafnir's long neck with his right hand. There was sickening crack as Chimera snapped Fafnir's neck in two. Chimera released his grip and the corpse of the dragon slowly slumped to the ground. Chimera stepped on top of his kill and declared his victory to the world.

Diana didn't even have the opportunity to dismount from Jason. The entire battle was over in less than a minute. Luke calmly picked up his radio, "Parsons, this is Luke. Fafnir has been eliminated. Prepare the Argos to head for Norway."

Luke yelled good job to Chimera, then tossed the kaiju one of his reinforcer cubes. He waited for Chimera to finish his reward, then directed the monster to follow him. Luke turned Jason around and he started heading back toward the truck so that they could get the Argos as quickly as possible. Diana was squeezing Luke when she heard him whisper, "I am coming for you, Melissa." The tone of his voice sent a shiver down her spine. All of the stories that she had read about Thor spoke of his anger on the battlefield. After hearing Luke whisper those words to his wife, she thought that Thor had no idea what true anger was but he was going to find out.

CHAPTER 42
NORWAY

Thunder and lightning streaked into the night sky, creating an incredible visual display. Thor was sweating as he continued to swing his hammer over his head. Creating a storm of such magnitude that it would affect the entire planet took a tremendous strain on the thunder god. Thor was perfectly in tune with the storm that he was creating. He could feel the Earth's electromagnetic field slowly shrinking by degrees. Soon the Earth would no longer be able to deflect the magnetic blasts coming from the sun. The blast would not directly affect most lifeforms on the planet. The animals and plants who lived on Earth would be unaffected by the assault but the humans' technology, their power, the very systems that they depended on to sustain their lives would be destroyed. Without power, the humans would die off in a few short years from hunger, disease, exposure, and dehydration. Thor felt as if destroying the humans in this way was a fitting punishment for them. It was through bending nature to fit their needs that they were destroying the world. Had they simply lived in harmony with the Earth then they would have been allowed to continue to exist. Now the very technology that humans were using to destroy the Earth would be taken away at which point the Earth would destroy them. Thor did not see what he was doing as an act of genocide. He simply saw his actions as returning the planet to its natural state.

Atlantic Ocean: The Argos

Luke and Diana were sitting on the observation deck watching Chimera as the monster was once more playing with his large ball in the holding deck. They had just come from the briefing room where they reviewed what was ahead of them. All of the information they had indicated that the Argos was heading to a battle which would finally end this war. During the meeting, Diana enlightened the crew as to exactly what they were facing in Thor.

In addition to being a god of thunder, Thor was also thought to be the strongest and most accomplished warrior of all of the gods. Legends spoke of Thor's prowess in battles. He had defeated countless monsters and giants. Diana mentioned that on two occasions Thor was said to have battled Jörmungandr, a serpent so large that his body encircled the entire Earth, to a standstill. As large as Chimera was, he was nowhere near as large as the legendary serpent that was unable to defeat Thor. Thor was also known to be the tactile leader of Asgard's army. The other gods Chimera had battled relied only on their raw power. If the legends of Thor were true, the thunder god would employ strategy as well.

When Parsons asked Luke if he and Chimera were ready for this challenge, Luke simply nodded. He had remained silent throughout the entire briefing. Diana had made a point to emphasize that their data suggested a possible portal that could be used to access Asgard and rescue Melissa. She had hoped that reminding Luke of this possibility would help to invigorate him but he simply continued to stare straight ahead.

When the briefing was finished, Luke walked out of the meeting and straight to Chimera's observation deck. Diana followed him and simply sat there in silence with him. She knew him well enough to know when he didn't need to talk but still needed company. Diana was perfectly content to sit with Luke until he was ready to talk or until the mission was ready to commence.

Chimera did a summersault in his holding bay and then he began laughing like a gorilla. Luke smiled, "The last time that I saw Melissa we were watching Chimera and he was doing the same thing. It was the first time that she saw Chimera in person and understood that he is more than just a monster."

Diana grabbed his hand, "He is part of our team and our friend."

Luke nodded, "He deserves more than a holding cell and an old hangar. Maybe once this is over we can find somewhere that he can roam freely like an island or something."

Diana laughed, "If he gets an island, you and your family will have to go with him. He loves you! Without you, he won't know what to do with himself."

Tears began to run down Luke's face, "An island, a desert, or wherever I don't care as long as she's there with me."

Diana hugged her friend, "We're going to get her back, Luke. We're going to get her back."

Parsons stood on the bridge staring over the ocean. He knew that the end of this war was just over the horizon. As a young boy, Parson's had idolized George Washington. During the Revolutionary War, Washington distinguished himself time and time again on the battlefield. His greatest victory came when he crossed the Delaware River to defeat a force far greater than his own. His victory in the Battle of Trenton saved a nation and changed the future of humanity. When he was a young boy, Parsons had often imagined the excitement that Washington must of have felt when crossing the river. At this moment, Parsons was crossing a body water to challenge a force far greater than him in attempt to save the planet and allow humanity to have future. It was not until this moment that Parsons finally understood that it was not excitement that Washington felt but fear. Despite that fear, Washington had to portray confidence to his men in order to spur them onto victory. With everyone on the Argos looking to him, Parsons tried to exude that same sense of confidence.

Toombs sat in his room alone trying to gather his courage. Up until this point, he had stayed aboard the ship when Chimera was engaging gods and monsters in combat. Now he was going to follow Chimera into a battle with a god that Diana said would be the most powerful being Chimera had yet to encounter. Toombs hoped that he would be able to avoid the conflict as much as possible. He had no desire to see Chimera battle Thor to the death. His only desire was to find the energy source that appeared to be a portal. If he found the portal, then he could go through it and hopefully find Allison on the other side. A few of the sailors had snickered when they saw him bring a mountain bike onboard. Physical exercise was not his forte, but he was pretty sure that with the bike he would be able to traverse from the ship through the forest and to the portal. From there, he hoped that the bag of explosives and firearms he had signed out from the armory would avail him long enough to find Allison and rescue her. Never in his life did he imagine that he could have a woman like her and he would be damned if some ancient gods were going to keep him from a woman like that. Toombs could feel the boat slowing down. He surmised that the ship must have entered the fjord which led into the forest. He took a deep breath, grabbed his bike and his bag, then headed for the front of ship. He knew full well that everyone would be watching Chimera exit from the back of the ship thus offering him the perfect opportunity to grab a lifeboat from the front of the ship and head ashore.

The sky was a dark gray from the ominous storm clouds over overhead. A light rain was falling and the sound of thunder could be heard in the distance. Luke and Diana were sitting atop Jason as they watched Chimera wading ashore at the edge of the electromagnetic field. This time there would be no piolet or SEAL team. It was just Luke, Diana, Jason, a couple of rifles, and Chimera. Luke nodded to himself as this thought crossed his mind. In the entire world, he did not have three friends that he would trust more when trying to save the world. As Chimera was coming ashore, Luke directed Jason to turn around. When the horse was facing the forest, they could see a dark vortex swirling in the center of the storm system. Diana shivered, "I guess that we know where we are headed."

Luke voice was like steel, "Parsons says that center of the Vortex is about five miles northwest of this point. We should find Thor there." Luke urged Jason forward then he gave Chimera the direction to follow him. Form the cover a nearby tree, Toombs jumped onto his mountain bike and began to peddle after the kaiju.

Luke remained quiet and focused as they rode through the dense forest. Diana respected his desire to remain silent and she simply held onto Luke, offering him as much support as she was able to. Diana realized that silence was for the best. Even if they wanted to communicate, they could barely hear each other over the ever increasing crashes of thunder combined with the sound of Chimera crushing dozens of trees with each step that he took. Diana wished that Chimera was able to walk through the awe inspiring forest without leaving a path of destruction. In all of her life, Diana had never seen such a beautiful landscape. The rain was increasing in intensity and Diana placed her hand over her eyes to shield them from the downpour. From the corner of her eye, Diana saw a bright flash. She tapped Luke on the shoulder and pointed, "Luke, head over there! I think we may have found the portal!"

Jason trotted over in the direction which Diana had indicated. As they passed through the trees, two stone pillars with runic writings on them came into view. There was a bright and colorful rainbow cascading between the two pillars. Luke pulled Jason to a stop in front of the pillars and Diana said, "The Rainbow Bridge. Luke, this is a portal to Asgard! We can use it to look for Melissa!"

Luke was silent for a long moment as he started at the portal. He took a deep breath, "Not yet. Melissa would want us to stop Thor first. We don't really know how long it will take before he makes Earth vulnerable to magnetic bursts from the sun." He reached down to his waist and grabbed Diana's hand, "Every fiber of my being is screaming for me to march Chimera in there and have him tear down whatever is on the other side until Melissa is returned to me. The only thing stopping me is Melissa because that's not what she would want. She would say to do what needs to be done. To protect everyone else first. She would tell me to make sure that our daughters are safe before I come for her." Chimera was standing behind them and waiting for a direction. Finally, Luke turned Jason back in a northwest direction and then he ordered Chimera to follow him. A sore, exhausted, and panting Toombs waited until Jason was out of sight and then he climbed off of his bike and walked over to the rainbow portal. He stood in front of it for minute and then said, "That bastard just left his wife to rot in there!" He gripped his bag of weapons tightly, "I am coming for you, Allison." Toombs then walked into the portal leading to Asgard.

Allison and Aiden were sitting outside Odin's throne room waiting to be summoned again when Allison's eyes suddenly lit up. Aiden questioned his sister, "What has happened? What do you sense?"

A sly smile crept over Allison's face, "It seems as if my fat little toad is braver and more resourceful than I had thought. Come dear brother, one way or another the opportunity we have waited millennia for is nearly at hand." Allison grabbed her brother's hand and began leading him to the Rainbow Bridge.

Chimera was following Jason when he suddenly came to a stop. Luke and Diana looked up at the monster through the tree cover to see him roar and beat his chest. After the deafening roar had ended, Luke shouted, "He sees something!" The couple looked ahead of them but the dense forest blocked there view of anything above the tree line. They were still staring when a massive booted foot came crashing through the top of the trees in front of them. They looked up to see a giant with a red beard swinging a hammer over his head that he brought crashing down onto Chimera's head. The blow sent Chimera crashing to the ground. He missed crushing Luke, Diana, and Jason by less than ten feet. Luke dug his heels into Jason urging him to run to his left. After they galloped for several minutes, Luke pulled Jason to a stop. They turned around to see the giant's foot stomping on Chimera's head. Diana spoke with sense of reverence, "I think that we have found Thor."

Chimera's face was being driven into ground as Thor continued to stomp on the back of his head. The kaiju could hear a voice screaming above him, "Today you die monster! For today you face Thor!" After a fifth stomp, Chimera rolled to his side and closed his powerful jaws around Thor's ankle. Chimera stood straight up sending Thor falling onto his back crushing hundreds of trees as he hit the ground. Chimera positioned himself above the god then he brought his fist down into Thor's face. Chimera was bringing his hand down to strike the god again when Thor's hand shot up and caught Chimera by the forearm. Thor roared, sat up, and then used his hammer to strike Chimera in the jaw. Lightning danced across the area of Chimera's face that the hammer had struck and the blow caused Chimera to go sprawling to the ground. The kaiju opened his eyes to see the forest spinning around him. In all of the battles that he experienced up until this point, no opponent had ever struck Chimera with such force.

Chimera lifted himself back onto his feet, turned to face Thor, and roared. With Chimera's hunched over posture, Thor was taller than the kaiju. Chimera's head only reached the point of Thor's chest where his bright red beard ended. Chimera lunged forward to attack but Thor moved quicker than the monster. The god stepped forward and smashed his hammer into the kaiju's forehead. Chimera stumbled backward and Thor pressed his advantage by using his hammer to deliver two more blows to Chimera's head. Chimera was losing his balance when he spun and used his tail to deliver a crushing blow to Thor's ribs. Thor was knocked to ground by the blow, allowing Chimera a brief moment to regain his balance. Thor had moved his body to a sitting position when Chimera unsheathed his claws and used them rake the god across his face. Blood flew across the forest as Chimera had gouged four deep cuts into Thor's face. Chimera continued to attack by using his other claw to cut Thor across his arm. The kaiju then delivered a viscous kick to the god's abdomen. Thor absorbed the kick then used his hammer to strike Chimera in the jaw. The blow stunned Chimera and the monster fell forward. Thor caught Chimera as he was falling and then in a show of unimaginable power the giant god lifted Chimera over his head.

Thor was holding the barely conscious kaiju above his head when he looked down and Luke and Diana, "Humans! Is this beast the greatest challenge that you can send to battle me? I am Thor, Prince of Asgard! I have battled frost giants, monsters, and even the World Serpent himself!" Thor laughed then he threw Chimera. The monster traveled several thousand feet before he came crashing back to Earth. Thor shouted again at Luke and Diana, "Humans, your champion has fallen. You have precious little time left on this planet. I suggest that you use it in prayer to your pathetic god. Let us see if his power can save you from Thor!"

Thor laughed and then he began to swing his hammer over his head causing the storm above him to send further lightning strikes into magnetosphere. Luke directed Jason to ride over to Chimera. Luke and Diana rode alongside Chimera's swollen face to see blood pouring out his mouth. Diana gasped at the sight, "He can't keep this fight up. Thor is two powerful. He will kill him." Luke stared at the kaiju in despair. It was obvious that Chimera was losing this battle, but he also knew that there was no other choice but for Chimera to fight on. Luke knew that in order for Chimera to continue the battle he had to properly motivate the kaiju, and this time a food cube would not be enough. Luke spun around in his saddle and then hugged Diana with all of his strength. He looked her in the eyes, "Thanks for all that you have done for me. You are my best friend and I love you." Luke then released Diana and pushed her off of Jason. Luke urged Jason to charge at Thor. As Jason was running toward the god Luke aimed his rifle at the exposed flesh on the Thor's leg. He fired every round into the god's legs and, while the attack did not harm Thor, it did get his attention. Thor sneered and then he kicked Jason out from under Luke. The mighty warhorse was reduced to a bloody pulp and Luke was sent flying into a nearby tree. Luke bounced off of the tree and fell to the ground. He was still breathing but it hurt like hell. He was sure that his ribs were broken. He opened his eyes to see the mangled remains of Jason and a tear began to form in his eyes as his whispered, "Goodbye my noble steed! You have earned all of the carrots in Heaven." Luke was blacking out when he looked to his side to see Diana running toward him.

Chimera was still lying on the ground when he saw Jason and Luke go flying through the air. The kaiju watched as two of the three creatures on Earth that he cared about were injured by the red-bearded giant. A wave anger overwhelmed Chimera's mind as simultaneously a surge of adrenaline coursed through his body. The kaiju roared and exploded off of the ground. He looked toward Thor who was smiling at him, "You still wish to battle? Good I was hoping for more of a challenge from—" Thor's bragging was cut short when his sensory organs were overloaded by a blast from Chimera's sonar attack. The god's body convulsed as Chimera charged at him. Chimera struck Thor with alternating blows from both of his hands. The god was still reeling when Chimera smashed his battering ram snout into Thor's face. Thor stumbled and then fell onto his back. Chimera stomped on the god's chest and then brought his face down to tear out Thor's throat. Thor saw Chimera's jaws coming to him and he used hammer to strike Chimera in the jaw. The blow snapped Chimera's head to the side but the monster turned his head back toward Thor and unleashed another sonar blast into the god's face. Thor's face contorted again as blood seeped out of his eyes and ears. Chimera pressed his foot into Thor's chest and then the monster delivered blow after blow into the Asgardian's face.

Diana watched as Chimera was beating Thor to death. She was trying desperately to revive Luke before the kaiju slew the god. The rain was slowing down as Thor was losing consciousness. Diana was shaking Luke when he moaned and opened his eyes. Diana screamed, "Luke, Chimera is killing Thor! You have to stop him!"

Luke sneered, "Let that bastard die!"

Diana grabbed Luke by the collar and yelled in his face, "If you let Chimera kill Odin's son, what do think he will do your wife?"

A wave a fear ran across Luke's face, "Grab the speaking horn and help me up!" Diana handed Luke his horn and then he leaned on her as he limped over to Chimera. Chimera continued to pound on Thor's face as the life was slowly slipping out of the thunder god's body. Luke lifted his speaking horn and screamed, "Chimera, stop!" The monster stopped and looked toward Luke. Luke knew that he had a concussion but he was sure that he saw Chimera smiling at him.

Diana gripped Luke tightly, "Tell him to tear off Thor's belt. It's what's giving him his extra size and strength. You can use me as a model to show him how to tear the belt off." Luke got Chimera's attention and then he showed him how to tear a belt off of someone by taking off Diana's unfastened belt. Luke then pointed to Thor and told Chimera to, "Tear off!" Chimera reached down and tore off Thor's belt. When he did so Thor shrunk back down to his normal height of thirty feet.

Diana was putting her belt back on when she said to Luke, "Tell him to pick up Thor. We need to get him to the Rainbow Bridge."

Luke pointed at the still breathing Thor and shouted, "Chimera, pick up!" When Chimera was holding Thor in his hand, Luke instructed the kaiju to follow him. With Diana's help, he began limping in the direction of the Rainbow Bridge. With the defeat of Thor, the storm clouds dissipated and the sun began to shine on the forest. Luke hoped that God had indeed heard Thor's challenge and this was a sign that this war was coming to an end. He also hoped that it was a sign that Melissa would be returned to him and their children safely.

CHAPTER 43

Toombs found himself envelope in a kaleidoscope of colors. His senses were reeling. He had no sense of direction and he felt as though he was both falling and soaring into the sky at the same time. Spinning out of control and standing perfectly still. It was beyond his mind's capabilities to comprehend what was happening to him. The sensation stopped as suddenly as it had begun. Toombs looked around to see himself standing before a magnificent city that looked as if it had been intricately carved out of oak or some other hardwood. A huge sword came down in front of him and Toombs looked up to see a warrior well over twenty feet tall standing in front of him. The warrior snarled, "Who is this mortal that dares to cross the Rainbow Bridge and enter eternal Asgard?"

Toombs was fumbling through his bag for something to try and defend himself with when he felt a thin and familiar hand place itself on his shoulder. He turned to his left to and to his astonishment and joy he saw Allison standing next to him. She was gesturing for him to kneel down. He quickly knelt down and she did so as well. She whispered, "Be silent if you wish to live." She lifted her head toward the guardian, "My humblest apologies, my lord. This is the man who had created the behemoth which defeated the Olympians and Marduk's sect as well. Lord Odin had asked me to bring him here to Asgard so that he may create similar creatures to help battle alongside Asgard's warriors during the coming Ragnarok. The storm that Thor is creating is interfering with my teleportation abilities; as such, I was forced to use the Rainbow Bridge to come to Asgard. This human simply slipped out of my grip during the journey."

The guard growled at Allison. "Take this mortal to the dungeon, nymph. Thor has engaged the behemoth in battle. Lord Odin will be watching this conflict with great interest. Once the battle is over I shall inform Lord Odin that you have arrived with this man."

Allison bowed and said, "Thank you, my Lord. I shall do so." Then she grabbed Toombs by the arm and led him toward the dungeon. Once they were out of the guard's line of site, she pressed Toombs against a wall, closed her eyes and imagined her one time lover Achilles, and then she kissed him passionately.

When she pulled herself off of Toombs, he was silent for a moment before he began firing questions at her, "What's going on here? That guard called you a nymph? I thought that you were a human. I thought that the gods had captured you to use you as one of their breeders. Who are you?"

Allison ran her finger along Toombs's mouth to silence him, "Hush, my love. What the sentry said is true. I am a nymph. Like all nymphs, I am servant to the gods. They use us as sex slaves and as their emissaries on Earth. They have forced my brother and me to abduct humans that they can use as breeders to create their new race of demi-gods. I was summoned here when we were making love. I dared not turn down a summons from Odin least I suffer terrible consequences." She stopped for a moment and looked off into the distance for dramatic effect. She sighed and then started to talk to Toombs again, "As nymph, I am tuned into people and their ability love." She smiled as she continued to spin her web of lies and partial truths, "In you, I saw not only a great capacity for love but also a man with the power to defeat the gods and free me and all of the other nymphs from their cruel oppression. You, who have the power to create a monster capable of crushing the gods and their beasts."

Her speech was cut short when a great roar spilt the sky. A moment later, Allison and Toombs heard a scream. They looked up to see the sentry who was guarding the Rainbow Bridge go flying overhead and crash into the walls of the palace. The scientist and the nymph ran around the corner to see Chimera standing at the entrance to the Rainbow Bridge. Luke and Diana stood in front of the kaiju. Luke was holding his speaking horn in front of him and shouting, "I demand to see Odin! We are here to negotiate the terms of surrender for Asgard!"

Allison grabbed a hold of Toombs hand, "My love, our hour is finally at hand! Answer me, do you love me and do you trust me?"

Toombs nodded causing both of his double chins to shake, "Yes, to both answers."

Allison kissed him, "That's exactly what I wanted to hear. The gods have used me as a slave for countless centuries and on Earth humans have overlooked your skills and ridiculed your appearance for your entire life. If I offered you the chance to have me and to rule both gods and humans, would you take that chance?"

Toombs's mind was reeling. This amazing creature was offering everything that he had ever desired. She was offering him the chance to erase all of his insecurities and validate his existence. To a man such as Toombs, there was only one answer. He nodded with a shine in his eyes, "Yes."

Allison pulled him in the direction of the dungeon, "Excellent! We must grab my brother and a few others before we leave this dimension and set our plan into action." Toombs didn't even bother to ask what their plan was, he simply followed Allison.

Luke continued to scream for Odin as Chimera stood behind him holding the unconscious Thor in his hand. Diana could see several gods cautiously watching them but none of them whom she thought could be Odin. Diana looked toward Luke and shook her head. Luke yelled through his speaking horn again, "Odin come out now or I will instruct Chimera to rip Thor in half, then I will order him to attack the city." The gates to the palace opened and a proud but defeated Odin walked through city streets and up to the invaders.

As was his way, the wise Odin took a long moment to consider his words before speaking. Once he had collected his thoughts, he spoke, "You have my son, and my city captive. As both father and king, I am at your mercy. What are your terms?"

Luke was struggling to look assertive even though every breath sent searing pain through his broken ribs and he was relying on Diana to hold him up. He glared at Odin, "Is my wife unharmed?" Odin nodded in reply. "Good, then you shall release her and any other human captives that you have to me." Once more Odin nodded. A wave a relief coursed through Luke's body at the thought of having Melissa returned to him. He continued with his demands, "You, and all other so-called gods, shall immediately cease to engage in any activities on Earth from now on."

Odin was silent for a long moment before replying, "You and your fellow humans are destroying the Earth and all other life on it. Would you have us idly watch this destruction?"

Luke took a deep breath, "After your attacks on Earth, we humans have learned to put our differences aside and work for the betterment of our species. I can assure you that we will work together to address how we take care of the planet."

Odin stared at Luke, "You do not know what you have done by defeating the gods. You see us as villains when in truth we have always strove to protect the planets which give life. By defeating us, you have put not only your planet but countless other worlds in peril from the Dark Ones who ruled over all reality before we defeated them. Without the gods, there will be no one to battle them at the coming Ragnarok. Your world will fall and they shall destroy all life on the planet before moving on from world to world until they have extinguished all life in existence."

Luke looked back to Chimera, "You defeated these Dark Ones and he defeated you. I think he can handle whatever they might throw at us." Luke growled, "Now bring me wife and the others!"

Odin turned to a god standing at his side and nodded. The young god went running to the dungeons.

Allison, Aiden, and Toombs were standing in front of the dungeon cells staring at Melissa and the pregnant captives. Allison eyed Toombs with ravenous eyes as she could see her plan coming to fruition, "How long will it take you to create another behemoth?"

Toombs shrugged, "With what I know from creating Chimera, I could have another fully grown Kaiju in roughly five years with the proper equipment."

Allison smiled, "Within ten years, the infants inside these women will be fully grown as well. Each of them will have strength comparable to the likes of Hercules and Gilgamesh." She wrapped her arms around Toombs, "Imagine my love, with twenty demi-gods and two behemoths at our disposal, no god, titan, or even Chimera could stand before us. The world would be ours!"

Melissa was listening to Allison speak from within the cell. She remembered Toombs from their brief meeting in Virginia. She could not believe that he was considering the blonde's offer. She tried to reason with the scientist, "Dr. Toombs, I am Luke Davis's wife. We have met before. Luke has told me that you are brilliant man. He said that without you Chimera never would have been created. Your creation has saved the human race! You are a hero! You can't seriously be thinking about taking this woman up on her offer."

Toombs sneered at Melissa, "All my life people have ignored or ridiculed me. It seems that most of the world has already decided that your husband is the hero of this war." He grabbed Allison, "I am going with someone who appreciates me, and my talents! Humans have nothing more to offer me but Allison offers everything that I could ever want!"

Aiden heard the sound of footsteps running toward the cells, "Allison, someone is coming we have to hurry!"

There was a bright flash which caused Melissa to shield her eyes. When she opened her eyes, she found that she was standing alone in the cell. One of the large guards came running into the cell and he scanned the room with a shocked look on his face. He yelled at Melissa, "Where are the other prisoners?"

Melissa shrugged, "The two blondes took them."

The guard cursed then looked at Melissa, "Are you the one who is the wife of the human that controls the behemoth."

Melissa nodded and the guard breathed a sigh of relief, "Come with me."

Melissa was unsure of what was going to happen to her. Had the gods finally decided that she had outlived her usefulness? She decided that whatever fate lay ahead of her she would meet it with as much bravery as she could muster. The guard led her down the crowded streets filled with the giant citizens of Asgard. After they had cleared a small hill, Melissa saw the awe inspiring form of Chimera standing at the city's edge. When she saw the kaiju, her heart leapt for joy because she knew that if the monster was here than Luke was not far behind.

She ran ahead of the guard to see Luke being held up by Diana. She sprinted past Odin and into Luke's arms. She embraced her husband and they both began to cry. Diana nudged Luke to remind him that Thor was still in Chimera's grasp. Luke directed the monster to put the down the defeated god. As Thor was being placed on the ground, he remembered that there were supposed to be other prisoners freed with Melissa.

Luke was about to question Odin on this fact when he saw the guard who had escorted Melissa back talking to the god king. Before Luke could ask a question, Odin stepped forward, "It seems that the nymphs have taken the other prisoners. I tell you on my honor that I had nothing do with this and I do not know their current whereabouts."

Luke nodded then he pointed to himself, Melissa, and Diana and gave Chimera the direction to pick them up. The kaiju gently scooped up the three humans then at Luke's direction he walked back through the Rainbow Bridge. After a disorienting moment, the three humans found themselves back in the forest. Luke directed Chimera to turn around and then he pointed at the two runic pillars with the Rainbow Bridge between them and he gave Chimera the command to destroy. With one swipe of his mighty arm, Chimera destroyed the portal between Earth and Asgard. Diana asked to be put down on the ground. She then quickly ran over and picked up Thor's belt. She dragged the mystical strap back to Chimera and Luke had the kaiju pick her up again.

From the palm of Chimera's hand, they could see the Argos waiting in the fjord, far off in the distance. Luke pointed at the ship and then he gave Chimera the command to walk.

For the first time in months, Luke and Diana felt as if they could finally rest. Melissa held Luke in her arms, "Where are the girls?"

"They are back in Virginia. My mother is staying with them. We will be able to call them from the ship. It will take us about four days to sail back home."

Melissa nodded, "Four days at sea will seem like an eternity until we get back home."

Luke looked up at his wife and his best friend with a big smile, "I am sure that the three of us can find something to keep us busy for three days."

The two woman responded simultaneously by poking him in his bruised ribs and laughing.

EPILOUGE
THE ARGOS ATLANTIC OCEAN

Parsons was seated by himself in the briefing room. He had spoken to Luke, Diana, and Melissa. He was fully apprised of the battle with Thor and of the events that had occurred in Asgard. He switched on the monitor with the live feed to president. The president's face appeared on screen and Parsons saluted him, "Good morning, Mr. President. I have your report on the events in Norway and Asgard."

The president nodded, "Go ahead, General."

Parsons brought his report up onto the screen, "Chimera defeated Thor and halted his attempt to alter the magnetosphere. My scientists tell me that it appears that the magnetosphere is returning to its natural state and I have in a request with NASA to confirm this. In addition to Thor's defeat, my team also entered Asgard where they were able to retrieve Mrs. Davis unharmed from the Asgardians."

The president smiled, "That's great news, general."

"Thank you, sir. Mrs. Davis reports that there were other women there who had been abducted and were pregnant with god-human hybrids. Mrs. Davis also states that the missing men were slain by the Asgardians. It seems that the nymphs responsible for taking these women in the first place also kidnapped them from the dungeons of Asgard."

The president's face grew concerned, "Where and why did the nymphs take these woman?"

"We don't where, sir, but we do know why. According to Mrs. Davis, the nymphs plan to use the hybrids in an attempt to subjugate humans to their will in the future. In addition to the missing women, Mrs. Davis also reports that Dr. Jonathan Toombs was working in conjunction with the nymphs. It seems that the nymphs want him to create additional kaiju to help them with their cause."

The president sighed, "This is terrible. Toombs was genius! Do we even have the ability to make more kaiju without him?"

Parsons shrugged, "I have forwarded his notes and equipment to some of the other top geneticists we have but Toombs was decades ahead of them in terms of his research. They are unsure if they will be able to create another kaiju." Parson's brought a new report up onto the screen, "Sir, Mr. Davis and Ms. Cain also report that Odin, the god king of Asgard, warned of a coming attack from what he called the Dark Ones, the beings who ruled the earth prior to the gods overthrowing them. Odin referred to the battle as the coming Ragnarok, the Norse apocalypse scenario."

The president nodded, "So it seems that even with the gods defeated we have two potential threats to deal with. How are we going forward at this point in preparation for these events?"

Parson's brought up a map of the base in Virginia and the area around it, "We have procured over two-thousand acres of woodland area for Chimera to live in. With the world aware of him, there is no need to keep him confined to a hangar. We have also cleared a path from this area to the ocean so that Chimera can have limited access to the ocean. Mr. Davis assures me that he can train Chimera to remain in this designated area where he will continue to train the kaiju for any upcoming confrontations."

Parsons brought another report onto the screen, "We have also recovered Thor's Belt of Strength. This item will be taken back to Virginia where it can be studied along with Apollo's Chariot and the Tablets of Destiny. Ms. Cain will continue to use her knowledge of mythology to assist our science team in determining how these items can be of use to us in future confrontations."

The president nodded, "Well then, general, it seems as if what we thought was the end of this war may only be the beginning."

Parsons nodded, "Yes, Mr. President."

THE END

ECK OUT OTHER GREAT
JU NOVELS

MURDER WORLD I KAIJU DAWN
by Jason Cordova
& Eric S Brown

Captain Vincente Huerta and the crew of the Fancy have been hired to retrieve a valuable item from a downed research vessel at the edge of the enemy's space.
It was going to be an easy payday.
But what Captain Huerta and the men, women and alien under his command didn't know was that they were being sent to the most dangerous planet in the galaxy.
Something large, ancient and most assuredly evil resides on the planet of Gorgon IV. Something so terrifying that man could barely fathom it with his puny mind. Captain Huerta must use every trick in the book, and possibly write an entirely new one, if he wants to escape Murder World.

KAIJU ARMAGEDDON
by Eric S. Brown

The attacks began without warning. Civilian and Military vessels alike simply vanished upon the waves. Crypto-zoologist Jerry Bryson found himself swept up into the chaos as the world discovered that the legendary beasts known as Kaiju are very real. Armies of the great beasts arose from the oceans and burrowed their way free of the Earth to declare war upon mankind. Now Dr. Bryson may be the human race's last hope in stopping the Kaiju from bringing civilization to its knees.
This is not some far distant future. This is not some alien world. This is the Earth, here and now, as we know it today, faced with the greatest threat its ever known. The Kaiju Armageddon has begun.

CHECK OUT OTHER GREAT KAIJU NOVELS

KAIJU WINTER
by Jake Bible

The Yellowstone super volcano has begun to erupt, ser
ing North America into chaos and the rest of the world in
panic. People are dangerous and desperate to escape th
oncoming mega-eruption, knowing it will plunge the cor
nent, and the world, into a perpetual ashen winter. But r
matter how ready humanity is, nothing can prepare the
for what comes out of the ash: Kaiju!

RAIJU
by K.H. Koehler

His home destroyed by a rampaging kaiju, Kevin Takahash
and his father relocate to New York City where Kevir
hopes the nightmare is over. Soon after his arrival in the
Big Apple, a new kaiju emerges. Qilin is so powerful tha
even the U.S. Military may be unable to contain or destro
the monster. But Kevin is more than a ragged refugee
from the now defunct city of San Francisco. He's also a
Keeper who can summon ancient, demonic god-beasts
to do battle for him, and his creature to call is Raiju, the
oldest of the ancient Kami. Kevin has only a short time to
save the city of New York. Because Raiju and Qilin are
about to clash, and after the dust settles, there may be no
home left for any of them!

Printed in Great Britain
by Amazon